A PARALLEL

TRUST

JAMES STODDAH

First Edition 2015

2QT Limited (Publishing)
Unit 5 Commercial Courtyard
Duke Street, Settle
North Yorkshire BD24 9RH.
www.2qt.co.uk

Release Partner: OUTLET PUBLISHING GROUP
Bulloch House, 10 Rumford Place, Liverpool. L3 9DG.
www.outletpublishinggroup.com

Requests to publish work from this book should be sent to:
press@outletpublishinggroup.com

This book is a work of fiction.
Any resemblance to actual events or persons, living or dead, is entirely coincidental.

Cover design: Kyle Wilson

Printed in Great Britain
Lightning Source UK Ltd

A CIP catalogue record for this book is available
from the British Library
ISBN 978-1-910077-52-8

ACKNOWLEDGEMENTS

No book release can happen without the help of a support network and I am eternally grateful to everyone who has helped me create this novel. It was particularly exciting to write and it wouldn't have been possible without family, friends and the professionals who have guided me, so thank you all.

Special thanks to: **Marilyn Wilson**, who helped look after me and the family; **Harley** and **Kyle** for anchoring me to reality; **Annette** and **Hannah Cartlidge** for their encouragement and putting up with my crazy ideas; **Karen Holmes**, my editor, for steering me through the writing process and teaching me to be disciplined and patient; **Emma Pritchard** for giving me faith in my own ideas; **Catherine Cousins** for the admin and absorbing the stress I create for her, and **Bruce Nicholson** for bearing the burden of my many emails when I'm in a pickle! Also my researchers and beta readers: **Steven Greening, Sarah Loftus, Georgia Barrett, Caitlin Lynagh, Chris Lord** and **Sarahjane Farr.**

– CHAPTER 1 –

My seventeenth birthday was the best day of my life. My Suzuki GN125 had been teasing me outside the dining-room window for three weeks as I wasn't able to ride it until I turned seventeen. My mother had bought it for me before she moved her new family to Carlisle in the summer. I had admired it daily and polished it vigorously until it looked brand new. I made mental plans for road trips up and down the country during my sixth-form holidays.

My first ride out had only been into the local town, Huntingdon, and back, I was unsteady at first. I had completed my compulsory bike training in the spring but hadn't ridden a bike since. The gears seemed more responsive and I pulled away too sharply on occasions but after about half an hour I nailed it. It must be in the blood. My mum is a biker, my granddad was a racer and my step-granddad won the TT before an accident ended his career.

I returned home feeling elated. I picked up the mail, so happy that I jumped up and down in my leathers. The house was empty. My father was at work and my brother was out. I wanted to go somewhere, any excuse to ride again, but I was hungry and had homework to finish. School started early the next day, or rather college as I prefer to say. The sixth-form building is attached to the same school I had attended since I moved in with my dad when I was eleven. It was still two weeks until half term. I thought my first major journey would be to see my mum.

I kicked off my boots and sat awkwardly on the sofa. My new leathers were not flexible enough yet; I was stiff and uncomfortable but reluctant to take them off. I sifted through the mail. There were birthday cards from my grandparents and an old delinquent friend, Denny, whom I had kept in touch with since primary school. There was also a small package. It had no name on, just the address; Heptagon House, Elsworth, Cambridgeshire. I thought it must be for me as it was my birthday. Inside was a memory stick. It wasn't in its packaging, just on its own. Still, it must be for me.

I got up and switched on the downstairs computer, then went into the kitchen while it booted up. The phone rang before I had put the bread in the toaster. It was Dad.

'Hey, Aril, I wasn't sure if you'd still be in or on your bike.'

'Just got in now.'

'How was it?' he asked.

'It was amazing. It rides really well. Had it up to seventy inside ten.'

'Wait, you what?'

'Relax! I'm joking. I kept at forty but it was awesome.' I love winding him up.

'Good. Remember rule number one?'

'Yeah, don't die,' I laughed.

My dad had never been keen on me having a bike. I spoke about having one for ages and I know I played on Mum's kindness. My dad didn't know about it until the last minute. My mum was moving her ever-growing family away and the bike was her joint birthday-leaving present. I would only see her now during major holidays. My dad had lectured me about safety. He had seen too many serious accidents to be confident about me having a bike.

I also have a defensive temperament sometimes. In the past, I would throw the game controllers if I was frustrated at a video game or aggressively give up on a task if I couldn't perfect it to my high standards. I need to prove myself. Rule number one was carved in stone. God help me if I came home dead.

We spoke for about ten minutes and made arrangements to meet with the family for a meal in the evening. I would have preferred pizza but he wanted something a bit more up-market. It was a double celebration.

After I ate, I plugged the memory stick into the computer. There was a single document called 'Heptagon House'. On opening, the message simply read:

52.8588   -0.6813   Red star. What is your name?

So this must have been for my dad after all. He runs an observatory about twenty minutes' drive from our house in the Cambridgeshire countryside. As much as I get my passion for two-wheeled independence from my mother, Dad is responsible for one of my other major passions. My bedroom is a mini planetarium: wall maps of the night sky from both hemispheres, mobiles of each planet from our solar system dangle from the ceiling, which is painted black with tiny glow stars. I worked with Dad to try and recreate constellations in their current positions. I would love to be an astrophysicist when I finish my education but I am struggling with mathematics at college so these good intentions could be limited by my abilities. I'd be more than happy to take over my father's job.

I was on a high all day from my ride out and felt confident about taking the bike in to college. I couldn't wait for the next day. I stayed at home as Dad was expected back early. I wrote thank-you letters for my presents, replied to the fifty-four birthday Facebook messages and smartened myself up. My brother, Harvey, returned from his walk. I thought he had forgotten my birthday but he entered my room with a smile and insulting card – as I would expect from him. Not that I was expecting the £50 voucher inside from the local bike shop. He knew I was looking to customise the bike. I was genuinely touched.

My dad, Dale Ousby, was exceptionally jolly when he got in. The observatory had just received funding for an extension of the facility and a new telescope. It was the culmination of two years' work. I was happy for him. He had worked late for many nights and had been travelling all over the world meeting with people. There had been one stumbling block after another and I was worried that it was taking its toll on his health. He hadn't been cooking, merely snacking, and anything worthy of calling a meal was a shove-it-in-the-oven thirty-minute plastic effort. No wonder he wanted to eat out at one of Cambridge's finest diners.

I don't do posh well. I have long brown hair which has grown past my shoulders. I like the alternative look, though have fallen short of the goatee or any piercings as yet. I'm not good with pain. I suppose I fit the biker stereotype but, as much as I like rock music, I have a broad taste in music. I like anything with a decent melody. Though I do play guitar and skateboarding is still a guilty pleasure. I put on a black shirt and my only pair of trousers that were not jeans.

I told Dad about the memory stick. He said he would look at it after the meal. He wasn't expecting anything and there were a number of red stars that it could refer to, but his observatory specifically investigated double stars. These are two stars that appear to be a single star – either because they are close or one is in the path of the other, even if they are light years apart. His observatory searches for and identifies them and their properties, and maps them for further observations by more powerful telescopes.

The meal rounded my day off perfectly. Marinated chicken breast with a feast of vegetables and tiramisu for dessert – the best meal I had eaten all year. It was good to see the family again too. My uncle and his family had travelled from Norwich and my grandma also came along. She was a card, a rebel in her day. She had successfully fought off two attempts from cancer to finish her off. She was a fighter and having none of it. I still visit her regularly and she makes the best bread-and-butter pudding on the planet.

I showed Dad the memory stick after we got home. He was puzzled. The numbers didn't look like the coordinates of the sky which are specific measurements in Right Ascension (RA) and Declination (Dec) and are usually in decimal degrees or even hours, minutes and seconds. These numbers were shorter, too vague. He suggested they were more like Longitude and Latitude coordinates. It was more likely to be: 52.8588 degrees North and 0.6813 West – a negative being west of the 0 degrees Greenwich Meridian line. We looked on Google Maps for an idea of where these coordinates could refer to and they were in England – about an hour's drive away in Lincolnshire. What would the red star have to do with it? Dad was puzzled. The location appeared to be in the middle of nowhere, possibly at the edge of, or very close to, a single-lane country road three miles south-west of Grantham. I made it my mission to ride out there on Saturday and take a look.

– CHAPTER 2 –

St. Louis, Missouri, USA

Dean Hatfield left the house shortly after noon. The office had called: a delivery van had broken down just off Highway 44, about fifteen miles out of town. It was urgent and they were flustered. They arranged for Dean to collect the parcel at the roadside rather than risk it being delayed. Dean reluctantly agreed as he was half awake and still fighting a hangover. The previous night had been his girlfriend's twenty-first birthday and he'd joined her celebrations. He had officially booked the day off, knowing that he could be suffering. One of the perils of working in a family business was that family was always priority over the job itself.

The traffic was busy getting out of town. Dean had thrown on a pair of blue jeans and a Cardinals top but made little effort other than a comb through his short, untidy blond hair. He would shave and shower when he got back. He was pleased his Aviators were in the car; the glare-back from the sun was not helping his thick head.

Forty-five minutes later, he was still stuck in traffic three miles east of Eureka. The road was gridlocked and he assessed from the noise of sirens that there was probably an accident up ahead. He decided to get off the highway at 269 and use local roads. He was getting lost and cursing traffic so he pulled over and phoned the office, ready to abandon the job. Luckily they were able to contact the van driver who left his GPS. Dean hoped he had enough charge on his Satnav to get there. Finally, after ninety minutes, he arrived.

'Sorry,' Dean said immediately to the man who came out the van, flustered. The van's engine was running.

'One of them days,' the man replied, looking up at the highway above them. 'I had to wait for garage to come and fix this anyway. Was praying this thing wouldn't overheat before you got here. I need your autograph,' he said as he walked around the side of the van to get the parcel. Or so Dean thought.

The man opened the side door then put his arm around Dean's waist and, that very second, another man lunged from inside the van and pulled him in. It happened so fast, there was no time to struggle. Dean rolled on the floor, making an involuntary yell as the van door shut behind him. He looked up to see a third man in a dark suit pointing a gun at him.

'Your cell phone Mr Hatfield. Now,' the man said, holding out a hand.

Dean didn't have time to think or assess anything and didn't want to argue with a gun. He handed his phone without a word, just staring at the gun, trembling.

– CHAPTER 3 –

I was up early that Saturday. I had already planned out the route. According to Google Maps, these mystery coordinates led to arable farmland but there was a small country lane very close by. The rides to college had been relatively uneventful, despite the odd car that had only seen me at the last minute. I was getting used to the feel of the bike now so I was confident about making the ride, in spite of my dad's worries.

It was quiet, too, even though it was a clear day. The Cambridgeshire countryside isn't known for being the most picturesque, even if the villages are quaint and typically English. The Lincolnshire countryside is the same. Lincolnshire is steeped in history but is virtually unknown compared to most other counties. It is probably most famous for stealing a 1,600 year record held by the Lighthouse of Alexandria when Lincoln Cathedral became the tallest building in the world in the Middle Ages. That was the only fact I knew about the place.

The big problem with being young and still on a provisional license was that I wasn't allowed on the motorways so I couldn't take the most direct route and my one-hour journey became almost two. Luckily I had a good memory for maps and directions, so I didn't get lost and found my way back onto the A1 without trouble.

I was doing well with the bike on the main roads but had

a scare just before my turn off into the countryside. A truck thundered past as I was slowing to turn without giving me much room and I could feel the bike being sucked into the side-wind. As a result, my turn was wider than I had allowed for and I found myself on the wrong side of the road. It was a miracle that there was no traffic waiting, otherwise I would have hit it. The manoeuvre unnerved me and I pulled over at a layby a few hundred yards down the road to compose myself. I could see how easily accidents could happen. I needed a bigger bike. It sucked being seventeen.

The lane was very narrow, little more than an access road for the farmers between the fields. The area around was so flat that it was hard to see anything beyond the roads and hedges, and even the hedges seemed somewhat arbitrary. I had worked out that the location point was about two miles west of the main road; that was a bit vague but I had noticed a cluster of trees on the roadside and that was my landmark.

I pulled up by a gate and decided to take a stroll. I was hot and the autumn sun's heat was being leached by the black of my leathers. I took off my helmet and left it with my bike. I could easily see anybody approaching and I wasn't going too far.

I didn't know what I was looking for but I enjoyed being out and having some freedom with my bike. I was still shaky from my scare at the junction though, and flashbacks of potentially bad scenarios burnt into my thoughts. I had to lecture myself to regain control of my wandering mind.

I wondered if I should have made this journey at night. Maybe I needed to look up to a red star from this point? Or did they mean the red planet, Mars? Most people look up to the sky and don't know the difference between stars and planets.

The road was completely empty. I thought it was probably only used by farmers tending the land. I could see the spires of a town in the distance, which I thought was Grantham. I had never visited the place but I would get some lunch there before heading home. I scanned each tree as I passed, looking for a red star that might have been painted on the bark. I kept thinking of the message and wondering why it would ask for my name.

I continued for about half a mile, looking up but also down into the wild grass and nettles of the undergrowth. The point on the map seemed to be on the south side of the road but I thought I should check the other side as I walked back to the bike, to allow for a margin of error. The trees were my guide but I had walked way beyond them now. By the time I returned to the bike I had found nothing. I stared at the sky, wishing that I had thought of coming later in the day with a telescope.

I looked back at the trees, contemplating a venture into the small wooded area. It wasn't so much the nettles that made me reluctant but that I'd seen too many horror films. I stood beside the bike with my helmet in my hand, looking into the wood, edging nearer all the time.

Something caught my eye. Just inside the wood, beyond the ditch, there was a little container at the foot of a tree. It was small, about the size of a drinks can. Curious, I edged further forward, and that's when I saw it. There was a small deep-red seven-point star embossed on the top of the container with an ellipse around it.

I felt a rush of adrenaline and hurried to the container. It looked fairly new, the kind of stainless steel can that you might use in a kitchen to store spices or sugar. The lid was hard to prise open because the damp had got to it a little, but eventually I separated it from the base. Inside was a rolled piece of paper and a pendant. The pendant looked old, antique, it was on a silver-coloured chain, possibly real silver; it had a grey stone that seemed to have a sheen to it giving it a coral or pearl effect, though it looked too grey to be a pearl. It was contained in an ornate wire cage. I unrolled the paper and read:

Good work. Leave me your name, you'll find a way. Do you have a dream you cherish? Something that you want to do so badly that you would do anything for? Curiosity is one of mankind's greatest traits. How curious are you? I have a treasure for you that would outshine your wildest dreams. 51.6517 0.5258 take this gift and you'll figure out when.

Treasure? An actual real treasure hunt? This is the kind of thing you only dream of. I read *Charlie and the Chocolate Factory* when I was about nine and used to fantasise about what it would be like to find the golden ticket. This was better still. This was personal. I surrendered to my curiosity in an instant. I was already thinking about how to leave my name. I had nothing on me with my name and no pen either. I really hadn't thought this through.

I stood up, looking around for inspiration. Just above the hollow of the tree but about 90 degrees to the right was a flat knot, as if a branch had been sheared at some time. I used my garage key to engrave ARIL on it as clearly as possible. I looked around for some sticks and found some small twigs. I grazed them with the key, which exposed the bark, making them white, and laid them into a recognisable arrow on the floor, pointing to the right. At the base, I leaned a bigger stick with the end sheared of at the top, which rested just under my engraved name.

I looked around me searching for cameras, wondering if anybody was watching. *Why was the memory stick sent to my house?* I had so many questions as I walked back to the bike. I couldn't wait to tell Mum; she would be jealous. It would have been good to do this together on our bikes.

I set off for Grantham, being extra careful when I slowed to turn. That incident had knocked my confidence a little and I was extra aware of the traffic, so I was pleased to park in the town. I found a café with seats outside and table service. I was glad to sit down, even if I was still restricted by my leathers.

I ordered food then tried to use my smart phone to work

out the new location. It seemed to lead south of home, near Chelmsford in Essex. It would probably take three or four hours to get there from here, avoiding the motorways.

I looked at the message and pendant again. *You'll figure out when?* Does that mean the next clue isn't there yet? I was looking at the pendant, wondering what the stone was, when my lunch arrived. The waitress was probably my age, if not younger.

'Who's the lucky girl?' she asked.

'Ah, nobody,' I replied, taken aback by her interest. 'I'm trying to work out what the stone is.'

She took the pendant from me and studied it. 'I used to collect gemstones. I should know but my memory is shite. It could be moonstone,' she suggested.

She continued studying it as I studied her. She was pretty, quite petite with very dark, almost black shoulder-length hair. She had faint freckles and very white teeth that drew your eyes to her smile. Her nail polish was black and silver which gave an alternative edge to her as well. Our attention was broken by a woman calling her from inside. 'Summer! Get a move on – I need you.'

She raised her eyes and handed the pendant back to me. 'Moonstone,' she said again. 'I'd put money on it.' She smiled again and went inside the café.

Summer? Was her name really Summer or was that a nickname? I was sure that's what the woman called her. This was turning out to be a good day.

I ate my lunch whilst checking up images of moonstones on my phone. It looked like she was right. They looked similar to my stone and mine had a bluish tinge to it in the light as well.

I looked up every now and then but Summer rarely came out, and she looked more flustered now when she did. I felt guilty, worried that she was in trouble for talking to me. I went inside to pay and made eye contact with her again as I was about to leave.

'You were right, I think,' I said as I was near the door.

'Of course,' she replied, smiling as she continued to clean a table.

***

The journey home took longer. The roads were busy and I was cautious. It was hard to think straight; my mind was jumping ahead of itself, wondering what the treasure might be.

When I got home, I just wanted to take off the leathers. They might look good but they were hell to wear in this heat. Harvey was home on his X-Box, hogging the main television, and he grunted in acknowledgement as I entered. I knew better than to disturb him in the middle of a boss fight but I was desperate to talk to somebody. My dad was still out at the observatory.

I had a shower and then sat on my bed in my boxers and dressing gown with a towel wrapped around my head. I looked up the coordinates in finer detail on my laptop. The location appeared to lead to a quiet country road close to Hanningfield Reservoir, about four miles north of Wickford in Essex.

When? When? When? I kept asking myself. I was supposed to use the pendant to find out when. But how? I heard a car pull into the drive and looked out of my window. Dad was back. I wrapped the dressing gown round me and sprinted downstairs. I couldn't wait to tell him my news.

I caught his attention the moment he walked in but I wasn't expecting him to have company. I froze as a neatly dressed woman followed him in. She was tall with long red hair, which was tied up in a loose bun. She was slim and elegant, pretty and... *Dad had brought a woman back?*

I completely forgot what I was going to say.

'Hey Aril, I'd like you to meet Eva.'

'Hey, um I'm sorry I've just had a shower.' I couldn't think of anything to say other than state the obvious. Dad went into the living room, seemingly oblivious to my shock. My parents split up more than ten years ago; in all that time he had never brought a woman home with him. Harvey looked up from his game and was much less tactful.

'Woah!' he said as caught sight of Eva. He removed his feet from the coffee table and stared at Eva as Dad made the introductions. Then he looked at me as I stood in the doorway with my mouth open.

'Eva is the new Operations Manager at Brayebrook. She will be in charge of overseeing the extension.' He laughed. 'I told you they'd die of shock.' He winked at Eva and they both went into the kitchen, offering us a coffee. I looked over at Harvey and he put his hand to his chest.

'I nearly had a heart attack then,' he joked.

'I know, right.'

I thought I would have to keep my secret a little longer but Dad asked me about my trip as he returned to the sitting room and handed me my coffee. I was hesitant at first; I wasn't sure if I could trust Eva. I decided to give him limited information.

'I found a container with new coordinates,' I said. I figured I could explain that much at least, without disclosing details of the note.

'Ah, a geocache' Eva said, smiling. She spoke softly with a slight accent, I couldn't place.

'What's that?' I asked.

'It's all the rage at the moment. My ex-boyfriend was into it. There's an app for it. It's a world-wide thing. You're supposed to leave your name and a gift and a possibly a clue to the next one.'

'Oh. Is it open to everybody?' I was disappointed. I had thought that this was for me personally.

'I think so. You can get a map online of where every cache is. There will be some near here, I would imagine. Some are very difficult to find.'

Maybe there wasn't treasure after all. I could have been anybody. I tried to think quickly. *Why would they have posted that memory stick directly to the house?* I explained about the pendant but not about the clue. Eva looked at it.

'This is quite a find. Most times there's nothing of any value. I wonder what stone this is.'

'Moonstone!' I said, excitedly. Summer's smile flashed into my mind.

'Of course,' she said. That was second time I had heard those words today and by two different females, both of whom shocked me for different reasons. I was still trying to hide my disappointment about geocaching. I thought this was a real treasure hunt.

I explained a little more. 'I'm supposed to try and work out from the pendant when the next geocache, or whatever it is, will be there.'

'A lot of gemstones are associated with various months. I know I'm sapphire,' Eva said putting her hand out to show off a sapphire ring. 'My birthday is in September.'

'Or it could mean the moon cycles,' my father said, finally entering the conversation, diverting quackery to astronomy as you would expect. 'Maybe the next full moon or new moon?' he added.

'Possibly.'

'How far is the next location?' he asked.

'Near Chelmsford in Essex. Under an hour by car, longer on the bike.'

'Moon day,' Eva interrupted. I looked at her, not quite knowing what she was getting at. 'Moon day? Monday? The days of the week are named after, or associated with, the solar system. Sun day, Saturn day.'

'Oh. I never thought of that. Even Wednesday?'

This made her laugh. 'Yes, even Wednesday. Wodenaz was a Germanic God in the Roman era and is associated with the planet Mercury.'

'Maybe look up the next time a Monday falls on a full moon?' Dad offered.

I excused myself, desperate to go and get my laptop and investigate. I needed clothes too. I was still a little shocked that my father had brought home a woman, even if she was a colleague. He was at ease with her. She seemed alright from first impressions. I checked the next full moon and though it wasn't Monday, it still felt right. For the next hour I looked up geocaching. Eva was right; it seemed to be a normal sort of hiding place and type of container though they all had a specific symbol, not a red star. I subscribed for a month and tried to locate the one I had just found, as well as the coordinates from the note I found inside. Neither of them seemed to be on the site. There were three geocaches within a mile of my house; one was on the way to college. I thought I would investigate sometime in the following week.

I returned to the family for dinner. I was warming to Eva. I think Harvey thought of her as a novelty but it was nice to see Dad with another woman, even if it was a bit surreal. After she left, I showed Dad the note. He seemed convinced it was a geocache sent as a prank, possibly to many different random houses in the area. Maybe he was right.

College ended early on Monday so I could go straight after college. It wouldn't take me too long. If I did find something then I would assess it. If it was just a carbon copy of the last cache, or if there wasn't any direct message to me and it seemed like a standard geocache, then I'd give up on it. But I *had* to know.

– CHAPTER 4 –

Columbus, Georgia, USA

Triana Perry couldn't believe her luck. Her three o'clock cancelled, which meant she only had one viewing today. She could set off early to Chicago for her long weekend away with her boyfriend, Milo. The viewing was about thirteen miles from Columbus in a small town of Cataula but she should be home by lunch.

She left Milo to pack up the car; the journey would take twelve hours but they had done it before. His parents owned a small lodge off Dune Acres on the banks of Lake Michigan. It had been nearly a year since they had spent a weekend alone together. Triana worked for her father's ever-expanding real estate empire. He had offices all over the Mid States and business was booming, despite the downturn in the property market. He had specialised niches for supplying contract work for power companies and lobbied political contacts to encourage growth in key areas of his own interest. Ashton Perry was a very influential man.

Triana was in charge of listing new properties for sale. She sold the company's services to vendors, measured up and took photographs and discussed valuations. She had done her homework before heading out to Cataula. Denney Road real estate was popular but she couldn't find previous owner notes on this particular property. She left a little earlier to tour the area and make a note of comparable houses.

She was a pro now. She had been doing this for six years but she had only been working in Columbus for eighteen months – since Milo asked her to transfer from the family home in Atlanta so she could be with him. He was a mortgage broker for the firm in Columbus. He already had a park-side property in the city, *Ashton Approved*.

Milo had been keen for this weekend away, exceptionally keen. Could this be the weekend he finally proposed? She was excited and eager to get the working day over.

Triana arrived half an hour before her planned meeting. She could see the property from the roadside but didn't pull in. She drove on, taking in the area. Most of the properties had private drives which distanced them from the roadside. It was very quiet, very flat and very private.

She pulled over at the far end of the town and checked her makeup in the mirror, reapplying her mascara. Her eyes were exceptionally blue today; she couldn't hide her excitement. She deliberated pinning her hair back or letting it fall, playing with it for a while, but opted for the pin because it looked more professional. She released a few strands either side of her temples so that it didn't look quite so severe. These wisps framed her oval face and she felt pretty for once; she was rarely happy with how she looked.

It was nearly eleven. Triana headed back towards town and into the drive of the property. There was a van in the driveway. Her first impression was one of disappointment. Unlike the other houses in the area, this property looked as if it had been neglected for years. A side window was broken and the garden hadn't been touched in months, if at all this year. Bags of trash and timber were dumped against the side of the garage, along with a mattress. The place probably wouldn't show well in photographs; they would have to tidy it up first.

Triana knocked on the door but there was no answer. She peered into the windows, which were dirty and full of cobwebs; the place seemed derelict. How could anybody live here? She looked at the van. There didn't appear to be anybody in the front.

'Hello,' she shouted as she walked slowly towards the van. There was no answer. The owners must not be here yet. She took out her camera and looked at the image of the property through the view-finder. Maybe it wouldn't look too bad from the side, as long as she didn't have the garage in view. She took a few steps back to capture as much of the building in the picture as she could. She was trying to think of a realistic value; she might need somebody to survey the brickwork to see if it needed rebuilding.

As she stepped back, a heavily-built man appeared from her left from behind an outbuilding and startled her.

'Miss Perry?' he asked.

'Yes,' she said, reaching in her pocket for a business card.

'Good,' he said. He swept his arm around the back of her legs, picked her up and carried her to the van. Triana screamed but the man didn't say a word, just kept walking. The side door of the van opened and he dropped her inside. Another hand grabbed her wrist as she reached for her purse. A man in a smartly pressed blue suit took hold of her purse as her robust escort closed the side door.

Triana was too scared to scream. She looked in disbelief at the two men who were now in front of her as she hastily shuffled back behind the front seats, cradling her knees.

One of the men took her phone from her purse, switched it off and pointed a gun at her. He spoke quietly and confidently. 'Shhh. We are going for a ride.'

– CHAPTER 5 –

Monday morning dragged. I had my plan of action and even prepared a packed lunch so that I could make my journey straight from college. The work was getting harder each week. I had always been good at mathematics and the sciences and achieved mostly grade As in my GCSE exams but A level was so much harder. I was warned but wasn't prepared as much as I thought I was. It's a bit disheartening to be told that everything you'd already learned was merely the foundations for a more complex truth. If I stand a chance of having a career in astrophysics then I need to master this, but my mind seems incapable and day by day my self-confidence is diminishing.

Maybe I was just too distracted. All day Sunday I was in dream mode, wondering what treasures could be discovered from my new obsession.

It took half an hour to get to my bike after college ended. One of my musician friends, Po (real name Poulan Saks), had been bugging me for weeks to join his band. He is a drummer-singer, extremely charismatic and frustratingly hard to ignore and, at that moment, he was a pain in my arse. Somehow I ended up agreeing to join his band in their next rehearsal on Thursday. I ended up feeling like I was his treasure. He was drowning in ego for getting me to agree. I just wanted to get on my bike!

I finally set off, feeling like a *Wild Hog*. Each journey was a new adventure and I had a genuine reason to ride into the unknown. I contemplated getting a camera to attach to my helmet. I'd seen a few video diaries on YouTube from bikers who documented their road trips. Their videos have hundreds of thousands of views and must make them a living from advertising and merchandise. I was kicking myself for not thinking of it sooner.

The journey was a nightmare. I had to avoid motorway sections by travelling on minor roads, so it was around three-thirty when I headed into the final section of country lanes in search of the next clue or cache or whatever. Again, a cluster of trees was my landmark. This road was busier than the one near Grantham, despite still being a narrow country lane, and there were more buildings and farms. There was a layby I could pull into not far from the location point but I was less confident about leaving my bike. I needed to be at the far end of the trees so I pulled in as close as I could, in the hope that I could see the bike if I needed to go a little further into the trees. I took my helmet with me. Luckily it was cooler today and overcast, so I didn't have to battle with the heat as much.

I searched for about twenty minutes without success. When I was researching geocaching I had noticed that the GPS coordinates were eight digits rather than six. My coordinates were more Ordinance-Survey based, so my field of exploration was much broader than it needed to be. Was I still looking for the same container I had left at Grantham? Maybe it was the wrong Monday or maybe I should have come later in the day. I was getting frustrated. As much as I loved the ride out on my bike, it was a long way to come for nothing. No, it was the disappointment that was bugging me. My imagination had carried me away and this frustration was disappointing. All the same, if I was right and there was something here, I would never forgive myself if I didn't look hard enough.

My legs ached. I still wasn't used to long bike journeys and I needed to sit down. I found a low branch and set my helmet aside so that I could think. I picked at small pieces of bark from my temporary seat, some covered in moss, and threw them to the ground in front of me. It had to be here eventually, it was just a matter of *when*.

My phone rang. I fumbled into my zipped pockets and found it just before it cut out.

I think my dad was as curious as me. 'Any luck?' he asked.

'Not yet, I've been down here half an hour. It's like looking for a needle in a...'

There was movement at the roadside. I was silent for a few seconds and stood up. There was an executive-looking car parked in the layby but that wasn't what alerted me. I was sure there was movement near the bike.

'Aril?' I heard Dad say.

'Hold up, Dad, I'll phone you back in a sec,' I whispered and hung up.

There was somebody at my bike. I knew it! I ran as fast as I could, my feet catching in the brambles. The car started pulling away before I reached the bike but I was relieved it was still there. A quick scan revealed no damage. By the time I looked up again, the car was too far away for me to catch the number plate. Maybe they were just looking at it but I could have sworn I saw the front wheel turn. I certainly didn't want to leave it again.

A small twig had somehow become lodged into the front wheel so I removed it, then noticed something as it landed. There was a stick on the floor in front of the bike with the bark sheared, just as I had done on Saturday. It pointed towards the trees but forward from the position where I was.

Curiosity guided me away from the bike again as I made my way back into the wooded area. About twenty yards in, I saw another stick pointing to my left. I continued a little further, looking around for any more markers, but there didn't seem to be any. I eventually came to the end of the wooded area and into a field. I thought I must have come too far by now. I turned back and that's when I noticed a stick propped up against a tree, in the same way that I had left one at the weekend. Yes, it had the end sheared as well.

I looked at the trunk and down below but there was nothing there. I walked around the tree, puzzled, before looking up. There was thin rope; it didn't look new and was a grey-brown that camouflaged it against the tree. I had missed it at first.

I pulled at it gently and saw the edge of a canister tied to the other end, resting in a hollow that had to be ten feet up. I gave the rope another tug and the canister came down. Thankfully the lid stayed on. It looked the same as the one before. By now I was shaking with excitement and had completely forgotten about the bike.

Inside, there was another rolled-up note and a pair of sunglasses. I opened the note. I was right; this was personal:

> *Aril,*
>
> *You have impressed me so far. Very nice work with the sticks, I like your thinking. You show good initiative. You are young, I gather, as well as clever. This is a bonus.*
>
> *There is a delightful irony behind your name, Aril. It is a mythological Etruscan version of the titan Atlas and he is paired with Phoebe, who governs the moon. Atlas carried the weight of the world on his shoulders. Do you, Aril? Do you ever feel that the burden of living prevents you from dreaming? I bet you've fantasised about this moment and about what treasure lies waiting at the end, about how far you will go. It's good to dream, Aril. Society takes away your right to dream, so never give up on your dreams. Never let them die. Let your heart and intuition guide you. Be creative, look to the universe with wonder and see yourself for what you really are.*
>
> *I need you to help me with my dream, Aril. In return, I will help you create yours. What price is trust, Aril? What value can it hold? Look outside*

*this hunt, look to the world for the bigger picture.
The sooner you piece the puzzles, the greater the
prize will be. Are you worthy of this legacy?
56.3911 –4.2136 You already know when.*

'Wow!' I just kept saying it over and over. I couldn't think of any other words. This was *real*.

I stood there, not knowing what to do. I didn't think I could put the canister back in its hiding place. I had to find somewhere else close by. Question after question demanded answers that I was too excited to be patient about. I felt I should leave a reply. Were these rhetorical questions or did he or she want me to answer them?

My phone rang and startled me. My dad of course, I felt guilty. 'Sorry,' I said immediately as I answered.

'Is everything alright?'

'Yes. I found it. The note is addressed to me personally.' I was talking quickly but I heard Dad say *Oh wow* as I continued. 'There are sunglasses and he speaks of helping him with his dreams and asks if I'm worthy of this legacy.'

I was still hyper and Dad tried to calm me. 'Slow down, soldier. Before you get too carried away or commit yourself to anything, we need to have a proper look.'

I took a breath. I knew he was right but I wanted this, wherever it led. It might be a mistake but at that moment it was a chance I was willing to take.

'I'm going to leave a note to say yes and come home before it gets too dark. I can always back out later,' I offered as a compromise.

'Fine. Don't leave it too long or you'll have rush hour to contend with.'

'OK, see you later.'

I had a pen on me this time but no paper. I found a petrol receipt in my pocket and left a note.

*I'm a dreamer. I'll be there Sunday. Somehow.
What's your name? Aril.*

I drew a star with an ellipse around it after my name. I felt compelled to leave something personal, I don't know why. The only thing I had on me was a guitar pick. It was my favourite so I hesitated but then thought it might show a shared trust. I dropped it into the canister with my receipt, then looked for a suitable hiding place.

It was difficult to find anywhere that was close enough and it started bugging me. I would need a ladder to shimmy up the tree to put it back where it was. *How did the canister get up there?* I looked at the stick that was propped up against the tree. It had a Y shape at the base. I had an idea. I tied the end of the rope around the canister again and hooked the Y of the stick close to its end. It took some doing, but I managed to get the canister back in the hollow at the top of the branch. You certainly couldn't see it. It took several attempts to unhook the stick without exposing the canister again but I did it. I left the rope dangling the way it was before. I propped the stick back against the tree but Y-side up to show that I had been there.

***

I was exhausted and hungry by the time I got home, just after seven. I had a few near misses and nearly got lost too. I was trying to pay attention to the road but the mystery was fragmenting my thoughts.

I hoped that the next clue would be closer to home. I was wrong. The coordinates took me to Scotland, near the village of Lochearnhead. I plugged in the direction online from Elsworth, avoiding motorways: 411 miles, 9 hours and 31 minutes.

I had a problem.

– CHAPTER 6 –

One thing more terrifying than a scream is the silence of fear. Martin Wildwood awoke in unfamiliar surroundings. His head ached and his limbs were stiff from the long ride in the van. His captors didn't entertain any questions, their voices as cold as the barrel of the gun they pointed at him every time he spoke.

The room was eerily quiet, claustrophobic and dark, the only light coming from two holes in the ceiling, which had been filled by plastic bottles with some luminous liquid inside them. They gave off a strange light, like weak fluorescent bulbs. He had no concept of time. He had no cell phone and wasn't wearing his watch. He couldn't tell if it was daylight outside. There were no windows; the walls were grey thermal blocks. But he was grateful there was a single bed, a small toilet and a hand basin.

Martin suppressed the urge to scream. His captors had made it quite clear there was zero tolerance for such efforts. *Any attempt to escape or draw attention will result in the gun being used – have no doubt.*

He was so scared he felt sick. How long had the journey been? At least eighteen hours. He only left the van on three occasions to relieve himself and each time the van had pulled over on a quiet section of the highway. All drinks and snack-food had been given to him inside the van. He thought he was maybe in Texas or California, but he could have been anywhere.

He wondered if anybody had realised he was missing. They might think he had gone away after his showdown the previous day. He knew he was renowned for childish tantrums. His father was CEO of a company in Des Moines, Iowa, which specialised in the production of GM foods. Maybe Martin had a selection of silver spoons that he grew up with, but he was rich, right? It was a privilege. He figured his captors were activists against his father's work. He needed to bargain with them. He had money; he could get them what they wanted or fund what they needed, as long as they let him out.

Maybe he should have realised something was wrong. He'd been stupid. When Blencarn, or O'Brien as he was referred to out of earshot, refused him time off for a golfing trip to Europe, Martin had kicked off. He cringed now, cursing his temper. When he got angry his brain shut down and a spew of verbal trash oozed out. He had left the lab threatening Douglas Blencarn with his father's wrath, claiming he was going anyway.

The European offer had come from a guy Martin had met at his regular Sunday golfing meeting. The man was staying in the area, apparently scouting for good minds and connections with an equally impressive golfing handicap to raise the profile of illustrious clients. Martin should never have agreed to meet him. The proposition was obviously too good to be true but common sense seems to work in hindsight when you're twenty-three. He had arranged to meet the guy near Willow Creek Golf Course. He was going to say yes and suffer the consequences later. The guy was even going to pay for flights and accommodation. They wanted Martin to make a speech about the company. Or so he thought.

When he arrived, he was still in a mood from his argument.

'Mr Wildwood,' the guy said enthusiastically as Martin approached him. 'Glad you could make it, I have somebody who would like to meet you.' He continued shaking Martin's hand then he led him to a transit van with a sliding side door.

The burly man who opened the door appeared to be the driver. Martin climbed inside where there were side benches. He sat down casually then looked up to talk to the men, only to have a gun aimed at his head.

'We're going for a ride Mr Wildwood. Just sit still, relax and don't say a word. Understand?'

'Hey, what's going…'

'Understand?'

Martin nodded as the safety catch was unclipped. He wasn't in a position to argue. 'Good. Now hand me your cell phone.'

Martin sat quietly throughout the long journey. His head was covered as he was taken from the van and he was led to this room. Now what? There was just this unbearable silence amplifying the ringing in his ears from the noise of the journey.

He felt sick.

– CHAPTER 7 –

I regretted committing myself to band practice not just because Po didn't let up on reminding me about it all week, but also because he was nudging me constantly to use our garage for further rehearsals. It was as if I was already a permanent band member – and I had no intention of being one. Maybe this was his ulterior motive all along.

Elsworth is a small village halfway between Huntingdon and Cambridge. The house is quite unique and full of character, which is why my father bought it. It was built in the shape of a heptagon; there are seven sides to the main building and all of the rooms are oddly shaped, which makes arranging furniture feel like completing a Tetris puzzle. The roof is like a chiselled dome with an attic room underneath, with skylight windows. Dad uses this as his private study-observatory.

I was banned from entering the room for about a year after my friends caused damage up there. It was a novelty I suppose, but I took pleasure in the attention I got from being the only boy in school with an observatory and powerful telescope. I used to have sleepovers when I was about fifteen, camping for all-nighters, watching the movement of the sky. It was fun, but we were clumsy; we broke the telescope's mount and my dad was not happy. Shame really, because I enjoyed it up there. It was a thinking space.

That last note had touched something inside me, like a spark of nostalgia, when it said to *look to the universe with wonder*. I do, frequently.

The garage is separated from the main house by a pebbled yard. It's never really used for the car; it's a mini bachelor pad. There is a pool table, dartboard and video game machine inside and the rest is used for storage. It would be easy to set up a rehearsal room there for the band – even the neighbours are not too close because all the houses on the lane are detached. But I just knew Po would abuse things; he was a control freak. I really couldn't join a band. Not right now.

Dad wasn't keen on the idea of me riding up to Scotland on my own. It would be a major trip because I had to avoid motorways. Even though it would be half term, and I was already planning to see my mother in Carlisle, it was still a long way to go.

I phoned Mum to explain everything to her. She was as excited as me, though also hesitant about the journey. She said she would phone my father and discuss a plan; she had an idea.

It was the last lesson of the day – physics in room L14. Po was in my class. I couldn't escape, I had to at least see out the band practice that night and then let him down gently. He knew I could play guitar. I could listen to a song and learn it in half an hour, without looking at the sheet music. When I moved in with my father, he paid for guitar lessons and I learned quickly; my tutor told him I was his most gifted student. After two years, the music school closed, but I'd learned enough by then and crafted my technique.

Po gravitated to me the instant the bell went. 'All set, bro?' he said, smacking me on the back with enough momentum to bend me forward.

'Yeah, yeah. I need to get my leathers, mind.'

'Great! I'll come with you.'

'Thought you might,' I mumbled sarcastically.

'Well, can't have you backing out now can we?' He knew me too well.

When we got to the hall, the rest of the band was already there and I cringed at Po's introduction of me to them. I was not the greatest guitarist this side of Jupiter, or even this side of town. Nor was I their saviour or, heaven forbid, their permanent replacement guitarist. I had to bluff.

'You know "Teen Spirit" don't you?'

Oh God, not Nirvana, spare me from this madness. 'Erm, yes but…'

'Great! You lead.'

I couldn't even argue. Of all the damned songs, he chose that one. I was in at the deep end. I played the opening riff and Po waited in anticipation for his epic drum-fill moment. He didn't disappoint. In fairness, the bassist played his part. I didn't know him well but Po had known him for years. They formed the band together with the former guitarist and a keyboardist out of school and had performed the odd pub gig. We followed the drum rhythm from that point but Po's fills were somewhat random. The others knew him well enough to improvise and adjust. I lost my way at times and deliberately fed the bassist some confused glances. He rolled his eyes and smiled.

This pattern continued for the next hour or so, covering a number of rock classics. At the end Po summarised. 'I'll give you a seven,' he said, twirling a drumstick between his fingers like a windmill.

'Cheers. Glad I fail. Can I go home now?'

'What? Seven is a definite pass. You just need practice. Consider yourself hired!'

'No thanks.' I grinned at him.

'Nah, uh! Mate, you're in. We should set up at yours over half term. We'll be the Gods of Godmanchester, God dammit.'

'Oh no. I'm up North anyway so that's not an option,' I said.

'Cancel it, Aril. This is more important. You will eat, sleep and breathe these songs.'

'Nice try.' I laughed. 'Maybe my dad will let you use the garage, but you'll have to find another guitarist.'

'Ah man, you're killing me,' he said. 'Ask Dale though and

we'll see.'

I didn't think for one moment that Dad would allow it but it was enough for now to pacify Po. Not that I expected to hear the last of it. I just wanted to get home and think of my plan for next week and work out how the hell I was going to get to Scotland by Sunday.

***

Eva was at home when I got back. Dad said they had to work late, so it was easier to work from home. Harvey had already warned me but I was still shocked to see her in the sitting room. She had a laptop on her knees and two files open to the side, taking up two seats of the sofa. She apologised.

'No, it's OK. I need to change. Where's Dad?'

'Kitchen, cooking.'

'Oh. I'll see if it's still standing,' I joked.

Eva laughed.

My father was indeed cooking. It smelt nice too – onions, peppers, courgettes, chicken. The radio was on quietly. This hadn't happened for years. I pinched myself on the arm and Dad saw. 'Very funny,' he said.

'Smells nice. When is it ready? I need a shower.'

'About twenty minutes. I spoke with your mother. She thinks you should leave after college tomorrow and stay with Denny in Bakewell. That way you have less travelling on Saturday. She reckons you should get a B&B in Scotland overnight Sunday so that you travel back down Monday and stay with her for the rest of the week in Carlisle.'

'I can do that. That will work.'

'I don't like the idea of you going that far, even to Carlisle really, but I have to trust you. Just remember rule one.'

'Yeah, I'll be careful. I don't want to die yet either.'

I hadn't seen Denny since Easter. He was a friend from my junior school and lived on the same street as my mother used to in Bakewell. He was my best long-distance friend. He wasn't the brightest spark, suffered from severe ADHD, but was a shit-hot footballer. He had already been scouted by Forest and had trials, even though there was no contract as yet. He was hopeful. I got changed and phoned him quickly to ask if I could stay. He was made up.

Dinner was surreal but I liked Eva more with each visit. I don't think Dad had spent as long as that in the kitchen since I moved here.

I spent the evening packing ready so that I could leave after college. It was only a rucksack but it was enough for a few days' essentials.

****

Denny pounced on me before I dismounted the bike. I was shattered. The ride had taken nearly three hours. He was desperate for me to take him on the bike and wouldn't understand that not only was it illegal – but also a 125cc bike would probably crumple under the strain of both of our weights. He didn't hide his disapproval either.

'How's football?' I asked quickly, knowing that he was distracted easily.

'It's all good, some guy's coming down next weekend to see us play Wisbech.' His face lit up with delight. 'We should annihilate them, useless suckers.'

Denny's room was chaos. The floor was covered in clothes, snack wrappers, plates and mugs. I stood in the doorway, embarrassed.

'Yeah I tidied it especially for you,' he joked, sensing my shock.

'I can tell. I'm surprised this isn't condemned as a health hazard.'

'It's been worse. You should have given me more notice. It takes me a week just to psyche myself up for it. You want a drink?'

I looked at the state of the mouldy mugs on the floor and shuddered. I shook my head and Denny laughed. I couldn't live like this; my room wasn't always tidy but it was my sanctuary and I never let it get half as bad. Plus Dad would go nuts if I didn't bring my mugs and plates down, so it was a routine I took for granted.

Denny plugged his iPod into the stereo and we talked over the music, catching up on old times. I told him about the hunt; he was jealous but echoed my excitement. He conceded that he wasn't clever enough to work out any of it but asked if he could join me if any clues led me close by. I agreed. As much as he is crazy, I like Denny. He is hyper but always happy and full of this bizarre optimism that seems to touch the people around him.

I didn't sleep too well, not only because of us talking into the early hours but because my makeshift bed was a folded quilt and sleeping bag on the floor. I was aware of rustling noises and visualised mice, rats or giant spiders that had been mutating from the spores in the coffee mugs. I hoped I would be awake enough to ride.

I left early on Saturday morning and stopped at the first roadside services for a strong coffee. The journey to Carlisle was picturesque over the Pennines and the undulating countryside was a majestic backdrop to the freedom of my road trip. It was everything I had imagined it would be. The elation helped to keep my senses sharp, though I did need to make more stops en route for more coffee and food. I could feel the cold in the air as I made my way further north. The autumn chill was a stark contrast to the Indian summer and I was relieved to finally make it to Carlisle.

***

My mother, Adel, remarried quickly after divorcing my father and her new family was growing biennially. We had four new half-siblings – to Harvey's disgust and he was often vocal of his disapproval. Mum was young at heart though and happy that I was following her family's biking tradition. We talked about the hunt and she was in awe; she wished she could join me on the mystery quest but her freedom was restricted by her young family.

This was the first time I had been to her new house – a four-bedroomed farmhouse on the edge of the city. Her partner's work had relocated north so it was a fresh start for the family and they were settling in well. Mum had dyed her hair again, this time a crimson red, and had a new tattoo, a sixth star to celebrate her sixth child, Keisley, who was now four months old and had fallen asleep in my arms.

Mum had planned out my route bless her, and even booked a guest house for me in Lochearnhead village. She had phoned all her biker friends to see if they knew of anybody in the area but nobody did so she had found the place online. There were a couple of Viragos parked in the drive on the website photo so she thought it must be a sign. The owners sounded pleasant enough, apparently.

I was looking forward to returning to Mum's house for the week after my trip to Scotland.

I never made it.

– CHAPTER 8 –

Scotland is beautiful. As soon as I crossed the border I felt a change in the atmosphere. It's hard to explain, more an intuitive feeling, almost like a release of peace and wonder. I had only visited once, on a school trip to Edinburgh by train, but had been too busy chatting with friends to notice just how enchanting the place is. Cambridgeshire is so flat that it's difficult to even see a horizon. I like the Peak District near Bakewell but it is busy and less tranquil. The southern lowlands retain their history, whispering their sacred stories through the trees and mountain tops.

The central belt was chaos. I got hopelessly lost in Glasgow and panicked as I unwittingly found myself on a motorway. Luckily the next turning was only a mile and I kept pace because of the general slow moving traffic. If the police spied me, I would be in serious trouble. Fortunately the next exit was the one I needed for the remainder of my journey north.

After an hour of riding through suburban Glasgow, the countryside opened up and the distant highlands appeared on the skyline, beckoning me like nature's majestic sirens. Then followed two hours of perpetual beauty: autumn leaves and rustic colours, shimmering lochs and waterfalls throwing liquid diamonds like confetti over the mountainside. I lost track of time, as well as my steering, on the bends winding their way round the jagged rocks framing the lakeside. I forced myself to focus on the road. I could feel the heat of the engine after long sections so stopped several times.

I reached Lochearnhead late afternoon. I found the guest house easily and was greeted by an older man with a grey beard; he was athletic in build and, surprisingly, had an English accent. He introduced himself as Henry Bainbridge.

Before I could step inside, he brushed past me and walked over to my bike. 'Nice,' he said.

'Erm, thanks,'

'You're brave coming all that way on this thing.'

'I wouldn't say brave, it's awesome to be able to. The ride was breathtaking.'

'I like your spirit,' he smiled and walked back to the house, finally inviting me inside.

It hit me then that this was the first time I had ever been away alone. I had cub-scout holidays when I was nine or ten, but they were different; the trips were supervised and though I was away from home, I had no responsibility. This time I had to cater for myself. The freedom was both exhilarating and frightening.

I sat down in a modest sized room with a bed, wardrobe, chest of drawers and window seat with small table in front. The window looked out onto the loch. I took out the note from the hunt and read it through yet again. It was still daylight but I resisted the urge to see if the next clue was already in place. I wondered what time it was likely to be there. I contemplated leaving at the crack of dawn and lying in wait to see if I could get a glimpse of the mystery man who needed my help to achieve his dream. Was it a man?

There was a gentle knock on the door.

'Come in,' I said, expecting Henry to walk in. The door had no lock; it was a typical country guest house as opposed to a hotel.

The door opened and all my senses surrendered in shock.

'My granddad forgot to leave these in the room,'

The girl walked in and placed a small pot of sachets containing coffee, sugar and milk on the side next to a kettle. She smiled. She was stunning: tall and slender with pale skin, long dark brown hair that curled over elegant shoulders and the deepest blue eyes I had ever seen, which smiled as her lips did. She had very light freckles. She looked Celtic and yet she spoke in a soft English accent. I couldn't help staring. Then I smiled back.

'Thank you,' I managed to say. I was worried that my cheeks were flushing. 'Just what I need right now too.' I was trying to be polite but I was dizzy with excitement and anxiety.

'I'm a life saver, I know,' she joked. 'Did you come far?'

'Um, Carlisle. Took a while because I couldn't go on motorways.'

'Yeah, it would. I'm jealous. I want to ride.'

'You should. It's the best feeling in the world!' I couldn't believe she was talking to me. She seemed confident and yet her own cheeks appeared to slightly pink. It was awkward, yet I wanted to press the pause button on time so I could just admire the beauty I was witnessing.

'I can't yet, I'm not seventeen until January. Already booked my CBT back home though.'

'You don't live here then?'

'No, I stay here in the holidays. I live near Manchester. It's nice here and gets me away from my mother and her boyfriend.'

Interesting, I thought. 'I don't blame you then.' I was about to introduce myself properly so I could find out her name when she turned to leave.

'I better go and help out downstairs. Enjoy your coffee.' She smiled and raised her hand as she left room.

'I will. Thanks.'

And I did. It was the best coffee I had ever tasted. I sat on the window seat looking out as the daylight faded. I tried to focus on the plan for the morning but I couldn't help thinking about Henry's granddaughter. I hoped I would see her again before I left.

Breakfast on a Sunday was between 8.30 and 10. If I had it early, I could go and find the next clue and come back to the guest house to collect my things before I went back to my mother's. That would only work if the clue was already there. I didn't know what time I had to vacate the room either. I thought I'd have a shower then go downstairs and ask. They might point me in the direction of a pub where I could get some food.

After my shower I smartened myself up a little then waited for my hair to dry. I was hungry now and it was getting late. I heard the television downstairs so followed my ears to the sitting room. Henry was there with a woman I assumed his wife.

'Excuse me,' I said quietly as I entered and was met immediately with warm smiles.

'Come in!' Henry called, waving me in. 'What can I do you for?'

'I just wondered if you knew of a pub or restaurant close by.'

'I think you're too late, kid,' he replied, glancing at the clock on the wall. 'All the pubs round here stop serving food at eight. You'll be lucky to find one unless you go in to Callander about half an hour away. They have takeaways there and an Indian restaurant.'

'Oh. I didn't think,' I said, embarrassed.

'You like pasta?' asked a voice from behind me. I looked around to see Heaven's Celtic angel in the kitchen doorway. 'I'm making myself some. I've got a stir-in sauce, it will only take a few minutes.'

I looked at Henry for approval. He was still smiling and waved me away. 'Go on,' he said. He must have sensed my delight at the suggestion.

'Thank you!' I turned to his granddaughter and said, 'You really are a life saver!' She laughed.

The house had a big country kitchen with small round spotlights lighting up the wood-fronted kitchen panels. There was a breakfast bar and a wooden table at one end with a fruit bowl full of perfectly ripe fruit that looked too good to touch. I wondered if it was ornamental.

'Come in, grab a pew.' She pointed at one of the stools in front of the breakfast bar. 'What brings you to sunny Scotland then?'

I didn't know her name, I had only set eyes on a couple of hours ago and for some reason, I didn't hesitate to tell her everything. I watched her face animate with genuine excitement as I explained about the clues and my hopes for the morning. I recited the last message word for word. The pasta nearly overcooked as she listened, merely interrupting with the occasional, 'Wow', Really?' and 'Oh my God!'

'Let me come with you,' she demanded. 'Please.'

'I don't think my bike would take both of us. It's about three miles from here.'

'That's nothing. We can walk.'

'Walk? I can't even remember what that is,' I joked. 'Are you serious?'

'Of course,' she said. 'I'm a life saver, remember. I'm also very observant and exceptionally proficient at multi-tasking.'

I wanted her to come with me but at the same time I felt as if I was betraying myself. Maybe my ego wanted to share this treasure hunt only with the creator. On the other hand, this beautiful girl was giving me a chance to spend time with her. I already realised she was intelligent. She was a carefree spirit like me, she was everything I could have dreamed of in a girl. I tried hard to think with my head instead of my heart.

So I agreed. She was ecstatic. I told her of my plan and she said there wouldn't be any rush to vacate the room at a strict time as I was their only guest. I said we would leave after breakfast, around nine. We ate our pasta while talking. I found out she was studying maths, physics and English literature for A Levels. Her mother and father split two years ago and she had lived with her mother and her mother's rich-but-psycho boyfriend. Her mother was everything she didn't want to be.

I told her about my family and my father and the introduction of Eva, guessing that we might see a lot more of her. An hour or more later, Henry entered the kitchen. I offered to wash the plates and he looked at me bewildered.

'We have a dishwasher. It's a high-tech establishment this,' he said with a wink.

'Does that include internet as well?' I asked, knowing full well a remote village in the middle of the Scottish-nowhere wouldn't.

'Of course,' his granddaughter said with a smile. I melted.

I thought I should leave them to it, feeling guilty that I had somehow invaded their private time. I was tired; it had been a long day. I told Henry that I'd be down for breakfast at half-eight, which was fine, and his granddaughter told him that she would be joining us.

As I was leaving, I turned around to her and she looked at me as if she was expecting it. 'Now we know each other, I don't suppose you have a name?'

'Unity,' she said with a giggle. 'Unity McClure.'

'Nutty by name, nutty by nature,' Henry added, unwisely, from the glare Unity gave him.

'I like it,' I said, trying not to laugh at Henry's joke. 'I'm…'

'Aril,' she interrupted. I must have looked shocked, 'I did my homework,' she added.

I swear my heart rate doubled when she said my name. 'See you bright and early tomorrow.'

'Night, Nutty,' I said, exiting the room and hastening back upstairs.

***

I slept well. I set my phone alarm for seven thirty to give myself an hour to get ready. I felt a strange excitement, not just for the hunt but because of the company. There was a little bit of guilt for abandoning the bike in favour of walking, but hey… I trundled downstairs at eight thirty and into the dining room. It was all quiet. I felt awkward sitting there at a small table. A white cloth was neatly laid over with cutlery and a plate but there was no sign of life. I got up and peeked inside the kitchen but it was empty. I hovered around for a few minutes before hearing noises upstairs so I returned to the dining room.

'Uh oh,' Henry said as he entered the room a few minutes later. 'Somebody forgot to put the clocks back last night didn't they?'

'What?'

'Clocks went back an hour last night. You're an hour early.'

'Oh.' I wanted the ground to swallow me up, especially as he took pleasure at my ignorance and his laugh alerted my hunting companion, who shouted down to her grandfather.

'What's so funny?' she asked, as she jogged down the stairs.

He didn't have to say, she realised instantly and laughed. 'You spanner,' she said. I dreaded to think of the colour of my cheeks. She sat down with me. Her hair was tied back and she wore no makeup and yet she looked pretty.

'Sorry, I look a state,' she said. I was speechless; if this was her in a state then God knows what she considered normal. 'My morning face is horrendous. I need coffee before the zombie in me takes over.'

'I know the feeling,' I said. 'I can't believe I missed an hour's sleep.'

'It's hilarious,' she said. 'You might as well stay down now, I'll put the kettle on.'

We had a leisurely early breakfast together. Henry cooked, Unity made fresh coffee and we talked about the treasure hunt. I had made a mental note of the location but was unsure if I would recognise the area on foot – I was relying on the milometer on the bike as my guide. We would have to improvise. Henry offered to drop us off but Unity declined. It was a crisp but sunny autumn day and she was looking forward to the walk. I nodded in agreement.

We arranged to leave at nine which gave Unity half an hour to freshen up. I didn't have a proper jacket as I had thought I'd be in my leathers, so ended up wearing a T-shirt with a black rock-band hoody over the top. Unity had a soft leather jacket, and had her hair down. She wore subtle eye makeup – I tried not to stare.

We set off and talked as if we had known each other for years. It was cold but pleasant, with only a light wind. I had worked out that at normal walking pace it would take about fifty to fifty-five minutes until we were close. There was no phone signal, so any GPS was ruled out. There was a particular house I had to look out for though, with triangular bay windows into the roof. I knew the location would be a few hundred yards beyond the site so we would have gone too far at that point.

The road was fairly busy. I could sense that we were both getting excited. My legs were aching but I wasn't going to tell Unity, she seemed full of energy and didn't miss a thing – plastic bags blown into trees, discarded cigarette packets on the roadside, she even checked littered bottles for messages. I recognised the section of road from the online street view map. We were lakeside; there was a thin strip between the road and loch with a line of trees. By now it was approaching ten o'clock and I wondered if we were too early. If so, what would we do in the meantime?

We walked on the grassy shore, looking for sheered sticks. There was a dense layer of freshly fallen leaves as the trees were semi-naked, undressing for the winter. I loved seeing the autumn colours.

Half an hour later, we were still searching. It had to be this section, we must be early. I was enjoying Unity's company too much to be frustrated. And being early, I was likely to glimpse the mysterious creator too.

The sun's reflection was glaring. I had the sunglasses in my pocket, my gift from the last clue. I put them on.

'Nice,' Unity said. 'I broke my Aviators a few weeks ago.'

'Shame. I wonder what the gift will be this time. The note said the sooner I solve the clues, the greater the prize will be. How am I going to solve the puzzles early if there is always a time delay between each one?'

'Maybe that's the mystery. Do you remember that big story in the news a while ago about that guy who set up an online treasure hunt in his will? He left like fifty million or something.'

'Yeah, I remember Dad telling me. Shame so many people were hurt though. I wonder if this will be something like that.'

We leaned against the trees, looking out onto the loch as we talked. We relaxed and stopped focussing on the hunt. I was aware that the morning coffee was filling my bladder though, so I hoped it wouldn't be too long before we made progress.

After a while we returned to the road to explore the trees on the other side. The area was heavily wooded up an embankment. Again, we scanned the area. There were clusters of mushrooms, which looked like they had been placed there to add to the fairy tale. The red shades were often confusing as we were particularly tuned in to the colour.

Unity let out a little shriek. I bounded over, but she was looking at the road. A four-by-four was coming towards us and started beeping its horn rhythmically. It was Henry. We jumped down the embankment and he stopped to greet us.

'I wondered how you were doing and if you needed an energy boost.' He handed us some chocolate bars. We were pleased to see him and both opened up the chocolate, speaking while devouring it.

'No luck yet,' Unity said.

'What are you looking for in particular?'

'Previous clues have been in a container with a red star on,' I said.

Unity was staring across the road as I explained to Henry where we had looked and about the sheared sticks that had been my guide before.

Unity crossed the road, looking at the tarmac. 'Here!' she called. There was a small red confetti star in the road. She picked it up.

'That's odd. I wonder if it's a coincidence. It could have blown here or been carried along by tyres,' I said.

Henry drove on a little, turned the car round then parked up before joining us as we looked for more stars. That's when he noticed another one on his back tyre. We walked in the direction of the area where he had turned round and Unity spotted another one. Henry found another in the grassy area next to the new discovery. We searched the area; the ground was thick with leaves.

Unity called out. 'Look!'

She pointed to a patch of ground which was sprinkled with confetti stars, there must have been twenty or thirty. I scraped away the leaves under them and realised there was a burrow hole, maybe a rabbit's. Inside, I could just about see the shining container. I let out an involuntary gasp of excitement as I pulled it out.

Unity was jumping up and down with excitement. Henry put his arm around her and they watched as I opened the container. Inside there was an ornate hairpin with tiny gemstones. There was another note.

> *Aril,*
>
> *Once again you impress me. You show initiative and desire. You are a dreamer like me, only we are the opposite ends of life. But I am still dreaming. You have come a long way this time but distance, like time, is an illusion. Everything is relative. You will understand that soon enough. Everything in the universe is just numbers. When is a circle a square, Aril? Think about that.*
>
> *You asked my name and I have been pondering the question. You see, even a name is relative. Do you call your mother Mom? So do I. However we are not siblings. As the weight of the world is your burden, so gathering sticks was mine. I am 'Hope' for want of any other name. However, I shall tell you the name I was born with and that is Clifton.*
>
> *Answer me this question next time, if you can. How would you get from Paris to Milan in 45 minutes?*
> *57.4866 –5.3091*
> *By the same time next week*

I read the note out twice as both my accomplices stared, wide-eyed. I felt I should leave something, some acknowledgement. I was trying to think of when a circle can be a square but the concept seemed ridiculous. Maybe I needed time to think – and that thought in itself seemed paradoxical in wake of Clifton's comments about time being an illusion.

I needed access to a computer, my phone was still out of signal.

Henry helped me phrase a note, which I scribbled on a paper bag he found in the car:

It is an honour to make your acquaintance, Clifton. I will think carefully about your questions. Keep dreaming. Aril.

We returned to the house in Henry's car. By now my bladder was critical and Unity confessed likewise. When we congregated in the kitchen again, Unity brought in her laptop. She punched the coordinates into the map search.

'Oh no,' I said, disappointed.

'It's much further north, near Ullapool,' she said.

'That's about a four-hour drive, maybe longer by bike,' Henry added.

There was no way I could travel down to Carlisle and then up to Northern Scotland on Sunday and back down to Cambridgeshire in time for college. Dad would go mad!

I could feel my eyes start to well and fought back the tears, hoping nobody would notice.

– CHAPTER 9 –

Fargo, North Dakota

It was one of those days. Douglas Fernwood wished he could have stayed in bed. He had been fighting a virus all week but there was too much to do. Bulk orders were in for Christmas and the factory couldn't handle them without help. He had been ruthless with squeezing maximum productivity for the price-war he had won, but was now racing to ship stock. He needed economical human resources from abroad so tomorrow's meeting was essential and he needed to prepare thoroughly.

Douglas had moved the business to Fargo from Chicago five years ago. Overheads were reduced by half, even allowing for extra distribution costs. He was the toast of the town too, employing more than one hundred staff, albeit on minimum wage. It gave the area a boost and he lapped up the attention; he was a *nobody* in Chicago – he was a *somebody* in Fargo. His son was a director now and his daughter had graduated with her business degree; she was going to run the accounts and HR in the New Year. For now, though, he needed help, quickly.

The phone rang shortly after nine in the evening. He was annoyed at the distraction.

'Is this Mr Fernwood?'

'Yes, make it quick, I'm busy.'

'This is Jamestown PD. Have you heard from Alexandria

Fernwood today?'

'Alex is on a business trip to Jamestown, she isn't back yet. Why?'

'A car, registered to her name, has been found abandoned in Nortonville, twenty miles south of Jamestown.'

'What do you mean abandoned?' Douglas was confused. Alex had been away following an important new lead for cheap fabric dyes.

'Her car door was open, her purse was still inside with her cell phone.'

'Oh no,' he said. 'What is she up to? Stupid girl,'

'There's something else. We need to speak with you. Can you come to Jamestown police station?'

Douglas was confused and fractious. Jamestown was an hour and a half drive from Fargo. He had to do this meeting in the morning: *curse her, she knows tomorrow is important*, he thought.

'No, I can't. I'm busy. Could she have broken down and been offered help locally?'

'Sir,' the voice interrupted, 'there's possible evidence of a struggle. We are going to get the immediate area examined. We need your help. I would prefer if you could see for yourself but otherwise we will send somebody round for you. We need to know who she was meeting, and where. Nobody locally seems to be aware of anything.'

Douglas resigned himself to the inevitable. He was going to have to improvise tomorrow. He needed to go to Jamestown. *A struggle?* His anger turned to concern.

'Thank you sir, we are at 205, 6th Street, ask for DS Hornsby.'

Douglas made his way to Jamestown immediately.

– CHAPTER 10 –

By *the same time next week.* Does that mean the clue is already there? I kept thinking this was a play on words. Henry made another coffee as we thought about plan of action. It was a long way to go if the clue wasn't there. This treasure hunt was becoming more complicated with each step. Maybe that's what Clifton wanted. I read through the message again, trying to answer his big questions.

'Why?' Unity finally spoke. 'I mean, why does this guy go to such lengths? Is he trying to lure you into a trap?'

'I don't know,' I confessed. 'Dad asked the same question.'

'If he wants to help you create your dream and needs help with his own, then there has to be more to it than just turning up clue by clue. How will that help him?'

'I get your point. He even said the sooner I solve the clues, the greater the treasure.'

'Clifton is doing all the work at the moment. You are merely working on arrangements and organising your own life to be there for the next clue.'

'You're probably right. Maybe that's what he means about distance and time being relative.'

'Also, why a girly hairpin? Does he know you have long hair or is there some other relevance, like working out what these stones are, like you had to with the moonstone?'

'Good point,' I replied. Summer's face flashed in my mind. It seemed so long ago now since I'd met her; Unity had even more wonder and mystery. I glanced at her again as she studied the hairpin. This was a new experience for me. I was aware of pretty girls at school but my head was in the clouds and I never thought of going out with them or that any of them would like me. I was a misfit biker with strange hobbies and obsessions. Unity was different and I felt at ease with her.

I couldn't get my head around a plan. I needed to get back to Carlisle; not that I wanted to – I already realised that I would miss Unity. I needed to make a decision soon if I was to head back this afternoon.

I was lucky in some ways that money wasn't an issue as both my father and my nan had given me £50 for each GCSE I gained above grade C in August. I still had more than £800 in my bank even after paying the insurance for my bike. Maybe I would stay with Henry again tonight and travel up to Ullapool tomorrow to see if the clue was there, then travel back to Henry's tomorrow night. I could spend the remainder of the week in Carlisle with my mum.

Henry told me it would be alright to stay and Unity seemed pleased with the idea. I had to clear it with my mum. Henry let me use the home phone as I had no mobile signal. Mum was reluctant at first and concerned that I could go all that way without any success. She suggested that I leave a note if there was nothing there, explaining that it was impossible for me to get back up again. I felt uneasy about that but agreed for her sake.

We continued chatting for a while in the kitchen. Unity was using her maths brain to figure out how a circle could be a square, playing around with pi and trigonometry, while Henry and I watched in fascination. I also had to think of how to get from Paris to Milan in forty-five minutes. Henry used Unity's computer and discovered the distance between the cities was about four-hundred miles, impossible by road or train in such short time. Even flying wouldn't be fast enough, allowing for acceleration and deceleration in take-off.

'What about military aircraft?' I suggested.

Henry searched online; there were many aircraft that were capable of speeds at mach-8 or 9 that could easily go the distance but again this was optimum speed. Even these aircraft were unlikely to leave Paris and land in Milan in forty-five minutes. You really would need help from NASA. Henry joked that we maybe needed a rocket and parachute!

The tiny stones in the hairpin were colourful but hard to identify. The best we could do was hazard a guess as to what they were.

Unity put her pen down, frustrated. 'My brain hurts,' she announced. We all laughed.

'Does anybody have Indiana Jones's number?' I said. 'We could do with calling a friend on this.'

'I doubt he would have the intelligence,' Unity said.

'Maybe we do need to look to the universe and see it in perspective. Even the distance between Paris and Milan wouldn't seem anything then,' I added.

'A space shuttle would do it,' Unity said.

'True, even the space station.'

Look to the universe with wonder. I liked Clifton, I hoped I would actually get to meet him one day.

***

A couple of hours passed. We weren't making much progress. I didn't want to impose on them again for food, so I made my way to a pub-restaurant just outside Lochearnhead Village. It was a beautiful afternoon, not a cloud in sight and no wind. I felt an urge to ride but there would be enough of that tomorrow. I don't think I had ever felt so excited. Everything was going right for me. I had butterflies every time I thought of Unity. I hoped she would want to stay in touch.

I enjoyed my food too. I had a window seat looking out onto the mountains further up the valley. I had brought a notepad and pen with me and I read back through the messages again. I made a list of observations: Clifton was obviously older, towards the opposite end of life to me; he was very philosophical and intelligent, and he called his mother Mom. That wasn't very British – could it be that he was European or American? I made a note to look that up.

I hoped the next clues wouldn't end up in Europe, especially with the random question about Paris and Milan. I wondered how I could help him with his dream. I couldn't help but think of the treasure being his empire – like Willy Wonka. Maybe this thought became my Achilles' heel. Maybe it prevented me from looking on and asking the right questions.

Back at the guesthouse Unity greeted me as soon as I entered. 'I wish I could go with you tomorrow,' she confessed. 'You're so lucky. I hope you remember us when you claim your millions!'

'Of course,' I said with a smile. I meant it too. I wished she was coming along with me. The freedom I had felt on my way up now felt like loneliness.

I spent the evening in my room, listening to music and writing a journal on my computer. I watched the sun fade over the loch and the moon slowly make its journey across the sky. If I was on the moon, I would be watching the Earth move across its sky, slowly spinning, exposing the shadow of night over Scotland as it disappeared from view for twelve mysterious hours.

***

I settled early and slept well. This time Henry was ready for me with breakfast. He advised the best route to take and where the nearest garages were for fuel. It was a long way to go, considering there was a risk that the next clue might not be there.

Unity joined me as I finished eating. She had printed out the route and some images of the area from Google Maps in case my phone signal was restricted. I thanked her before I left shortly before nine and she waved me off.

'Good luck!' she shouted as I donned my helmet. I raised a thumb to acknowledge her. 'See you later.'

Thus began a somewhat painful but inordinately beautiful journey north through the Scottish Highlands. The bike kept going regardless of the steep rises and falls of the roads as they winded through the mountains and valleys. I had to pull over to cool my legs because of the heat of the engine, but I was chilled by the passage of the autumn air as I rode and my fingers felt like ice blocks at times, in spite of my gloves.

By one o'clock, I was finally on the section of road I needed. The landscape had flattened a little but the road was desolate. I knew I should look about two miles north-west of Loch Dughaill, not far from a z-bend in the road. I pulled over and began my search. I looked either side of the road for any clues. In an hour of searching, only one vehicle passed by. I scoured every tree, every ruffle in the undergrowth, and kicked away at the leaves for a few hundred yards either side of the road. I denied the obvious for as long as possible: *It's not here.*

What was I to do now? I didn't want to abandon the hunt but it was impractical to continue. I was clueless and *clue-less* and couldn't see how I could return to this area. Should I stay locally and check daily? I really wanted to see my mum, too.

At the very least, I needed to leave a note to let Clifton know I had been here. I looked around for somewhere to leave one. I was hoping to find a bottle or discarded cigarette packet but compared to the road at Lochearnhead, this was litter-free. I saw a piece of chipped slate on the roadside. I had brought a fine tipped pen with me so I tested to see if it would work. It did. I wrote:

> *Clifton, I took a chance and came here, too early it seems. I have college next week but will try to return, I don't yet know how. Military aircraft might get me from Paris to Milan in time unless momentum from above, say a space shuttle or*

missile? What is your dream? How can I help?
Aril.

I still had some of the confetti stars I'd collected from the roadside the day before, so found a space to bury the slate at the base of a tree that had a little inlet. I doubted it would stay dry but the pen might stay on it for a while. I sprinkled the stars and found a couple of sticks that I could shear like I had done last week. I left one propped up against the tree and hoped it would be seen.

I was trying to think of a plan on the ride back. I would have to go to Carlisle and see Mum. Maybe I could still come back Saturday and hope that the next clue would be there by then. I'd have to travel back to Carlisle late and then home to Elsworth on Sunday. It would take sixteen hours' riding over a couple of days.

I stopped for food on the way back, by now very tired. I looked at my phone and saw five missed calls. All from Dad. I was not relishing the thought of telling him my new plan; he would not be happy.

'About time too!' he said, the moment he answered.

'Erm. Hi.'

'Aril, your friends are driving me nuts!' I was confused. 'They've been here all day – you could have asked me!'

'Oh, Po?' I had forgotten to mention about Po using the garage for rehearsals.

'Yes, Po. And his merry men. They told me you had agreed to them using the garage. I didn't give permission, Aril. You can hear them all over the village.'

I tried not to laugh. I could picture the scene. When Po sets his mind to something, the idea becomes a runaway train. I didn't feel the timing was right to mention my progress. Not that Dad would listen while he was so angry.

'I'll phone him now and tell him to pack up. I didn't give permission, I told him I would ask you. He was bugging me all week. I forgot to say. I can't believe he set up.'

'Do it, Aril. If I had known that from the beginning I

wouldn't have let them anywhere near.'

Then he hung up. I stared at the phone for a few seconds before bursting into laughter. Only Po could drive a grown man to the point of insanity. I dreaded phoning him but it had to be done. On the third attempt, he answered. It took three minutes before he took breath so I could tell him the bad news. I actually felt bad, he was so hyper.

'You've got to go, mate,' I said. 'Dad's going to explode. I never said you could set up.'

'You can't stop us now, we're on a roll. We need this week.'

'Sorry, Po, they can hear you all over the village.'

'They're getting a free gig, we should charge them,' Po retorted, not grasping the seriousness of the situation.

'Jeez, I'm like five-hundred miles away, in the middle of nowhere and Dad's on my back. Just go, will you? I'm sorry to step on your awesomeness but you need to find some other village to torture.'

Po fell silent for a few seconds, a first. I genuinely felt bad. Then he said, 'Can we use your roof?'

'Jeez!' I shouted, shocked. He was winding me up.

'It's OK. We're finished here today anyway. Shame though, it's perfect.'

I somehow agreed to tag along next week at college and see how they were getting on. Then I set off for the final leg back to Lochearnhead. The sun was starting to set but at least it was just one long road back now.

My eyes found it increasingly hard to adjust to the diminishing light; it was as if the road was slowly fading with the darkness. My headlight was switched on but it didn't seem to be making much difference. I had to stop. That's when I realised that the headlight wasn't actually working. I fiddled with the switches but nothing worked. I thought the bulb must have gone. Typical. I was still about eight miles shy of Lochearnhead and it had been a while since the last village.

I checked my phone. No signal. I started to panic.

Was there ten more minutes of light? Was that enough

to get back in, I wondered. I had no option but to chance it. My tail light was working, so at least I could be seen from behind. I could see the road ahead but not very well and I didn't know whether I would see potholes. I would have to ride slowly but that would take more time. One thing was certain: I had to make that decision right away because every minute mattered.

The first four or five miles weren't so bad but the light faded fast. I could make out the silhouetted peaks of the mountains against the ash grey of the skyline. My problem was the glare of oncoming traffic. I had to slow to a near stop every time a car approached. About two miles from the village, the last of the light finally surrendered. I stopped with the engine running waiting for traffic to come behind me and light my way enough to see ahead for short bursts. Going so slowly, I could feel the draft of every vehicle suck me towards them each time they passed. I had never been so terrified.

Then the inevitable happened. Less than a mile from Lochernhead, while I was using the light of a vehicle behind me, I made it up to 20mph. A car came into view ahead of me. I was temporarily blinded and slowed down quickly but must have caught the edge of the road. I felt some bumping as the car behind thundered past me and threw me further off balance. I put my feet down to steady me but my foot hit a rock or raised soil and next thing I knew I was falling almost sideways from the bike. I landed with a skid and heard the bike clatter behind me. After the oncoming car passed, everything went dark. I waited for the pain as my body tensed in shock.

My right arm and hip hurt but it wasn't so bad that I couldn't move. I was lucky. Thankfully my phone had survived. I used the torch to take in my surroundings. The bike's engine had shut off; it was on the roadside behind me resting on its side. I picked it up so I could inspect it. There looked to be a dent in the tank and the front wheel and forks were out of line. There was no way I could ride it.

I walked it in the direction of the village, using my phone torch to see the road. Typically, not a single car passed for ten minutes. I ached, the bike was heavy and I could feel it pulling on my back. I was worried that I would lose balance and it would fall away from me. I was stressed and upset and I had no idea what to do next.

I finally reached the pub-restaurant where I had eaten the day before. There was a small car park at the back. I wheeled the bike in. I couldn't walk it for the remaining mile or so to Henry's house. I went inside the pub and explained to the manager, who was very kind and allowed me to leave the bike there.

A local offered to take me to Henry's; I felt embarrassed but he insisted. The man, whose accent was so Scottish that I couldn't catch his name, chattered for a minute or two. I smiled and nodded and tried to be polite, but he could have been speaking in Mandarin or Martian for all I knew. I tried to react to the tone of his voice and hoped he didn't think I was rude. He beeped his horn as he pulled in and Henry came out to greet us. They obviously knew each other so Henry waved me inside while he spoke.

I must have looked a state. Unity's face dropped the moment she saw me. 'Are you OK?' she asked. 'What happened?'

'Either news travels fast or you're an intuitive genius,' I said, trying to joke, but was feeling woozy. 'I killed my bike.'

'Oh no!' She looked genuinely concerned. 'Did you find the next clue?'

'No, it wasn't there. I left a note. I hope Clifton finds it.'

'Awe, shame. OK, you need a coffee. I'll put the kettle on.'

I winced as I accepted her offer. I seemed to ache everywhere. I told Unity that I would be down in a few minutes. I needed to get out of my leathers. I turned to the stairs and then became disorientated. I was aware I was shaking and suddenly felt nauseous, as if I was about to pass out.

Unity sprinted over to me as I let go of my helmet, which

clattered to the floor. She steadied my balance and led me a few paces to a wooden chair in the hallway.

'Shock,' she said. 'You need sugar now. Don't move!'

I didn't say a word, but sat with my head in my hands, breathing short sharp breaths. I didn't want to be sick. I felt so embarrassed. She must have thought I was a drama queen.

'Here, drink this.'

Unity handed me a glass of Coke. I wanted to guzzle it down quickly but my fear of being sick forced me to be careful and sip it. She sat on the stairs while I told her about my day and my fall. Henry returned and told me I was white as a sheet. I was still shaky but feeling less nauseous, though obviously I still didn't look right. He wanted to call a doctor but I refused. I just wanted to sleep.

'I'll take a look at your bike tomorrow,' Henry promised. I thanked him and apologised for being a nuisance. Unity rolled her eyes.

After about twenty minutes I was starting to feel better. Unity said the colour was returning to my cheeks. She ordered me upstairs to bed and said she would bring up a coffee in ten minutes. I tried to tell her that I would be fine but she was a determined angel.

Upstairs, I removed my leathers and inspected the damage. I had a huge bruise on my hip. My right arm ached but there was no bruising that I could see. My back hurt from wheeling the bike. A bath might have been the best thing but I felt so tired. I stripped to my T-shirt and boxers and climbed into the bed. It was bliss.

Moments later there was a gentle knock. 'Are you decent?' Unity called softly.

'Well, I'm under the covers, if that counts.'

She entered the room carrying a tray and wearing a smile that warmed me. She sat on the edge of the bed. There were two mugs of coffee and a plate of chocolate biscuits on the tray.

'How are you feeling now?'

'Better for being back here,' I admitted. For some reason I

felt shy with my confession, so I looked down quickly. 'A few bruises but I didn't break anything.'

'You were lucky. What will you do now?'

'I don't know. I'll need to get the bike fixed.'

'Looks like we could have the pleasure of your company a while longer then,' she said.

I laughed. 'I wouldn't say pleasure. You've already saved my life three times.' I hoped my smile was as genuine as the appreciation I felt inside for her company.

'Oh, I have something to show you,' she said, then leapt up excitedly and left the room. She returned a few moments later, carrying a big white cardboard box. I must have looked so confused. 'That's got your attention,' she said.

She placed the box on the bed and faced it towards me. It had two adjacent panels cut out and a host of things on display. She told me to watch. There was a sugar container, two small canes, some string and two torches. She made a cross with the canes then tied them together. It looked as if a single cane had been snapped in two. She tied a loop of string around each cane, and attached the container on its side to the other end of each loop. When she lifted the canes it suspended the container in the air. She delicately balanced the canes over the top of the box. I was mesmerised. When the container was stable, she took her torch and shone it at the front of the canister so that it created a circle shadow on the wall of the box behind. She gave me the other torch and told me to shine on the container from my 90-degree angle. Projected on the back, it cast a shadow – an unquestionable square.

'Woah!' I said sitting up further so that I could see the circle and square together.

Unity sat there with a smile on her face, looking at her makeshift scientific creation. 'Hold it still,' I said. I reached for my phone and took a picture. 'You really are a genius!'

'Of course,' she said, turning off her torch and smiling with pride.

'Everything really is perspective when you think of it like

that. I don't know if I'm more impressed with the illusion or your scientific skills.'

'What do we do with this though? How will we help Clifton?'

'Good point,' I replied, noting her *we* comment.

'Anyway you should sleep,' she said. I had been distracted from my pains with Unity's incredible piece of theatre. 'I hope you feel better tomorrow.' She gave another warm smile as she collected up the box.

'Thank you,' I said. 'You've turned a pretty rotten day into something kind of wonderful.'

'Ah, it's nothing. Glad you're back in one piece.'

I waved as she left. Her hands were full so she left the door open. When she returned a few moments later, she waved goodnight as she closed it.

– CHAPTER 11 –

I upset Mum. I didn't mean to. I know she was worried about me and I know she wanted to see me but there was no way I could stay with her. Henry looked at the bike and assessed that it was fixable but he would need help. Thankfully he owned a small trailer, so he took the bike to a garage in Callander. They could get the parts we needed in twenty-four hours but it would take another day or so to fix. I had no option but to stay.

Henry took pity on me and only charged me a tenner a night until the bike was fixed. I offered to help around the house as I felt guilty but he threw out the suggestion immediately. 'You're hardly in a position to lift a mug, let alone lift a hoover or spade,' he joked. 'These things happen.'

'I'll reward you handsomely when I claim the treasure then.'

'Deal,' he said.

I was still sore. My arm ached more than I let on. Maybe I should have seen a doctor but I was stubborn. I spent most of the next two days talking to Unity. As well as being intelligent, she was highly creative. She showed me her sketches and paintings that she did to pass the time and I helped her with her homework. She made sure I was fed and watered, and timed my painkillers like a trained nurse. I suggested that as a career for her.

'I thought about it but I think I'd care too much. I don't

think I could detach myself from the patients. If somebody died who I cared about, I'm not sure that I could handle the trauma.'

'What do you want to do then?' I asked.

'Something constructive, not too monotonous. I don't know. I haven't set my heart on a particular goal but I do want to go to Uni. What about you?'

'As a kid, I wanted to be an astrophysicist or cosmologist. I'm struggling with maths though, so I might have to drop it next year. It's what my dad does, I've learned a lot from him.'

'Clifton couldn't have chosen a better person for his game really. The passionate son of an astrophysicist.'

'I know, right.'

Clifton's hunt was proving difficult now. I certainly didn't relish the thought of making that journey north again; maybe the fall had knocked my confidence with the bike. I thought about Unity's experiment with the circle and square perspective and asked her if she had any theories herself.

'It's obvious Clifton wants you to think. He talks about relativity and perspective, like Einstein. I wondered if this could be a clue as such. Do we have to work out how Einstein would get from Milan to Paris?'

'That's cool. Maybe you're right.'

***

By the Thursday evening, Henry was confident that the bike was safe enough to ride again. The garage was going to check it over the next day. I thanked him, I really appreciated his help. I had to think of what to do next. I told him that I would eat at the pub that night; I was feeling guilty that they were feeding me, but I also wanted to thank the manager again and leave some drinks' money for the local Samaritan that had helped me.

I returned before it got dark. It was a beautiful clear night again. I still hadn't thought of a realistic plan but one thing I knew was that I either had to abandon the hunt, or sacrifice college on Monday. I had more movement in my arm but I was still sore. It would be an uncomfortable journey home, regardless of whether I took a detour north.

At Unity's request, I joined the family in the sitting room. I hadn't spoken much to her grandmother but she was nice. She had mobility problems, but I didn't want to pry. She liked to talk though and, much to Unity's embarrassment, I heard tales of her childhood visits. She was a mischievous little girl, for sure.

The news came on which sparked further conversations. It was the driest autumn on record and Unity began to rant about global warming, criticising the sceptics. I listened and nodded, agreeing with everything she said. Dad would love her. There was an abduction reported in America, some business tycoon's daughter. Though Unity's grandmother was compassionate, she was damning of society and increasingly tired of all the bad news. Henry was much more philosophical.

'It's only the bad stuff that makes the news because it's different from the norm. Most people are good. Most people want to live peaceful, happy lives.'

Something in her grandmother's eyes revealed a despondent objection as if something in life had taken away her faith in humanity. Unity saw it too but I don't think she realised I had noticed. We watched the rest of the news in melancholy silence.

'You fancy a walk?' I suggested to Unity. I was restless and thinking about Clifton and how we were supposed to be helping each other. I wanted to look at the night sky for inspiration.

'Sure,' she said, leaping off the sofa immediately. 'We might need those torches though.'

I laughed.

We didn't walk far, just a few hundred yards down the road, and stopped at the bank of the loch. There was a chill to the air but otherwise it was pleasant. The sky was bragging the stars' splendour with pride.

'You know how small we are?' I asked, looking up.

'I know numbers, but it's hard to grasp perspective when you think of the universe.'

'That's true. Many people never look up and think. Many don't care. I can't help it though, I really want to know and understand.'

'I wonder how many stars are out there.'

'Dad says there are more stars in the observable universe than there are grains of sand in all the beaches in the world.'

'You mean we can see them? Like with telescopes?'

'Yes. There are hundreds of millions of stars in our galaxy alone, and hundreds of millions of galaxies, and around every star there are multiple planets orbiting.'

'You think there's life on other planets?' she asked, looking at me instead of the sky.

'Yeah, no doubt about it. There would be either no life at all – anywhere – or there is life in abundance. All we are at the end of the day is a whole load of elements that interact with each other. Those elements are everywhere throughout the universe.'

Unity looked back up at the sky, silent for a while.

'I wish I could travel out there and do a Star Trek,' she joked. 'Better still, time travel, get myself a Tardis.'

I laughed. 'We time travel every day. It's easy, we are doing it now.'

'Yeah, yeah, I know. The light from the stars we see is millions and billions of years old and most of those stars don't exist now, blah blah,' she giggled.

'Right principle. Though most of the stars you see out there probably do still exist as they are within our own galaxy. Even the North Star there.' I pointed. 'It's only about 320-odd light years away. But yes, many of the distant objects that my dad watches are millions of light years away and the powerful NASA telescopes can see light that is over thirteen billion years old.'

I was thinking of Clifton again. I had this overwhelming feeling that the treasure hunt was for Dad. He had sent it to our address. *Why?* Had he just got lucky or was it meant for Dad all along?

'Clifton is a physicist or astrophysicist,' she said, reading my mind once again.

'I was just thinking that. I wish I could talk to him.'

I was inspired now. I started wondering about the history of all the stars we were watching. All that light had its own story, just like me. Like Clifton. Like Unity, who was standing next to me, barely visible but was lighting up my world. Our shoulders brushed but we were both relaxed enough not to move away.

'Clifton wants us to see something we're not seeing,' she said.

'I think it's my dream,' I replied. 'He can't help me until he knows my dream and I can't help him until I know his. I think that's the treasure.'

I knew then she was looking at me. I could feel the gentle warmth of her breath on my jaw. I reached my fingers out until they found hers and very lightly took her hand.

'Come on. Let's get back in,' I said. She didn't resist.

***

Around noon the next day I was in my room, looking out of the window, indulging in my favourite new pastime – thinking. I had updated my journal and showered. I still had no idea what to do, or whether to abandon Clifton's hunt. I liked it in Henry's house. I was going to miss Unity too. I was trying not to let myself get too emotionally attached – trying to keep my thoughts practical – but my mind would ping thoughts off the logical walls of my brain until they found her again.

The notion of *love* has always been a myth. It's what artists sing about or writers write about. It is fairy tale. An illusion. Real people never feel it, it is the *idea* of love that's appealing. I wasn't in love… I was going to miss her company.

I heard a familiar sound as I looked out my window. I

looked to the right and saw a bike pull in. It was Henry. On my bike. I ran down the stairs and outside to greet him.

'I didn't know you could actually ride!'

Henry took off his helmet; he had a roguish smile on his face. 'There. Good as new,' he said, dismounting. 'It's been a while since I've ridden something so small.'

He walked over to the garage and opened a double door. I stood there, mouth open in shock. There were four bikes: a Virago, Norton, Triumph and Harley-Davidson. The garage wall was decorated with framed photos of Henry on various bikes.

'You race?'

'I used to. I made a living out of it thirty years ago. An accident ended my racing career but I still ride. So did Grandma. We've toured the world.'

I was in awe. Mum would love this and I couldn't wait to tell her – her intuition had been right. We stood in the garage trading tales. I told him about my own family; Henry was aware of my stepfather, who had won the Isle of Man TT races.

We went in the house and Henry made coffees. The parts cost £120 but he refused to accept any money for the time he'd spent fixing the bike. I was getting agitated because he had spent the best part of two days repairing it. My conscience was as stubborn as I was.

'I do want you to see if you can claim this treasure though,' Henry said. 'From a biker's perspective, this is the most exciting thing I could imagine. The thrill of it is probably greater than racing. Anyway, I have a plan.'

At that moment Unity entered the kitchen. It was the first time I had seen her all day; she didn't look as if she had been up long.

'Hey. I couldn't sleep last night,' she said wearily. I couldn't tell if she looked troubled, or if it was just pre-coffee, morning-afternoon blues.

'The bike's fixed,' I said enthusiastically.

'That's nice,' she replied, walking to the toaster without

looking up. She was definitely troubled. I could sense the unlocking of more unfamiliar feelings. *Disappointment? Compassion?* I didn't know if she was upset with me; maybe I shouldn't have taken her hand last night. I think Henry immediately noted the tension.

'I was just telling Aril that I have a plan. I was waiting until you came down before suggesting it. I have to take you back home on Sunday. I think Aril's done enough riding for one week, but it would be a shame to abandon the hunt now. How about if Aril covers the fuel costs, I take you back up North tomorrow and we make a day out of it? Then Sunday we put the bike on the trailer and I take you both back to Manchester and Aril rides from there to Cambridge? That way he'll be back in time for college Monday and you can still keep the hunt going.'

I felt excited but extremely guilty. This was perfect for me. Unity seemed to brighten a little too and she said 'yes' for me.

'Thank you, and yes on one condition,' I said. 'I pay a full rate night for tonight and tomorrow and I buy a pub lunch for us all en route tomorrow. It's the least I can do.'

Henry laughed and rolled his eyes, but agreed.

***

Our adventure began early Saturday morning. I rode shotgun in Henry's Range Rover and Unity perched herself on the back seat, leaning forward between Henry and me as we spoke. The skies were grey but the countryside still retained its splendour, the remaining leaves surrendering themselves to the breeze, occasionally falling on the windscreen.

'I used to call these "rebel days",' Henry said. 'I worked for a forestry company in Galashiels and my boss also rode. Every now and then, maybe once every six months or so, I'd come into work and he would say, "Rebel day, Bainbridge". Then we would take the day off and ride like tourists, sometimes wouldn't get back until midnight. I used to love those days. It feels like I'm being a rebel now.'

'I sure hope the next clue is there,' I said, feeling guilty.

'I don't mind either way. It's something different, some excitement to break up the monotony of life.'

I sensed that reawakening of excitement in Henry. He was a man at the other end of life who had supressed his dreams, for whatever reason. Maybe retirement had given him the surroundings he had always wanted but *living* had ended. He was in a queue, waiting for death, reluctant to move in case he missed his place. He used to race; he must have enjoyed the thrill and excitement. Maybe this hunt was Clifton's rebellion. Henry had boxed up his dreams neatly and labelled them obsolete. Maybe Henry was envying Clifton and his existential crisis and was now fiddling the latch on the box that confined him, opening it up one last time.

'Every day should be a rebel day,' Unity said. 'Not that every day should be an adventure but every day you should do something memorable. That was the day I did that thing … and that was the day we did this thing.'

'Ideally, yes,' Henry replied. 'That's the spirit of youth that adulthood squeezes out of you, because the routine of life makes you forget it until it's too late. So make sure you keep that inside you, Nutty. You don't have to end up like your mother or your grandmother. She let the accident kill her; she resents life because she can't get back what she had, instead of making the most out of what she has. She's trapped in a prison cell of regret for one mistake.'

'No chance,' Unity said, with a determined smile.

Henry was a good storyteller. Unity and I heard tales of his life and travels, including a year in Brazil, and anecdotes of snakes and crocodiles that didn't exactly promote a desire to visit the Amazon rainforest jungle.

We made good time to the location. I hoped I would be able to retrace my steps easily and remember where I had left my message for Clifton earlier in the week. I thought I recognised the area but the fresh scattering of leaves had distorted my memory. It was colder too and the grey clouds rolled over the mountains formed a curtain of impending rain.

We walked along the road for a few hundred yards. I was sure I hadn't gone this far but Unity seemed to be following her intuition. She was right. She sprinted towards a tree with four sticks sheared at the end leaning against a tree at a ninety-degree angle to each other; they looked like landing supports for a spacecraft. I caught up quickly and Henry jogged along behind me. This definitely wasn't where I had left my message. I wondered if Clifton had missed it. There were no confetti stars this time, no rope dangling from the tree, so we scanned the ground, kicking at leaves, trying to detect any burrow holes.

'You need to see this,' Henry said, looking up at the tree. We joined him and he pointed. Drawn in paint on the underside of a branch was a red star. It was about fifteen feet up.

'How the hell…'

The tree wasn't too wide so I considered climbing it. Unity could tell my thoughts and warned me off, which made me feel slightly more inclined to try it. Maybe it was childish flirtation. I jumped to the first knot and gripped the tree; I could feel the bark crumble over me as I shimmied to the next one.

'Careful, you spanner!'

'Wait a sec,' Henry said. His eyes were tracing the branch. I hung about six feet in above ground, hugging the tree like a koala.

Henry noticed a fork in the branch as it descended. There appeared to be a rag nestled inside with cotton strips, like laces, dangling down. They were still out of reach but the end of the branch wasn't. He went to the end and pulled it down, lowering the branch as much as he could. Unity took one of the sheared sticks and could just reach the rag; she hooked it and eased it down. I watched, still clinging to the tree. She looked over and laughed.

I let myself fall, as elegantly as I could, then ran to them.

Inside the rag was the familiar canister with the red star on top. Inside that was a brass disc, which looked like a spinning top and engraved on it were the letters 'W.C.G.C.' There was also a note.

Aril,

I commend your persistence and hope for your sake you return here. I apologise for your wasted journey. I couldn't be more specific. Though time is the ultimate ally, timing often presents itself as an enemy.

You ask my dream. I have always been a dreamer and have followed every one, but my final dream was taken from me by the greed of the few. I want to look on to the world and know that I have made a difference. People may believe that I do wrong but in fact my motives are the exact opposite. Everything is perspective and we have to fulfil a trust. Time is a luxury no longer afforded to me. Where I once planned in decades, I soon planned in years, then months and now weeks.

I want you to tell my story, Aril. Inside that, all of your own dreams can be realised.

You drive from Paris to Milan, Aril.

What is your dream?

54.7585 -2.5810
One week

I could feel the relief instantly in all of us. Unity cuddled Henry's arm.

'Drive?' Unity began. 'How do you drive from Paris to Milan in forty-five minutes?'

I shrugged, reading Clifton's note again. Did he want to know my dream now or next time? I didn't even know what I truly dreamed. Right now it was solving the puzzles to find out the prize – but if my prize was the fulfilment of my dream then I needed a dream. Was it money? That seemed so anti-climactic in the midst of all this intrigue. What would I do with money if I had it, I asked myself.

'He mentions trust again,' Henry said.

'And perspective,' Unity added.

I looked at his present. I thought it might be a brass button without the pin; it looked almost like a medal. The motif was ornate and cut into the brass with the letters engraved. I wondered what they stood for. There was no signal on any of our phones to check the location of the next clue. I had to think fast; the rain was closing in and we were cold. We went back to the car to discuss my reply. I couldn't think of a specific dream, certainly not one I cared to share.

I wrote a reply this time with a pen and paper, courtesy of Unity.

> *Clifton,*
>
> *I am sorry to hear your dream was taken. I hope I can help you to get it back. I dream of security and my own time to explore the world and to understand the secrets of the universe. I know it's vague but I'm young enough to let my sense of wonder guide me.*
>
> *What is your story?*
>
> *I need to invent a car that travels at 600 miles per hour to make that drive!*
>
> *Keep dreaming, Aril.*

I included a printout of the photograph I took of Unity's circle-square experiment.

The rain began as we tried to replace the canister. Henry pulled down the branch and I looped it, wrapped in the cloth, onto one of the sticks and tried to guide it back into the fork. It took several attempts as it catapulted out when Henry released the branch. The third time was lucky. I left only three of the sticks propped up against the tree, so Clifton would know we had been then we headed back to the car.

We were drenched but full of laughter as we made our way back.

We checked for a phone signal en route and eventually Unity's phone sprang to life. The next clue appeared to be halfway up a mountain in Cumbria, not too far from my mum. I had to think this through.

– CHAPTER 12 –

I upset Dad, I didn't mean to. I was in too deep now with the hunt and it was becoming my priority, even over college. I couldn't switch off, I couldn't stop thinking and I was uninterested in my college work. All I wanted to do was reminisce about my week in Scotland.

I was nervous riding back from Manchester on Sunday. The accident had knocked my confidence and I was relieved to make it home. Henry had dropped me off at Unity's house in Disley, near Stockport – thankfully the right side of Manchester for my journey home.

Unity made me promise to come back and visit sometime and left me her number and social media. I felt an unfamiliar emptiness as I left that made my stomach coil. Having spent a full week in her company, I was used to having her around. We made a good team, bouncing ideas off each other, helping each other.

I asked for Friday off college. I spoke to the teachers and asked for work in advance. I was a good student so they agreed. Dad wasn't happy and, having said no, was disappointed that I went over his head but I had to get up to Cumbria; I couldn't abandon the hunt now. Mum still didn't want me ride all the way in one go and suggested I stay at Denny's again, but I had better plans.

On Tuesday night I played on the X-Box with Harvey, catching up on all the gossip. Dad had been spending a lot of time with Eva but seemed happy, and the expansion work had already started at the observatory. Dad had been working late most nights. I hadn't had a chance to explain the new developments from Scotland to him. Harvey was jealous of my treasure hunt; I felt a bit guilty for not including him but he couldn't drive and had no intention of learning, so it was hard to involve him. I tried keeping Unity a secret but we were texting and finally Harvey's curiosity got the better of him.

'I can tell that's a female.' He gestured to my phone, grinning.

'That obvious, huh?'

'Yup. You've got that gormless smile every time you read it.'

'Get lost. It's not gormless and she's just a friend.' I could feel my cheeks flush.

'Yeah, yeah. Does she have a name?'

'Unity.'

'Ministry of stupid names. Aril and Unity; sounds like a law firm.'

'Cheers, bro.'

I turned on his character in the game and blasted him into oblivion. He stared at me, outraged and I burst into laughter. 'If you need a lawyer, give me a call,' I said, springing up from the sofa.

He threw a cushion like a Frisbee, which caught me plum on the back. 'Direct hit!' he claimed, restarting his game.

I felt the urge to go upstairs, chill in the attic and keep the sky company, if it was visible. It wasn't but I sat in the dim light, looking up anyway. Clifton had his dream taken from him and needed my help, and in his dream was mine. He didn't actually say what his dream was. He just wanted to know he had made a difference. Was he being philosophical? Did he only *plan* in weeks or did he only *have* weeks. I had this uneasy feeling that he was dying. Maybe that's why I needed to solve the clues quickly because he was running out of time. I was confused and even more so by his comment about driving from Paris to Milan.

I heard the door go. I had heard the car pull in so I knew it would be Dad and called out so that I didn't make him jump.

'Hey, you OK?' he said.

'Just thinking. I want to help Clifton and I don't know how. I think that he's dying.'

'He certainly travels a lot. Do you think there's any connection to these places or are they just random quiet roads?'

'Good question. I hadn't thought about that,' I replied, spinning the disc from the last clue in my hand like a top. 'I need to meet him. I need to talk to him face to face. Maybe I need to maintain a vigil at the next clue.'

'I still think you need to be careful. These things don't just happen. You could well find you become sucked into a very costly commitment to this guy.'

'If he ever asked me for money, or it seemed like a scam, I would back off immediately. But I don't think it is, Dad. There's a sadness, a voice of wisdom. I want to trust him and for him to trust me.'

'I know what you're saying, just be careful. No more missing college either.'

'Yeah, I know.'

I left Dad alone and got ready for bed. I wanted to believe Clifton, I didn't want to be wary but Dad was right. I sent Unity a good night text before I settled and tried to let my mind switch off for a few hours.

***

On Thursday Po collared me early, reminding me of rehearsals after school. I was hoping he had forgotten, but no chance. I didn't have my guitar but I knew I could get one from the music room. It was the last thing I wanted to do but I was becoming a recluse and it hadn't gone unnoticed so I had no option.

My playing hadn't improved much either. I usually played

my guitar through the holidays but hadn't this time and my timing seemed off. Not that Po noticed; he hammered the drums with a smile on his face as if he was playing Wembley Stadium in front of a cheering crowd.

'Getting there,' he said, after our hour was up. 'A few more weekends at yours and we will be invincible.'

'Yeah, about that. It's not going to happen. Dad's not interested.'

'Talk to him. Stress the urgency.'

'This is Dale Ousby we are talking about! My dad will just ground me and change the locks. It's not gonna happen.'

'Ah man, we need a place. We can't do this once a week. We need some gigs too. Maybe the Fox and Hare pub can let us play and rehearse.'

'Maybe, but don't count on me to play. I'm all over the place at the moment.'

'Some guitarist you are! We need commitment from you, you gotta practice like your life depends on it.'

'I'm not in the band, remember? You can't even sack me.' I laughed.

'Ask your dad again. Tell him he can choose the hours.'

'I'll try but don't hold your breath.'

Thankfully that seemed to be the answer he needed. I wanted to get home and pack. I had a busy day ahead.

***

I left on Friday morning after Dad had gone to work. He knew I was stopping on the way; I told him I was going to see Denny but I knew I had the whole day to get to Carlisle. I hadn't actually approached Denny; in fact, I made my way to Disley. I had been in touch with Unity all week and she had been doing her own investigation. She was taking the afternoon off school as she only had *games*. She often bunked off Friday afternoons and her mother didn't mind.

I had a clear journey and the bike behaved, so I reached her home half an hour early. I didn't knock but parked the bike outside and went for a walk through the village. It was an affluent area of suburban Manchester with a lot of spacious houses; there was a monument in the middle of the village but the tranquillity was spoilt by the roar of traffic on the busy main road.

My radar must have been tuned in because I saw Unity as she rounded the corner two hundred yards away. She was in her sixth-form uniform, hair tied up and she buried her face in her hands in embarrassment as she saw me.

'Oh no!' she said, as she came within range. 'I was hoping to get changed before you arrived.'

'Don't worry, you look cute.' She raised her eyebrows and shook her head. Her cheeks were crimson. I smiled; it was good to see her again. She let me into her house, a large building with four steps leading up to the front door. Inside, a small hallway had two doors to each side: the house was separated into two two-storey flats. It was designed to look like a single house from outside. Unity led me to the right into the kitchen then put the kettle on.

'You wait here I'll be back in a moment. I need to get changed.'

I waited, feeling a little awkward after the kettle had boiled. I was tempted to make the drinks but was shy about poking around in someone else's kitchen. Unity came down wearing light-blue jeans and a cream jumper. It looked so soft I had to fight an urge to hug her. Her hair was down now but she had an ornate pin clipping the left side up above her ear which exposed her cheek on one side.

'Pasta?' she said with a smile. Déjà vu.

I smiled and nodded. We talked about the hunt and shared our thoughts as she cooked.

'I think Clifton is dying,' I said. 'I think that's why he only plans in weeks now instead of years.'

'I was looking online for Cliftons. It's not a common first name and I wondered if he was famous. I didn't find anybody I could relate to, though.'

'Dad wondered if the locations were specific instead of

random. Clifton obviously travels a lot. Do you think he drives at six-hundred miles per hour?'

Unity laughed. 'I looked up W.C.G.C. and the only thing I got was Wimbledon Common Golf Club. Do you think that's where he's based or where a clue might end up?'

I had forgotten to look it up and felt stupid. 'It could be. Maybe we can find out online if there's a Clifton who works there.'

'I'll get my laptop after we've finished this,' she said.

We ate our pasta in the living room. Unity put the television on to fill the silence. Her music tastes were the same as mine; she channel-hopped to find the rock channel and we both spontaneously showed our excitement when Young Guns started. She wanted to see them when they toured. I said I'd come with her if they played Manchester.

Unity collected her laptop from upstairs and sat beside me while we searched the Wimbledon Common Golf Club website. There was no mention of any Clifton. I compared the font on the logo to the one on the disc: it looked different. We searched for more WCGC and found many: Winchester Canyon Gun Club and Washington County Golf Club were both in America but we still looked to see if the logo was the same.

'The Westcliff Centre for Gifted Children?' This struck a chord with Unity and it made sense. The logo wasn't the same but it wasn't too far from where I had found the second clue. We felt we could be on to something.

'I need to see him. It's bugging me. How can we talk in riddles from such a distance?'

'Maybe suggest it next time you leave a note,' she said.

'I have to. I really can't see what more I can do with the information we have. I do all the things he asks. I can't jump a step ahead because he's controlling the timing.'

We went for a walk through the village. Her house wasn't far from the grounds of Lyme Park, a deer park and mansion owned by the National Trust. She knew a way to get in without paying. We walked along a field and through a small turnstile, away from the public footpath where the river narrowed.

'Usually you can't get across here but it's been so dry we can just jump it and rejoin the road at the other side of the ferryman.'

So we did. Unity cleared it further than I did. I was impressed.

'Long legs come in handy sometimes,' she joked.

We strolled around the park for a few hours, talking. I wished she was coming with me; a car seemed a more practical prospect now than a bike. I wondered how fast I could get my driver's licence but then insurance would be way too expensive. We talked about the hunt, asking the same questions and juggling ideas and theories.

'I still can't fathom out why Clifton's doing this,' she said. 'If he didn't know you but sent it directly to your house, he must have meant it for your dad.'

'Dad doesn't think so. He thinks it was random. So does Eva.'

'Then was it the house? You said the house has a unique design, heptagonal, isn't it?'

'Yes, true, it could be the house.'

'Could it be that it has some connection with a seven-sided coin? Like a fifty-pence or twenty-pence piece.'

'It could be. I wonder if we can find a way to link the clues that way.'

'I'll look at it tonight. Will you stop here on the way back down on Sunday? I really want to see the next clue.'

I looked at her and she stared back with puppy-dog eyes. I laughed. 'Any excuse,' I said, and then cringed in case I sounded too pathetic. 'The more great minds we have on this the better,' I added, quickly.

She laughed. 'I think I might buy a foldaway map and plot the locations. Can you email me the earlier points from before Scotland?'

'Yeah, sure, I'll do that tonight.'

We headed back up the road out of the park. I knew I

needed to set off soon as there was still a long way to go to Carlisle.

I agreed to coffee before I left and drank it in the kitchen. Unity seemed as determined as I was to solve the clues and understand Clifton's dreams. She came outside to see me off and waited while I donned my helmet and sorted myself out for the ride.

'Good luck tomorrow,' she said as I turned the engine. 'Text me when you find it.'

I put my thumb up to acknowledge her then waved before setting off. I could see her waving in my mirrors. I turned the corner and felt that feeling again in my stomach. It was like an emotional emptiness that made me numb. A physical pain, not a psychological one; it really gripped me.

It was a lonely journey to Carlisle. The light was fading by the time I reached the A6 for the long ride north but my headlamp was working this time. I still struggled to adjust to oncoming traffic, which made me nervous. I couldn't wait until I could ride on the motorway, it would be so much easier.

It was nearly eight when I reached Carlisle and was greeted by my extended family. It was a relief to get the journey over – as much as I loved to ride, it was exhausting. My bike deserved a medal for holding out; 125cc bikes are rarely expected to do such distances. My legs were throbbing.

Mum had food waiting for me and she was pleased to see me after I had missed her the previous week. I told her about Henry and his bikes and racing history. She said she would send an email to thank him personally and recommend his guest house to her biker friends.

'Would you mind if I joined you on the ride tomorrow?' she asked.

'No, that would be great.' I'd hoped she might be able to but my stepdad wasn't always able to babysit because of his work commitments.

'Where is the next clue located?'

'South-east of here towards the Pennines.' I unfolded a

map I had printed out and showed her.

'Oh. Hartside Pass, it's a biker's paradise. Hairpin bends every few hundred yards.'

'I hope my bike can handle it,' I said.

'Only one way to find out,' she grinned.

After the kids had gone to bed and the house was quiet again, I emailed Unity the information she needed. I looked for some significance behind the heptagonal designs and wrote out a few theories to chew over.

My thoughts turned to my own dreams and how Clifton's dream could help mine. He wanted me to tell his story. How could I do that when I knew nothing about him? I was hoping his note would enlighten me.

***

Mum and I left the house around ten on Saturday. She followed me so that she could limit herself to my pace – I must have seemed painfully slow for her Suzuki GSR. I had memorised the route but it went through many country lanes and it took a while for my confidence to grow. I nearly lost control of the bike a couple of times because of animal droppings on the tarmac so I was relieved when we reached the main road to the pass. I knew the clue would be located as the road began its incline and I hoped it was before too many hairpin bends.

I pulled over as the road started rising; there was a parking bay on the other side of the road and I needed to look at the map again.

'I don't think it's far from here,' I said to Mum, as she stopped her engine.

'Let's do this on foot, then,' she suggested.

It was difficult to walk along the road because it was fenced both sides and the mountain was quite steep to the right. The road was narrow and busy, being a main trans-Pennine route.

'All the previous clues have been amongst trees.'

'No trees at all here. Are you sure this is the right section?'

'I think so.' I looked around, confused. It was hard to be inconspicuous here. Clifton was bound to have had witnesses when he made the drop. We walked up and down the road for a while. I wondered if I would see a red star on one of the fence posts.

As we made our way back up towards the bikes, one of the posts caught my eye. I pulled myself up the embankment then helped Mum up. One of the fence posts had been sheared at the top and the barbed wire on that section had been cut. The fence wasn't high so we climbed over. The hill was steep but there was an area of rocks close by that you couldn't see from the roadside. I immediately saw a small red star which looked like it had been drawn in marker pen on a rock. The overhanging main rock provided a sheltered inlet and I saw the canister nestled firmly inside. Mum found it hard to hide her own excitement. I loved this part.

Inside the canister was a white shoelace; it didn't look new. There was a note too:

> *Aril,*
>
> *Once again I underestimated you. Well done with your circle-square experiment. Your edification is significant. When I was a little boy, I wanted to be an astronaut. Later, I wanted to study beyond the boundaries of travel and to take my mind to the very edge of our known existence. Your generation fascinates me, Aril. People like you give me hope. All of our dreams are woven into the fabric of time. You must follow that dream. Do whatever it takes to get to that point. We all need a trusted cordwainer when the path ahead looks rocky but you must trust in yourself. You will find out my story and you will tell it as my lessons will be told by others.*
>
> *52.1587 0.0188*
> *Dies Saturni*

I felt humbled again but still no nearer fathoming out what I was supposed to do. *Dies Saturni?* The phrase troubled me.

I looked at my phone and laughed. Clifton must have found every signal dead-spot in the UK. Mum was animated, asking questions, but I wanted to think about phrasing my reply to Clifton.

She examined the shoelace. 'It's definitely been worn,' she said.

'These gifts have got to mean something.'

I sat on the rock, with my pen and notepad, thinking about what to say. There was no particular reason for leaving my own note but I had hundreds of questions. I needed to meet Clifton.

Clifton,
Thank you for your kind words, I'll do my best.
I have so many questions. I think we should meet, if that's OK with you. I will help you tell your story. Are you an astrophysicist, like my father?
Look after yourself, keep dreaming.
Aril.

I replaced the canister under the rock.

The valley below looked so vast, the Lakeland fells rising in the distance. I took a moment to take in yet another inspiring view before we climbed the fence back to the road. I couldn't wait to update Unity.

We made our way back to Carlisle via Penrith where we stopped for some lunch. Clifton hadn't used negative coordinates again, so I assumed they were east of the meridian line. I had signal on my phone now so punched in the coordinates. They led to Cambridgeshire, very close to Dad's work. I was relieved not to have to travel far next time and thought it would be the ideal place to meet Clifton.

I looked up *dies Saturni* and found out it was 'Day of Saturn' or 'Saturn's Day' – Saturday. Perfect.

– CHAPTER 13 –

McKenzie, Tennessee, USA

People were arriving from all directions: news vehicles, reporters, police; unfamiliar chaos in a city so small. Something was wrong. An ever-growing crowd of locals stood at the entrance to Bethel University, loose tongues sharing speculative gossip. Had somebody been killed? Was it a shooting? More than a hundred reporters were waiting for the scoop. As Congressman Linden Keld walked out onto the stairs with his wife Edina, together with the Police Chief and City Attorney, the cameras clicked and buzzed in a frenzy of activity, each reporter hustling for attention. It took minutes to regain control.

The Police Chief spoke. 'At ten thirty this morning, one of Bethel University's youngest and brightest students, Daisy Keld, was lured away in what appears to be an organised criminal act. She was picked up by a black Mercedes, which was later found abandoned on Austin Peay Memorial Highway, six miles north-west of McKenzie. We have no reason to believe she has been harmed at present but we must find her quickly. We are appealing to witnesses who might have seen the car or seen Daisy transfer to a different vehicle. Daisy Keld is fifteen years old, five-foot-three with shoulder-length, dark brown hair with honey streaks. She was wearing blue jeans, a purple jumper and black suede boots, and she had a cream three-quarter length coat with a furry hood, though she was carrying it as she entered the car, not wearing it. A man and woman were in the car. We believe Daisy knew them or had met them before. If anybody knows, or saw, anything at all, please let us know. We are putting an AMBER alert on this and we have a helpline number which will be in the press pack we'll be handing out shortly. Linden Keld would like to say a few words.'

Linden Keld stood forward, his arm around his wife, forcing her into the spotlight with him as the cameras continued to click. His voice was loud, projecting to the back of the crowd; he wanted his words to be heard. Edina Keld looked scared and anxious.

'Daisy is a child prodigy. She graduated from high school at fourteen and has been at Bethel University since the summer. God gave her the brains and the wisdom in her youth to handle the social responsibility of university life. She would not have willingly gone with people if there was any way she thought she was likely to come to harm, so she must have trusted them. We need your help to find her. We need your prayers so that her faith can guide her and keep her safe. The Lord will know the reason why she has disappeared and we need to call on His help to find her fast. I will do whatever it takes and draw on whatever resources we have to get her home safely. Daisy, if you see or hear me now, phone home … and if you can't, keep praying and know we're coming to get you.'

The cameras continued flashing as Edina cried. The couple's body language was starkly different: Edina looked frail and distraught while Linden was determined and resolute. He was a billionaire at the top of the political ladder and had the House of Representatives under his thumb. He showed no doubt that his faith would ensure his daughter's safety and serve justice on her captors.

– CHAPTER 14 –

My mind can be loud in the calm and quiet of night. I couldn't sleep. It was three in the morning and my brain would not switch off. I was starting to worry whether I would be fit for the ride home in the morning. I didn't know if it was the adrenalin from the hunt or anticipation of seeing Unity again that was disturbing me.

I had phoned her to update her on my latest discovery. She said she was on to something, she would show me tomorrow. I was thinking about the gifts. I had thought that they were specific but a shoelace was too random, it had to have more significance. I started thinking metaphorically. Was each clue a lead towards the next? Like the hairpin being a prelude to the hairpin bend of Hartside Pass? Then there was the acronym WCGC: did C stand for Clifton? It was obviously a 'treasure' hunt because Clifton had already mentioned the treasure.

Mum, Dad and even Henry's adult brains were no wiser than mine. Most of the intelligence work had been done by Unity so far. I had an urge to buy a huge whiteboard and write the clues out visually like you see the detectives do on TV.

I was awoken by three hyperactive siblings using me for trampoline practice. It was eight thirty and I was exhausted. Mum made a cooked breakfast and I washed it down with two giant mugs of fresh coffee before saying my goodbyes and heading off. It was nice to see her again and I was pleased I had been able to involve her in the hunt.

I felt the cold as I rode; the mild autumn was giving way to winter and even my gloves and leathers couldn't shield me from the cold. I stopped at a roadside café near Lancaster to warm up.

I made it to Disley early afternoon. Unity must have been looking out for me because she came leaping out of the house before I had dismounted the bike.

'Hey,' I said, acknowledging her smile. 'I'm freezing!'

'Come in, I'll stick the kettle on.'

I followed her up the stairs and into the house. I noticed she had straightened her hair and I felt bold enough to compliment her.

'Aw thanks. I used to straighten it all the time but I've got lazy recently, especially since I've grown it long.' Then she pointed at the table at the end of the kitchen. 'Park yourself there. I'll make a drink then show you my discovery.'

I was curious. I hadn't met her mother yet in the three times I had been in the house. I asked where she was.

'She's out again. I'm not complaining. She does this all the time.'

Unity made the coffee then joined me at the table. There was a folded road map of the British Isles on the table and she opened it and spread it out in front of us. I instantly saw her markings and said, 'Woah!' before she even spoke.

She chuckled. 'I knew you would notice,' she said.

She had marked out the locations of the clues and drawn a line between them. It resulted in a straight line running south-east to north-west.

'I bet you any money the new clue is on this line too,' she said.

I didn't have to look at Clifton's note, I could see that Little Eversden was on the line she had drawn. 'Look!' I said, unable to contain my enthusiasm. 'So is my house.'

The line went through the area of Elsworth where I lived; surely this was deliberate. I put my arm around Unity, gave her shoulder a squeeze and said, 'Well done, you!' then released it quickly, realising what I'd done.

'You're welcome. It wasn't hard work. You would have done it yourself eventually.'

'Now we need to work out what do.'

'I think the treasure will be on the line somewhere. Maybe we need to look at the gifts and find a connection – maybe to other places on the line.'

'Good idea.'

I had all the gifts together in a freezer bag in my rucksack. I emptied them on to the map and we studied to see if we could make any connections to the place names. We spent two hours looking for any association between the gifts and places on the map. Unity started in Scotland and worked down while I started from Wickford and worked up. If there were connections they were certainly cryptic; there seemed little that was obvious. We had to be on to something though – there was no way it could be a coincidence.

Unity had typed out all Clifton's messages, made notes by each one and printed them off so that she could look at them too. By five thirty it was getting dark. I still had a two hour or more ride home so I knew I couldn't stay too long, but I was enjoying our investigation.

'It's a shame you don't have to come back up north for the next clue,' she said.

'You could always come down to Cambridge by train. I can see if Dad can pick you up and take us to look for the clue.'

'I'm not sure I'll be allowed, but I can ask. I want to.' She looked pensive. 'We can talk during the week though.'

'Yes, we should,' I replied with a smile. 'I suppose I should start making tracks to get back before Dad sends out a search party.'

'I suppose.'

I packed up my rucksack and got my helmet as Unity cleared the table. She had done well, we were finally on to something. I could let Clifton see the progress we were making and I had a full week to think without travelling. I hoped Unity would be able to come down because she deserved to share the rewards. I no longer felt this was just between Clifton and me.

'I need to tell Clifton about you,' I said, unsure of her response.

'You don't have to. He might not like it. I trust you.'

'I just feel bad about it. You've done so much work.'

'You've done the hard work with all the travelling and it's cost you a fortune in fuel, food and accommodation.'

'Yeah, I know – but still. I couldn't have done it without your help. Maybe Clifton should know that.'

She shrugged.

I walked to the door and thanked her again. She looked away with half a smile then came outside to say goodbye.

'Maybe see you next week then,' I said, before putting my helmet on.

'Fingers crossed,' she replied.

I started up and pulled away, waving as I did, and I watched her waving in my mirrors.

That familiar pain lasted all the way home.

***

I showed Dad the latest location in the morning before I went to college and explained about Unity's discovery.

'That's about half a mile down the road from Mullard Radio Observatory,' he said. 'We were there only last week.'

'Small world.'

'Not that small. He's up to something, your new friend.'

I had a thought then which bugged me. I had to think of my words carefully. 'Eva said her ex-boyfriend used to Geocache. You don't think this could all be one great big prank aimed at you?'

'What do you mean?'

'What if the hunt was always meant for you? The idea of these distant clues being to get you as far away from Eva as possible? Maybe set up by her ex?' Dad laughed. 'I'm serious, Dad. You introduced Eva on the same day I found the first clue. She knew all about geocaching.'

'It's not her ex-boyfriend, don't worry. You could be right that the initial clue might have been for me, mind.'

'I think Clifton is an astrophysicist too. It makes sense.'

'I still have warning bells about him. I'm glad you don't have to travel for the next one. Do you want me to come with you for that?'

'Erm, yeah, about that. Would you mind going via Cambridge?'

'Cambridge? Why?'

'I offered for Unity to join us, the girl that's been helping me. She's nice, you'll like her.'

He laughed and ruffled my hair. I hated that when I was ten, and it was twice as bad at seventeen. I cringed.

'Yes, that's fine. Are you two an item?'

'No, she's just a friend.' I was trying not to let my cheeks flush.

'OK. No, it's fine,' he said as I started to leave for college.

I was tired. My mind had never been this active before and I hadn't slept well so I knew I had to take control again soon because my personal goals would suffer if I didn't get my grades at college. I hadn't done my homework. My tutor called me in at lunchtime because a lot of the teachers were concerned that I'd seemed preoccupied the previous week. I couldn't believe that I had forgotten about my homework. I had to discipline myself to catch up during the week. At least this gave me an excuse to keep Po's demands to a minimum – not that he didn't try.

By Wednesday night I had caught up with most of the backlog of my work. I kept up with Unity on social network sites but she knew I had to prioritise college work. She was still hoping to join me at the weekend but her mother had not given a definite yes. I didn't want to pressure her so didn't push it. I allowed myself to think about Clifton for a while. I hoped that he would allow me to meet him, even if it would spoil his mystery a little.

Unity had a theory; her maths brain had been working. She had measured out the exact half-way stage between the most southerly and northerly locations from the clues. The location was very close to the previous Cumbrian clue. She had been looking for patterns between the distances but there weren't enough clues yet to formulate any data to draw from. I felt guilty that she was doing all the brainwork.

I settled for bed, still thinking. Why was Dad so confident that Eva's ex-boyfriend wasn't responsible? I liked Eva, from what I saw of her, but I didn't like coincidences. I hoped that she wouldn't end up hurting him or the work he had devoted most of his adult life to.

Avoiding Po was impossible on Thursday. Having made excuses all week not to approach the pub with them, I couldn't avoid the regular Thursday practice at college. I didn't want to be in the band but Po's pressure was relentless. I was a few minutes late turning up and expected a lecture but instead Po came running up to me and thrust both hands on my shoulders saying, 'Guess what? Guess what?'

'You're retiring?'

'We've got a gig!'

'What? Where?'

'Fox and Hare. They'll let us rehearse once a week in return for a gig once a month. I just got the call now!'

'That's cool. You'll need to find yourself a guitarist quickly then,' I said with a smirk. He shook my shoulders viciously. 'You, Aril! You are our guitarist. A guitarist that needs to practise hard.'

This was an unnecessary distraction right now. I regretted agreeing even to rehearse. The idea of playing live *did* appeal to me though, in some strange way, so I was reluctant to dismiss it straight away. Po immediately noted that and smiled.

'No promises and I might be away, so don't rely on me. I'm standing in for now, OK?'

'Anything you say.'

Po leaped up on to the stage and grabbed his sticks. I strolled behind and took my time to set up and thus began an hour of noise.

After we finished, he was desperate to get me to ask my dad again if we could use the garage. I didn't want this any more than Dad would. I told him I'd ask one more time but I sure didn't want him over on Saturday.

I spoke to Unity on social media on Thursday evening. She said that she was going to come down on Saturday. Her mother hadn't agreed or disagreed and every attempt she made to talk to her had failed. I helped Unity book the tickets; she would reach Cambridge just after half past ten and I said I'd pick her up from the station.

I was pleased but anxious about how Dad and Harvey would react to her. I chose not to tell Harvey for now. I secretly hoped that he would be out for the day.

***

I was up early on the Saturday morning. I showered and tidied myself nervously. Dad agreed to be taxi. We had a clear run into the city and were early, so we bought a hot drink from the café stand at the station.

Unity was first to step off the train. I saw her before she saw me and told Dad to wait while I greeted her. She gave me a warm smile. She had straightened her hair again and wisps were gently catching the wind as she walked.

'Hey, how was the journey?' I asked breaking the ice. I had an urge to hug her but I knew Dad was watching.

'Boring,' she said with a giggle. She had a tie-dyed messenger bag with her. We both wore blue jeans that looked as if they had been cut from the same strip of denim and were both wearing black leather jackets. Dad noticed and the first words he said as we approached were, 'Twins!' Unity laughed.

'Pleased to meet you,' Dad said, holding out his hand. Unity smiled and shook it. 'Let's go hunting then,' he continued, as we made our way out of the station to the car park.

We made polite conversation on the way out of Cambridge. Unity was fully prepared and had printed out the location of the next clue. She asked Dad what he made of the hunt.

'Whoever is doing this seems organised and intelligent but I don't understand his motives and that makes me wary.'

'I suppose so,' Unity replied, glancing over to me. 'We could do with hiring proper treasure hunters. Shame they don't exist.'

'We should set up a treasure hunting company,' I said enthusiastically.

'There is one, actually,' Dad said. 'Do you remember the famous case of the online treasure hunt a few years ago?'

'I remember you told me,' I said.

'The couple set up their own private investigation company. They do a lot of tracing of lost relatives for legacies or property ownership. They even track down bad debtors who do a runner owing money. We probably wouldn't be able to afford them, though.'

'Shame. We could do with professionals.'

I was excited as we approached our destination. It wasn't far from Dad's workplace. We passed the Mullard Radio Observatory and pulled over about half a mile beyond it. The road was quite busy and the land typically Cambridgeshire – flat fields, most of them already harvested ready for the winter.

I was relieved that Dad and Unity were getting on OK. She had an ability to communicate at an intellectual level with people much older than herself. I had a feeling that she had learned a lot about life the hard way, but she had this energy and positivity about her. I felt proud of her in Dad's company.

It seemed to be a ritual, spending half an hour searching for clues. There was very little here and it seemed hard to hide anything – I couldn't even see any sticks to guide me. Unity was hyper-focussed on looking for confetti stars as we walked either side of the road. There was a small ditch with a few bushes but little else. The undergrowth was full of rubbish though, which slowed our progress a little. Dad was drawn into both the excitement and frustration that seemed familiar to me now.

'Maybe Clifton made a mistake?' Unity muttered.

'A mistake?' I enquired.

'Maybe he meant a minus. Could it be in a fold in the note? We could be in the wrong place.'

She was right, it could be. I took out the note again from my bag and had another look. There didn't appear to be a minus there but maybe Clifton had genuinely forgotten to put one in. I had a phone signal so put the latitude coordinates west instead of east, and the location pointed to a field the other side of Great Eversden, only a few miles away. The field had a hedge with three trees there. It seemed perfect. We went back to the car to try again.

It was awkward getting to the field. There was a single dirt-track lane which was so narrow that there was nowhere to pull over and park. We followed it as far as we could and eventually Dad had to turn the car round by driving into another field. We headed back towards a small hamlet and parked there. We had to do the rest on foot; it wasn't too far and thankfully I still had a phone signal. This was more like a place Clifton would use, though it was off the line, albeit not far. We headed across a recently ploughed field to the hedgerow that was our landmark. We looked for a place to cross and had to double back on ourselves a little. Eventually we were in the small meadow looking for Clifton's clue again.

Again, I looked for sticks and hollows, Unity looked for confetti stars and Dad looked up into the trees and along the hedgerows. An hour passed as we studied the hedgerow for a few hundred yards before heading back to the trees again. I was confused now and a little embarrassed. I think Dad's enthusiasm was also waning.

'It's not here Aril,' he said. 'Maybe your request to meet him has scared him off?'

The thought had crossed my mind but I didn't want to be

disappointed in Clifton. I felt that we had an understanding, so I shrugged. Unity was kneeling down looking at something. I joined her.

'There's a symbol here,' she said pointing to a stub from a fence post that looked as if it had been cut off. It was barely visible above ground. The symbol had four small squares with a circle inside; the bottom right square looked a bit like a flag and the top left looked like a cross with a dot above. I looked around but couldn't see anything. I took a photo of the symbol on my phone.

Unity pulled at the post stub and it came up quite easily. Underneath was a container – not the same as the one Clifton usually used – and it was dirty. I opened it and there were a number of items inside. I pulled out the piece of paper while Unity explored the contents.

'This is different. It's a list of names and more coordinates, all eight-figure ones.'

'This isn't Clifton,' Unity said. 'It's something else.'

'Could you have found an actual geocache?' Dad asked.

I searched for geocaching on my phone and instantly recognised the symbol. 'Yes, it is, you're right.'

'This is addictive,' Unity joked. Her smile was wide, she was enjoying herself.

'Uncanny that the symbol is a circle inside a square made up of four squares,' Unity said. I knew what she was thinking.

'OK, it's not here. Maybe we were in the right place from the start?'

'Let's head back there now and give it one last try. Maybe we're early, or misread the clue somehow. If we can't find it, let's get some lunch somewhere and try again later,' Dad said.

We made our way back to the car. Unity's phone went and she looked at it but declined the call without saying a word. I didn't mention it but I began to worry in case she hadn't told her mum where she was after all.

We returned to our starting point. It was difficult to pull over on this side of the road so Dad let Unity and I out of the car and drove to a layby further up. After Unity declined a second call I asked her if she was alright.

'Yes, it's just my mother.'

'She does know you're here, right?'

'She will remember, eventually.'

'Ah, Nutty, I feel bad. You should tell her.'

'No, I don't want to. She'll ruin my day with another scene. She was drinking last night, she wasn't listening.'

'Could you not phone Henry and explain to him? Maybe he can get a message to your mum.'

'That's an idea. I never thought of that. He knows how my mother can be.'

Unity walked on a little ahead to make the call while I looked again for clues and waited for Dad to catch up. Maybe there was a chance of seeing Clifton if we really were early. I was secretly pleased that the clue wasn't off the line. As much as the type of location made sense, it threw out our theory and I wanted prove to Clifton that we were making progress.

The moment Dad caught up, Unity called. She beckoned us over while still on the phone to Henry. 'Look!' she said, 'there's another one there.'

She held out a red confetti star and pointed to one on the bank. She ended the call and jumped in front of me. We didn't see any more stars for a minute or so, then I saw a small sheared twig pointing to my right. I followed the direction a few yards and saw another star. I called Dad and Unity and showed them my find. Then I noticed more twigs on the ground, five of them pointing inwards like a star, with a scattering of confetti stars in the middle.

'Damn. This wasn't here before. I know we walked along here,' I said, realising that if we had stayed, we would have seen them.

'Just our luck.' Unity obviously thought the same.

I burrowed under the stars and felt the metal of the canister. At least we had found it. I opened the lid. Inside, there was a watch, gold, with a thin linked strap. The time was wrong: it was showing seven o'clock. I wasn't sure if it was still ticking. I found Clifton's note inside so I read it out.

Aril,

Your father is an astrophysicist, is he? My, my, it's a small world. Clever deduction, though. I consider myself an altruistic cosmologist. I love our planet, Aril. Life is a wonderful thing, be it the life of a human being, a glow worm or giant oak. The existence of life and how our complex living machines have evolved is something beyond remarkable. The fact that all these things break down to atoms and sub-atomic particles is even more fascinating. How does a cell know what to do? What event enabled atoms and particles to give life as they do? Our study of evolution starts at the very heart of physics and into the very cosmos. I want to look onto the earth with wonder. I sometimes feel I've come down too soon.

Meeting you will be a pleasure, Aril, but there is still much to do and little time. Have you worked it out yet? You need to find me to know my story but above all we must trust each other. We have a parallel trust; I trust you Aril and <u>you must trust me</u>. Your life is on the line as my death is.

Nova philosophiae planetarum et artis Criticae Systemata Adumbrata

Cold pease porridge in seven days, Aril. You already know when. Bring all the gifts with you.

We were all silent for a moment. Dad's face was like a ghost and Unity looked confused.

'I don't like this anymore,' Dad said. 'I don't like his language.'

'I don't read it like you do. I don't think he means it literally and I don't think he's threatening me.'

'You can't trust him, Aril. I have warning bells.'

'No, you don't get it. He means my life as in the things I want out of my life. My dreams. His death is on the line because he is at the opposite end of life and wants me to help tell his story after he has gone. It's a play on words, he does that!'

Dad turned away. I looked at Unity; she had her head down and she must have felt awkward. I let Dad walk on a bit and I went over to her. 'Do you read it like I do?'

She took the note from my hand and read it herself. 'Your dad could be right but I don't think so. I think you're reading this right but if you were my son, I'd probably be worried too. We need to leave a reply.'

I thought honesty was the best policy.

> *Clifton,*
> *I made the mistake of bringing my father in on this and he is worried that I could be in danger with your 'life is on the line' comment. I've worked out the line but have no idea yet where to find you. I do trust you, I hope you trust me.*
> *Life is incredible, I will never take it for granted, not mine nor any life around me.*
> *You take care, Aril.*

I apologised to Unity as we walked back to the car to join Dad. She tugged on my arm and said it was OK as we climbed into the back seats.

'I've had an idea,' Dad said as we returned to the car. 'I won't tell you just yet, in case it isn't possible, but let's trust him as far as trying to work out where and when the next clue is or if he actually means to meet. We'll make a decision about what to do after that.'

'That's a good plan,' I said, relieved. I caught a tentative smile from him and relaxed. I reached for Unity's hand and gave it a gentle squeeze.

'I think this is a girl's watch,' she said, trying to put it on her own wrist. 'There's no slack in the links so whoever wore it must have had very slim wrists.'

The time was still showing seven; I assumed that had to be in the evening. Pease porridge rang a bell. I used my phone to search the phrase.

'Pease porridge hot is a nursery rhyme. I thought it was.'

'Pease porridge hot, pease porridge cold, pease porridge in the pot, nine days old, some like it hot, some like it cold, some like it from the pot nine-days old,' Unity sang, red-cheeked and with an innocent smile. Dad joined in for the final line. 'It used to be a clapping song with my friends.'

'Nine days? Didn't Clifton say seven?'

'You're right, he did.' Unity looked at the note again. 'We need to look up this foreign language quote again, it's probably Latin,' she said, checking her own phone, cursing quietly to herself as she mistyped the words.

She was still trying to type when we reached my house. Unity's train wasn't until six so we had a few hours to kill and we were all starving. I hadn't even opened the car door to get out when a beat-up van pulled into the driveway. My heart sank as Po leapt out from the passenger side door.

'At last! We've been driving around for an hour,' he said. 'Hello Dale, did Aril ask if…' His words tailed off as he caught sight of Unity getting out of the car and he stared at her, then me.

Dad spoke to break the awkwardness. 'No, he didn't and no, you can't. Not if you want to make a noise. I have work to do and don't want to be hearing your racket.'

'Dale, Dale,' Po said, walking up to him putting his arm around Dad's back. He looked so clumsy – Po is four or five inches shorter than my father. 'We already have our name in lights, our first gig is the weekend before Christmas. Aril needs to practise his guitar. You have the perfect place. This is his destiny. He will make so much money he can look after you when you retire. You can consider the inconvenience an investment.'

At this point, even though I wanted the world to end, it was too comical not to smile. Unity walked over to me, also giggling. 'You play guitar?' she said, quietly.

'I do but I don't want to be in Po's band. Sorry about this,' I whispered.

She laughed.

'Poulan,' my dad said, brushing off Po's arm.

'Yes, sir?'

'Nice try. But still no,' he said, laughing. 'I'm sure there will be a field somewhere where you can annoy the wildlife. A farmer might even use you as a scarecrow, but in this quiet village they are not cultured enough for your racket.' He walked into the house.

'I told you,' I said to Po, as he stood dejected. His brother was watching from the driver's seat and I assumed the others were in the back.

'I'm disappointed in you, mate,' he said. 'You're supposed to back me up. This is life or death.'

I did feel a bit sorry for him because the band obviously meant everything to Po and I wasn't interested, my heart wasn't in it. 'You know what he's like. Plus you don't do yourself any favours with your arrogance. I know it's just Po-talk but my dad thinks you're rude.'

Po stood with his arms out and palms up and an actor's expression of disbelief and hurt at the mere suggestion. Robert de Niro would have been proud. 'You hurt me, bro. I'm not arrogant.' He looked at Unity and pointed. 'Do you think I'm arrogant?' He raised his eyebrows waiting for her response.

She laughed. 'Drummer,' she said and even I looked at her.

Po held out his hand to her to shake it. 'Poulan Saks,' he said. 'Friends and enemies call me Po.'

'Unity McClure,' she said in return.

Po's eyes were transfixed. I felt uncomfortable so had to say something. 'So when can you rehearse at the pub then?'

'Starting next Saturday, but it has to be morning as they open at twelve and we have to stop by then.'

I couldn't commit myself because I didn't know when I might meet Clifton but I wanted Po out of the way quickly so

I nodded. Thankfully his brother wound down the window and asked what was happening.

'Denied, bro, I'm coming.'

Po took Unity's hand again and said, 'Pleased to meet you.' Then he walked backwards towards the van, pointing at me as if his fingers were guns. 'And I'll talk to *you* on Monday, ciao!'

The van made a U-turn and Po wound the window down as we waved. 'By the way, how did you know I was a drummer?'

'Cause all drummers are arrogant!' Unity shouted as the van pulled away. I collapsed into laughter and Unity wore a smug expression on her face and the warmest smile I'd seen yet. I high-fived her then we walked into the house.

Luckily Harvey was out. Po was bad enough; I didn't like the idea of us being wound up further. Dad had made tea and was buttering a French loaf and had cheese and ham ready on the table. I sat at the table with Unity and apologised again for Po.

'That's the third time you've said sorry today.'

'Sorry,' I said, almost as a reflex. Unity looked at me and grinned, holding up four fingers. I had to change the subject quickly. 'What about that Latin, did you look it up?'

'Yes, I couldn't get it to translate but it's a book, apparently.' She thumbed through her phone to get the details. 'Written in 1723 by Eusebius Amort, a Bavarian philosopher.'

'This has just got very weird. We have a nursery rhyme that contradicts his own instructions, a Latin quote from a Bavarian philosopher nearly three hundred years ago and no coordinates. We only know the day and time.'

'Not to mention enough trust to put each other's lives on the line,' she added.

Dad joined us and asked to see the note.

'*Nova philosophiae planetarum et artis Criticae Systemata Adumbrata.* Let me see.' He spoke slowly. 'Er, outlining the … er … new philosophy for the art of planets and critical systems?' It's definitely Latin. If this guy really didn't know

I was an astrophysicist, then this couldn't have been for me after all.'

'I thought that, but the house is on the line. So I suppose it could be a coincidence,' I said.

We ate our food slowly, refilling our mugs while dissecting Clifton's note line by line. It did look as if he was a positive man, deeply in love with life. If the watch was genuine, it was worth a lot of money, maybe £500 or more depending on where it was bought. It had a few scratches on it so it wasn't new. It was definitely a lady's watch. Dad was still wary of the 'life on the line' quote. I was more worried about letting Clifton down.

As it approached five, I knew we had to get Unity back to the station. I was glad she had been able to come down but worried that she might be in trouble at home. When we were in the car about to leave, Harvey returned. He saw Unity and me in the back and Dad asked him to come with us but he was exhausted and declined, thankfully.

Dad drove us to Cambridge Station and stayed in the car while Unity and I waited on the platform for her train. She asked if I could type out the clue so that she could add it to her own notes. She looked anxious as the train approached and I asked her if she was alright.

'I'm fine,' she said. 'I've enjoyed today but it's horrible getting back to reality. Do thank your dad, he's nice.'

'He's a pain most of the time, but I will.'

'He cares for you, which is more than I can say for my mother.'

'You can come down here any time, you know. I've enjoyed today too. Even if you did have to encounter Po.'

She laughed. 'I can't get over you playing guitar – you should do the gig.'

'I'll think about it. You should get on the train.'

Unity opened the door and got inside. She waved before closing the door and thanked me again.

I waited and watched as she found her seat. That gripping pain in my stomach had already started. As the train pulled away, she smiled and waved and I did the same until she was out of sight, then went back to the car. By now the pain was intense. I loved seeing Unity but I hated the aftermath.

Dad must have been able to tell from my body language. 'Yeah, that's the worst part,' he said. Then he pulled away.

– CHAPTER 15 –

At college on Monday I got a text from Dad telling me to go straight home afterwards as he had arranged a meeting. I assumed it was to do with his work.

The rumours had already started courtesy of Po. I had been asked three times about my 'girlfriend' even before I saw him. My language to him was unusually profane.

'Who is she, then? You never told me about her and we're mates. No wonder you keep standing me up.'

'She's a friend from Manchester, helping me with a science project of my dad's,' I lied.

'She's hot … or hadn't you noticed?'

'Oh, I've noticed, but she's untouchable. So don't get any ideas!'

I've no idea why I said that. I don't know if I was being over-protective towards her, knowing Po the way I do, or simply trying to divert the gossip. After all, we weren't an item and she was just a friend.

'She's taken, then?'

'Something like that.'

'Shame.' Po pulled a rubber-faced look of disappointment. I laughed.

I wasn't surprised at the rumours. Po was the most vocal person I knew, which is why I hadn't told him about the hunt. He was the last person I'd want to know about it. The rumours continued throughout the day.

Back home I was greeted by Harvey as I pulled into the drive. He was on his way out but warned me that I had visitors. I heard voices as I entered the house and opened the sitting-room door gently to let Dad know I was back.

'Ah good, come in,' he said.

A man and a woman were in the room with him and they stood up to acknowledge me.

'Aril this is Thomas and Lucy Riley, private investigators.'

They both offered me their hand to shake. *Private Investigators?* Was I in trouble?

'I phoned them this morning and explained about your hunt. They thought they should see you immediately as you are working to a timescale. They've come from London to see you.'

I wasn't sure what to think. I realised that I needed assistance, but how would these people be able to help?

'Aril, this is the couple that helped solve the online treasure hunt that I was speaking about in the car on Saturday.'

'Oh, oh wow!' I was in the company of professionals – this changed everything.

'We haven't agreed to take on the case yet but it certainly is a curious one. We thought we should speak to you first,' Thomas said. He was casually dressed and clean shaven with high cheekbones and a defined jawline. Lucy looked a little younger, with shoulder-length light brown hair and friendly blue eyes.

I left them briefly to collect the clues and gifts from my room while Dad explained to them about each clue in turn and went through Unity's discoveries. They seemed to be very much into it; I had a feeling they were hooked. I liked their enthusiasm but felt guilty that Unity wasn't with us.

'You've done extremely well to get this far. I am not surprised that Clifton was impressed,' Lucy said.

'The latest clue is difficult. Dad's worried that I could be in danger.'

'Yes, he explained that to us. It's hard to tell from the tone in the message but your father is right to be wary. We have seen enough deception to know you should never be complacent,' Lucy responded.

After a couple of hours, Dad asked if they felt they would be interested in the case. Thomas motioned to Lucy, palm up slightly, and I watched her smile and nod.

'OK, this is a different sort of case and I understand that there could be a time pressure,' Thomas said. 'I'm not sure if you know of our background but we have an exploration fund set aside for cases like this which we pay for ourselves.' Lucy handed us a printed pamphlet as Thomas continued. 'It might be easier for us to base ourselves in Cambridge for a few days. If it turns out that there is something of value at the end of the hunt then we will ask for a twenty-per cent cut from any assets received, after any taxes. If there isn't, then we will ask for direct costs only and not for our time, and we will cap that at £350 as long as we don't have to travel outside of the British Isles. Is that OK?' Thomas was looking at Dad as he mentioned the money but I answered.

'Yes. Yes, that's OK, I can pay that myself,' I said.

'What I suggest, in that case, is that we meet here after your college ends tomorrow and we will go through everything with a fine-tooth comb.'

'That will be good, thank you,' I said, relieved.

They stayed for another hour, discussing formalities and then asked about the unusual design of the house.

'I always like houses with character,' Dad said. 'This house was built in the early seventies by an Asian businessman. There are seven sides, seven turrets, seven bushes in the garden and even seven coloured tiles in both the kitchen and bathroom. I think it was his lucky number.'

'Interesting,' Thomas said.

'Seven clues too,' Lucy added. I liked her thinking already.

'We need to start there,' Thomas said, standing up ready to leave. I noticed he stood awkwardly, shuffling slightly as he walked, as if he had a limp. 'We will look into it in the morning and see what we can find before we meet up tomorrow.'

After they left, I thanked Dad. I realised this was the idea he had had in the car after the last clue and it was genius. I couldn't wait to tell Unity. I phoned her as soon as I went upstairs.

'Really? That famous couple?'

'I know right. It felt weird you not being here. They're coming tomorrow to discuss it. I wish you could be here.'

'You could always ask if I could join via Skype if you have your laptop,' she said.

'Yes. Good idea, I'm sure they will agree. It's no different to you being in the room.'

Why didn't I think of that? I was even more excited now.

***

The rumours continued in college the next day until it got boring and I was cursing Po and his big mouth. I did commit myself to band practice on Thursday, though I hoped it wouldn't interfere with meeting the private eyes. There was so much work on at college that I hadn't really had time to think about the latest clues. I was doing homework until midnight the previous night and I spent my lunch break in the library doing more homework so that I would be able to devote the evening to the hunt.

Thomas and Lucy were already at home when I got back. Dad had cleared the dining-room table and Lucy had a folded map similar to Unity's. I explained about Unity and asked them if it was alright if she joined us via Skype. Fortunately they didn't mind so I called her and they welcomed her. She was in her sitting room, I recognised it from my visits there. I didn't want to take up space at the table so pulled out a chair and placed a box and some cushions on it and put the computer on top. Unity could see Lucy in the middle with Thomas and I either side, and see the table even if the angle wasn't too good.

I marked out where each clue was on the map, as well as my house, and Lucy joined the dots to form the straight line, as Unity had. They had been able to find out a little about our house online. It had been included in a list of follies which were written about by an author from Nottingham. They had ordered the book and written to the author via his website but were yet to receive a reply.

'I think the number seven has some significance,' Thomas said. 'We don't know if this latest clue is the final one, but it's certainly the seventh and it is different.'

'We think this is why he chose Heptagon House as his starting point,' Lucy continued. 'It wasn't a coincidence, he planned for this line to go through the house.'

'What do you make of Clifton? What's your assessment of him?' Unity asked. I was glad she was involving herself.

Thomas had been reading through the clues and writing his own notes as Lucy was mapping. He spoke. 'He is intelligent, creative, knowledgeable about Britain, sure of his own capabilities but thinks that he is not liked by everybody. If he has knowledge in cosmology or astrophysics, then he's probably worked in this field. So this is a line of investigation we need to pursue.' Thomas didn't look up as he spoke; it was as if Unity had triggered a question in his own mind and he was answering himself out loud. 'I think he plays golf too.'

'You do?' I asked.

'Yes, this is a golf marker,' he said holding up the disk. 'We need to visit Wimbledon Common Golf Club and ask around.

'Oh,' both Unity and I said in unison. 'We did look that up online but the logo was different so we didn't think it was a lead.'

'It might not be but it's the obvious starting point.'

We continued for an hour, going through every clue, looking to see what we might have missed. There were some random lines that didn't make much sense in context: *Look outside this hunt; the price of trust; the randomness of the Paris to Milan question; the significance of the red star; needing a cordwainer; his story to tell; finding him and come down too soon.* These were ambiguous but seemed deliberate. The other thing was the gifts: there was nothing obvious that connected them. The first two were day markers but the rest didn't seem to have a meaning, especially as Clifton told of specific days in the notes. We also needed to find the significance of the Latin book. Lucy had tried to find an English translation but couldn't. Most confusing of all was the nursery rhyme because it appeared to contradict Clifton's own instructions.

'It seems to be a thing, these ambiguities in the clues,' Lucy said. 'I have a feeling that Clifton has studied previous cases, possibly even our own hunt for Professor Jason Chadwick's legacy. It's been well documented.'

'Why?' Unity asked. 'Why do people even set up these hunts?'

'They are rare,' Lucy said. 'Often it's a way of leaving a legacy to someone worthy if they have no heirs or kin. Some people leave their estate to charity and others like to be more creative. It takes a lot of effort to organise though, so it's usually the more affluent that try. It could be an attempt to be remembered. I think that's what's happening with Clifton – he wants to be remembered for something – hopefully positive. He certainly wants you to tell his story, Aril.'

'I gathered. We need to find him first, and before it's too late.'

'We will,' Lucy smiled. 'He wants to be found.'

Dad made a variety of pizzas which we shared. Lucy told Unity to eat. At first she said she had eaten but Lucy stared her down and Unity smiled, rolled her eyes and said *fine* and returned ten minutes later with soup.

We continued work. By now Thomas and Lucy had written up everything and taken photographs of the gifts. They also had a plan of action for the next day. Unity remained online the whole time, explained her own thinking and detailed her science experiment. She also thought it was worth investigating some of Einstein's work because Clifton had spoken about perspective and made reference to things being 'relative'.

Thomas and Lucy left shortly after nine. I liked them. They seemed to be on our wavelength and were able to do the research better than Unity and I, especially with school and college. Though that got me thinking; if Clifton was so keen for me to succeed with my dreams and goals, you would think he would allow for the fact that I had college. Unless he was expecting an adult to follow the clues – but then adults could have work commitments.

Unity stayed on Skype for a while after our new allies left so I asked her what she thought. 'I like them. I can't believe we have professionals on this now.'

'Glad you could be with us.'

She had been online for more than five hours and apart from the odd trip to the kitchen had stayed in the sitting room the whole time. There had been nobody else around. I asked where her mum was.

'She's with lover-boy, she'll be back soon, unfortunately. Glad she stayed out and didn't bug me,' she said.

'Ah. OK, is it a regular occurrence?'

'Like clockwork, and then she'll come home drunk and pretend to care, then make me tidy up her crap. Then I'll go to bed. I'll get myself up in the morning, go to school and by the time I'm home she will be out again. We're passing strangers.'

'Sounds really rough,' I said. I genuinely felt for her.

'It's nothing, I'm used to it. That's why I like going to my grandparents in the holidays.'

'Yeah, I don't blame you. You have the coolest granddad on the planet.'

She smiled and agreed. I would hate to live like that. Unity was so bright and always fun to be around. Some people become a clone of their parents, especially when circumstances are bad. Unity was the opposite; she'd decided that she didn't want to be like her mum and, instead of carrying a chip on her shoulder, she was positive and brushed it off. She dismissed the bad as an inconvenience and carried on. That took courage.

We finished the call shortly afterwards as she had homework and I needed a shower. I was pleased that there were professionals involved and that Unity could still be included. I hoped I wasn't betraying Clifton and he wouldn't think I was cheating. I wanted him to trust me just as I needed to trust that my life was not on the line – or was that the test?

– CHAPTER 16 –

Thomas and Lucy Riley returned to their hotel in Cambridge. Lucy felt a nostalgic excitement like an electric pulse in her veins. They had been waiting for a case like this for years. Their company was doing well and some of their investigations had been steeped in mystery, but it was usually historic. They had found lost heirs to fortunes and uncovered lost paintings and jewellery, even traced family lines of former royalty. This was the first intellectual mystery they'd had since leaving the Metropolitan Police Force to start their own company.

Lucy could already feel a psychological bond forming with Clifton, their new host. There was always the worry that this could lead to danger, like the Chadwick case when Thomas was shot three times and nearly lost his life. He still carried the physical and emotional scars. But this hunt seemed genuine. Clifton was alive and overseeing this treasure hunt personally. He was a positive man, in love with life, and showed respect for Aril. Lucy liked Aril too. He and his friend had been clever and innovative in their reading of the clues and yet hadn't got carried away. They reminded her of how she and Thomas were in the early days.

'I don't know about you, but I'm already hooked,' she said, as they entered their room.

'Yes, I've got a good feeling about this,' he replied, turning toward her to kiss her forehead.

They had booked a large room with a desk as they were basing themselves locally. It overlooked the River Cam with a view over Midsummer Common, not far from the city centre. It was dark but the streetlights illuminated the city. They sat on armchairs, either side of an oak table, looking out the window, their maps and notes unopened for now.

'We've got a lot to do if we're going to solve this in five days,' Thomas said.

Lucy nodded in agreement, enjoying the lights of the city. 'I think we should visit the library tomorrow and see what we can find there. They might have this Latin book too, or a translation.'

'Maybe we can use the University Library; we might even find somebody to translate it.'

'Of course, good thinking.'

Thomas looked towards Lucy and she smiled. They had been through a lot together. She had nursed him back to health after the shooting and no longer took life for granted. All her time with Thomas was precious, even the boring days at home when they would listen to the radio and attempt crosswords while lounging in their pyjamas. Maybe Clifton had the same respect for time and for *being alive*. She felt they were already a team.

They got ready for bed, discussing their plan of action, then put the television on to catch up with the news. Expectations were high for a Christmas sales boost, a sign that the economy was strengthening after years of slow growth. In America, some billionaire congressman was pleading for his daughter's safe return after a kidnapping.

'I bet you it's a ransom job,' Thomas muttered.

'Usually is,' Lucy replied. 'It must be terrifying for a parent to go through such anxiety. You couldn't put a price on your daughter's life. You would pay anything.'

'That's what these criminals rely on.'

Lucy sighed. She had seen the price of greed over the years and the knock-on effect. She still had nightmares, reliving the trauma of finding Thomas after the shooting and those desperate days and weeks that followed, when it was hit-and-miss as to whether he would pull through or walk again. Their windfall meant nothing back then. What use is money when you're dead – or have nothing to live for? Lucy turned the television off and snuggled into Thomas.

They were alive – and back in the hunt.

– CHAPTER 17 –

I was late for college. It was the first real taste of winter and I realised my bike didn't like the cold. I needed to buy it a winter-warmer to keep the frost away. I think Dad was relieved; he didn't like the idea of me riding on the ice. He dropped me off for my bus on his way to work but I still missed the first lesson.

Our physics lesson was different today: we watched a live-stream of preparations for the first manned trip to the moon in forty years. It was a privately funded mission, with the help of NASA, taking off from the Kennedy Space Centre in Cape Canaveral. They hoped the landing would mark the fortieth anniversary of the Apollo 17 landing. I was fascinated; there was so much more to the organisation than people knew.

A documentary followed and it was optional to stay or go for lunch, but most people stayed. The mission had been hit by so many complications and was originally going to be a NASA funded project, using a hybrid fuelled rocket system, but the funding was withdrawn during the recession. Commander Leslie Peterson and his team persevered and he was going to be the first person to walk on our natural satellite this century.

I couldn't help but think of Clifton. There could be no better viewpoint to look on to the world from than from the moon. From anywhere else in our solar system, Earth would appear no more than a *pale blue dot*, as astronomer Carl Sagan once said. From the moon, you would still be able to see Earth's full glory – a miracle of life and beauty. This thought haunted me all day; I felt humble to even exist in this vast cosmos.

Dad picked me up from college. He knew we had another evening with our guests so left work a little early to save me catching the bus and waiting around.

Thomas and Lucy Riley arrived shortly after six. They had been in library most of the day. I called Unity on Skype so that she could be included.

'We've tracked down the architect of your house. It was designed by request from a businessman in 1970 who sold it three years later. We've traced the owners' histories in case a Clifton once lived here, but there is no name like that at the Land Registry,' Lucy explained, looking down at her notes. 'We think that there is a connection to the number seven though. It could be that the house was initially targeted for that reason.' She talked fast. She turned another page and continued, 'Eusebius Amort, who wrote the Latin book was born in Bavaria on the 15th November 1692 and died 5th February 1775. He was a teacher of philosophy and theology. He spent most of his life in Munich. We've printed out as much information as we can find but haven't yet been able to make a connection.'

'What we are doing is getting together as much information as we can and then we'll hopefully piece together the real message Clifton is trying to give you,' Thomas added.

They used the table to create a think-board. Everything was photographed, each gift, clue and note, each with a corresponding number to mark on the map. Index cards were handwritten with a bold black marker pen to highlight any ambiguities. They had even printed out my photo from Unity's science experiment. Seeing it all laid out like that made my stomach churn with excitement; it was real – this was a *real* treasure hunt with *real* treasure hunters.

'We contacted Wimbledon Common Golf Club,' Lucy

said. 'It's not one of their markers but they confirmed that is what the object is. We need to search online for other courses – it could come from a private club.'

Thomas suggested going through every town and village on the line. I told him that Unity and I had done that but he said the map wouldn't show everywhere; we really needed to follow an online map, where we could zoom in on the smallest hamlets. We could keep an eye open for golf courses that way, too.

'I'll do that, if you like,' Unity offered. 'I'll document the name of every place on the line and send it to you to reference.'

'If you could, thank you,' Lucy said.

I felt a bit useless so had to think of what I could offer. They had brought a computer with them so I still had Dad's to use.

'Do you want me to check for golf courses with the initials WCGC?'

'That will be good,' Thomas said. So I did, while they talked, throwing ideas and theories around.

The shoelace seemed the most puzzling of the clues. The moonstone and sunglasses had served their purpose, the hairpin had a weaker connection and the watch appeared to have a time connection. The golf marker hinted at another place but the white shoelace was a mystery. Lucy looked for any connection she could find. It was obviously worn – not brand new but not as worn as my own Converse laces. There were dirt stains and bends in it as if it had been previously threaded in a shoe.

'It must be a sports shoe, like a trainer or golf shoe,' Lucy said.

'Golf shoes would be my guess,' Thomas replied. 'It would make sense.'

'He mentioned needing a trusted cordwainer when the path ahead was rocky. Could it be connected? I mean who uses that term nowadays?'

'True, it's something else we should look into.' Thomas

wrote notes.

I found a list of British golf courses. These included West Chiltington Golf Club, West Cornwall Golf Club and Wellington College Golf Club, none of which were on the line but Thomas took notes to see if they could recognise the marker.

I spotted something else by accident. 'World Corporate Golf Challenge. It's held all over the world but next year it's in Scotland, Loch Lomond,' I said. Thomas came to over to me.

'That's interesting. It's not on the line but definitely worth investigating. See if there's recent history of it elsewhere in Europe, like Paris or Milan.'

I had a thought then as to whether Clifford meant 'drive' as a golfing term when he was explaining the Paris–Milan riddle.

Lucy was already on to it. 'Great minds think alike,' she said. I loved working like this. We were a team. Dad wasn't with us all the time as he was working but he offered his thoughts occasionally and kept the kettle warm. Eva had not been over for a while; she had endless work meetings and had been travelling all over the country.

Unity eventually finished her research. She sent a list of around three hundred villages and towns that the line crossed – or were very close to. It was getting late so Thomas and Lucy saved the list in order to go through it the next day. They also wanted to go through every line from Clifton's messages that seemed ambiguous. We needed to move faster if we had any hope at all of finding him on Saturday. It had been a productive evening though: there were new lines of enquiry for them to investigate.

I saw them off and headed upstairs with my laptop. Unity was still online and again I had noted that she was alone all evening.

'Thanks for your help,' I said.

'No need to thank me, I enjoy it. I'm glad I can be of use.' She smiled and looked relieved. I was proud of her – another alien feeling I was getting used to.

After we said goodnight, I finished my homework then settled into bed. My mind was racing so it took a while to sleep. *Where am I supposed to meet Clifton?*

***

It was hard to concentrate on the Thursday. I was too excited about the hunt and couldn't leave the clues alone. I had a separate notebook and had written out all the clues and our train of thought. The lessons were a blur as I wondered how Thomas and Lucy were getting on. I couldn't wait to get home but reality bites when you have a friend like Po. There was no way I was going to get out of band practice. I was pleased that my bike had worked in the morning – at least I could go straight home afterwards.

Po was told we had a half hour set. We spent the first ten minutes deciding which songs to perform. As the gig was the weekend before Christmas, he wanted to make a Christmas theme of it and even suggested we dress up in red suits and white beards. Luckily nobody bit the bullet and we decided on finishing with a Christmas classic instead – which would be a 'punked-up' version of 'Stop the Cavalry'. We improvised and it sounded dreadful. Po loved it! I really didn't want to do this gig. Still, I had raised my skill level to eight out of ten and Po was delighted. I would probably have to let him down on Saturday morning but I wasn't brave enough to tell him yet.

I got home and managed to finish my tea before Thomas and Lucy Riley arrived. I felt their excitement instantly. We cleared the table and I called Unity on Skype. She was already waiting.

Thomas and Lucy started laying everything out on the table again as Dad made drinks.

'We have made progress today, but we might have to change our theories,' Lucy said. 'There is another nursery rhyme with cold pease porridge and it mentions a place.'

'Really?' Unity and I asked in unison.

Lucy smiled and opened up her book. '"The man in the moon came down too soon and asked his way to Norwich, he went by the south and burnt his mouth, with supping cold pease porridge."'

'But Norwich isn't on the line,' I said. My uncle lived there and we had often visited; it was to the east.

'No. That's the problem,' Lucy replied.

'*Came down too soon?* It must be. I thought he was referring to being born too soon to understand the evolution of life from matter.'

'That's deep,' Unity said, laughing. I blushed.

'There must be a reason why he diverts,' Lucy said, still looking at her notebook. 'He also said that his name refers to gathering sticks – which it doesn't – but the man in the moon does, according to 'Numbers' in the bible. A man was cast to the moon for gathering sticks on the Sabbath. That is what the nursery rhyme refers to.'

Lucy opened the map. 'There are two golf courses in the south of the city but they don't share the initials. The only link is that the World Corporate Golf Championship is also at a De Vere course, which is one of these two.'

'We think the link is too tenuous,' Thomas added.

'So there's no indication of where?' I said.

'No. We've been looking for something obvious in the town, even searching due south of it.'

We all stared at the map for a while, confused. Maybe *man in the moon* was the reference point but that still didn't indicate a meeting place. We looked at the other clues and spent a while making anagrams from the first letter of each location, wondering whether the mention of Norwich introduced the 'N' for a reason.

'We checked the names of all the towns and villages on the line from Unity's notes but again there were no obvious links. The other golf courses didn't recognise the marker either,' Lucy said.

'We wondered whether the shoelace could be a shoe string

and if there's a metaphoric connection to "on a shoestring" meaning low-budget,' Thomas said.

Unity added her thoughts. 'We need a reference to the moon, like lunar, or a reference to moonstone or Monday in any town or area – even a road name.'

'Yes, that was our thinking during the day,' Lucy said. 'We even looked into the names of pubs and restaurants to make a connection. He certainly likes to be cryptic, our Clifton.'

'We were wondering about the significance of the red star too,' Thomas said, 'Possibly a connection to Mars?'

Dad overheard this and immediately jumped in. 'Antares,' he shouted as he re-entered the room with a fresh brew. 'Mars is a planet but Antares is a star, a supergiant red star nearing the end of its life. It's the brightest red star you can see with the human eye. It was also the name given to the lunar landing modular on one of the Apollo expeditions.'

I could feel that we were onto something. We started investigating online for connections, especially to Norwich. After an hour or so the excitement diffused into frustration.

I noticed Lucy had been staring silently at the wall for a few minutes. 'Are you OK there?' I asked.

'Antares, the red star is nearing the end of its life. It's not a literal clue, it's a metaphor,' she said. 'We are on the right lines but we could be looking at this upside down.'

We all stopped, waiting for her to say something else, but she didn't. She looked at the map again, took a ruler and started extending the line beyond the north and south locations. Unity seemed to be on her wavelength.

'Look outside this hunt, Aril. Look to the world for a bigger picture...' she quoted Clifton. Lucy smiled.

'Smart thinking,' Thomas said, and put his hand on Lucy's shoulder.

Lucy extended the line to the south coast and upwards to the western isles of Scotland and made a note of the main town names. Unity offered to do a more in-depth search using the online maps, as she had the previous night. Lucy accepted and thanked her. I looked through the list of village names that we already had, trying to make a connection to Antares. Thomas seemed to be in his own world, reading his notes and adding more.

'Check the most southerly point first,' he said. '*Came by the south* is a line in that nursery rhyme. It could be more significant than Norwich.'

'It intersects with Hythe in Kent,' Lucy said.

Just then Unity gasped. 'Hey guys, go online and check where in Hythe the south point is.'

The most southerly point was Princes Parade, a beach road. A canal separated this from the main road but north of that, less than a hundred yards was 'Cliff Road' which bordered a golf course. It was narrow and secluded, even though there were houses on it.

'Surely this must be it,' I said. It *had* to be on the line; if Norwich had no significance then the *south* had to. Otherwise there was no reason to reference the nursery rhyme twice, as Clifton had done. We studied the area in more detail.

'There's a layby on the beach road,' Lucy said. 'It's not impossible it could be there but the Cliff Road location fits in with the clues. There's a cul-de-sac off the road and a wooded area beside that with no houses.'

'At seven in the evening it will be dark,' Thomas said. 'I wouldn't like to venture into a wood alone even at that time.'

'I think he wants to meet,' I said.

'Maybe he lives there,' Unity said.

We stopped what we were doing, all thinking the same thing. Were we right? And if so, what could we expect? Dad was probably wondering if I was likely to be in danger.

'We need a plan,' Thomas said. 'Dale, if we monitor Aril from a close distance, will you allow him to do the meeting?'

'I should be there too.'

'He hasn't actually told me to do the hunt alone or not to tell anybody so I don't think he'll mind if I'm dropped off. It might be a bit awkward if somebody is with me, though.'

'I think we should take two cars. One to be close to Cliff Road where the likely meeting is, and the other to observe the layby on Princes Promenade. We can stay in touch by phone. Aril can also phone if he has to meet Clifton and go somewhere else,' Lucy suggested.

Thomas agreed. He suggested having a number on speed-dial that I could hit surreptitiously if I felt I was in trouble; if that number rang, they should come to the rescue immediately. Dad agreed.

It was probably a two-hour drive but we decided to leave at three; if we were early, we could stop locally and get some food. Unity didn't say a word. I knew she was probably hoping she could join us but we were unlikely to be back much before midnight and certainly too late for a train home.

'I feel bad not including Unity in this plan,' I said.

'I don't think I'd be allowed anyway,' she said. She looked disappointed.

It didn't seem right without her. I was cursing her mother; she didn't have much right to deny Unity freedom when she obviously provided very little support for her in general. I looked to Dad and he nodded.

'You can always stay here Saturday night. There's a sofa bed in the observatory.'

Unity paused then said, 'I want to, but I don't think I'll be allowed. I'll ask though, if it's OK with your Dad.'

He stepped into view so that Unity could see him. 'Would it help if I spoke with your mother and explained?' he asked.

'I'm not sure. Maybe. I'll see if I can catch her sober tomorrow. If I try tonight when she's had a few, I'll get nowhere. Thanks though.' She smiled.

We printed out street views of the two locations in Hythe as well as road maps. Thomas and Lucy were going to stay in Cambridge but were not planning to come to the house on Friday; they would arrive around two thirty on Saturday but if they thought of anything else they would call. They wanted to see if they could get a better insight into Clifton's own dreams that he needed my help with.

Thomas and Lucy left shortly before ten. I thanked them again. I was pleased with their help and it did look now as if

I would finally meet Clifton. I wondered how we would help each other. As much as I was excited, I realised how nervous the prospect made me.

Unity stayed online and I talked to her briefly before settling down to sleep. Once again there had been no sign of anybody in the house all evening.

'You must be pretty lonely. I take it you've got friends you can hang around with too?'

'I've a few good friends but I tend to see them on weekends instead of evenings as they live nearer town. I'm not lonely, I like my own company. I prefer it like this. I'm lucky really.'

'Strange definition of lucky!'

'No, it's cool. I'm happy as long as I avoid confrontation.'

Something in her eyes made me doubt her sincerity. She liked her own company but was this by choice or familiarity? She had to come on Saturday, it wouldn't be right otherwise.

'Well, I really hope you can come Saturday. We can pick you up again and drop you off Sunday.'

'Yeah, I'll try. I'll hurry home at lunch and see if I can get back before Mum goes out again.' She smiled and I was relieved. Her eyes regained their optimism.

We said goodnight and I settled for sleep. I was tired and nervous and yet more excited than I had ever been in my life.

***

Thomas was pleased with the evening and proud that they had been able to make headway. There was still a way to go but something niggled him: why would Clifton arrange a meeting after all this mystery and intrigue? A meeting could have been arranged at any time. Though there was nothing in these clues that hinted that there would be anything sinister, Thomas was cautious. It was right to supervise Aril. He made a mental note to check the street to see if he could find a Clifton on the electoral roll and, if there was, look into his background.

'You're not convinced, are you?' Lucy said, soon after they

returned to the hotel.

'No, you're right, but I don't know why.'

'Do you think we've found the right place?'

'It would be hard to find anywhere better following the last clue.'

'What do you make of the girl?'

'She's bright, that's for sure.'

They settled for bed and checked the news again. They weren't missing much. Thomas liked the days when there was little bad news because some gems would come up that normally wouldn't make the headlines. There were developments in the case of the congressman's missing daughter. Her abductor had made contact. Thomas could read between the lines, he knew the hidden language of the police liaison officers – there had been a ransom demand. The congressman was as determined as ever to get her home safely.

'Well at least there's no drama with this case,' Lucy joked as she snuggled contentedly into Thomas, turning off the television.

She was wrong.

– CHAPTER 18 –

I left it until the last minute before having to decline or commit to band practice. Unity had missed her mum after school and knew she would have to either talk to her late Friday when she was drunk or early Saturday when she had a hangover. Neither prospect was thrilling. I had to leave at nine for rehearsals so asked her to phone me if she was heading to Cambridge and I would leave early.

As it happens, I slept in. Po's call woke me – not that I could let him know – but I was in no mood for riding to Godmanchester with a guitar on my back. I let him down and understandably suffered his wrath. Nice start to the day.

It got better still half an hour later: Unity called to say her mum wasn't going to allow her to come after all. She sounded upset. If I'd had a bigger bike I would have set off and collected her, and we could have rode off like rebels into the unknown. I told her I'd text her and keep her updated as much as I could. I felt that empty feeling again and I hadn't even seen her this time. I hated her mum; I know it was wrong of me but I couldn't help it. Unity deserved better.

I moped around for most of Saturday morning, still nervous about meeting Clifton but excited to learn his story. Harvey was feeling left out. I told him he could come down with us but he didn't want to abandon his gaming mates – more bosses to kill.

When Thomas and Lucy arrived, they brought us up

to date on their own findings before we set off. They had checked the local area but couldn't find a Clifton living there. There was nobody named Clifton registered to the local golf club either. I was warned against getting into a car and they told me to be sure I mention that my father was close by. It wasn't that they had any reason to distrust Clifton but they wanted to make sure that I had control of the situation. They were still unsure what to make of his dream. They felt that he wanted to feel he made a difference, he obviously had a faith, he wanted to look on – they assumed he meant from heaven – and know that he'd made the world a better place.It's just as well we left early because there was a hold-up en route that slowed us down. I travelled with Dad, and Thomas and Lucy took their car. We reached Hythe shortly after six and stopped in town to eat before making our way to the location. We drove around for a while first. There were a number of parked cars and a scattering of people about; some walking dogs, some who looked like businessmen who Dad thought were likely to have come from the golf course, and parents playing with their kids.

Thomas and Lucy drove to the promenade so they could keep an eye on the layby area. Dad parked a hundred yards down the road from the group of trees we had determined as the most likely meeting place. I made sure I had the gifts with me – and my phone – and headed out at five to seven.

I made my way to the wooded area near the entrance to the cul-de-sac. I looked into the trees but there wasn't much light. Hopefully the clue wasn't in there. I waited on the corner for a few minutes, looking in all directions. There were still a few people about and I was trying to be inconspicuous. There was a small fence with the top shaped like a diamond which made it impossible to sit on but I rested a foot on it. As seven o'clock passed, I wondered if I was in the wrong place. Had Thomas and Lucy spotted anything at the layby on the promenade?

How much more time should I wait? I shone my phone torch into the trees. It didn't throw out much light but I wondered if it would be enough to pick up any sheared sticks leaning against a tree. That's when I noticed something, just inside the wooded area towards the first bank of trees, something pinned to a tree trunk. I was curious enough to ease forward a little. I knew Dad could see me at a distance so I gestured to him. I hoped he could read my body language.

It looked like a piece of paper torn from a small notepad on which a small star had been drawn with pen. I inched nearer. I was right. My torch picked out a red star. I looked below and around the tree then unpinned the piece of paper. On the reverse was written in capitals: 'UNLUCKY FOR SOME' with the initials *T.M.*

Odd. This was not like Clifton's work. Somebody must be playing games with me – or maybe it was a red-herring and I was in the wrong place.

I returned to the road side with the note in my hand, intending to return to the car and discuss it with Dad. Within seconds there was chaos. A van pulled up and people were running towards me from the cul-de-sac. I froze as I found myself surrounded by men. One grabbed my arms and pulled them behind my back; another frisked me and threw me against the side of the van. The man holding my arms tugged on them with such force that it hurt. I looked towards Dad. He was getting out of his car, talking on his phone. I was terrified. It all happened so fast and not a word had been spoken.

My pockets were emptied. They had my gifts, phone and wallet. Eventually the man who'd frisked me spoke, reading my licence. 'Mr Ousby?' he asked.

'Yes. Don't hurt me!' I was shaking, trying to stay composed but there were tears in my eyes.

Dad ran up to us. 'Leave him alone. Let him go! I've called the police.'

'Sir, we *are* the police.' Dad looked shocked. 'And you are?' the man continued.

'Dale Ousby, I am Aril's father.'

The man held up Clifton's gifts in the freezer bag. Two

other men approached Dad and said they needed to search him too.

'Aril Ousby, I am arresting you on suspicion of conspiracy to kidnap and extort,' said the policeman. Then after a brief pause, looking at the gifts: 'And theft.'

I felt my legs give way. I was propped up against the side of the van as I was handcuffed. The man continued reading me my rights. My world crumbled.

– CHAPTER 19 –

Thomas and Lucy Riley drove up and down Princes Promenade a number of times before realising that the layby they wanted to monitor was the only place to park. They behaved like tourists and walked along the promenade. There was still fifteen minutes until a possible rendezvous.

The first thing they noticed was that there was a footpath running from the layby and a big sign stating *Hythe Imperial Hotel and Golf Club.*

'I never saw that on the map,' Lucy said.

'Too much of a coincidence. I think this might be the actual meeting point.'

'Maybe we should call.'

They walked to a bench across the road. They could hear the sea lapping the shore. There was little breeze but the air was cool.

'Let's give it five minutes or so,' Thomas said.

A car slowed just past the layby, then pulled in, parking half on the pathway. As the bench was facing the sea, Thomas had a better view when he looked to the left while talking with Lucy. He asked her to keep looking at him so he could see what was happening over her shoulder.

'No movement yet,' he said after a couple of minutes.

'Maybe he's looking out like we are,' Lucy suggested.

At seven o'clock exactly, the doors of the car opened. Two men dressed in suits got out and looked around. They walked towards the layby and past Thomas's car, glancing inside. Thomas wondered what to do: should he call Aril or speak to the men? They waited a little longer.

'We need to find out what's happening,' Thomas said.

He phoned Dale. 'No sign of anyone here,' Dale said.

'I think they're here. Two men, professional looking, in the layby. There's also a hotel golf club at the entrance to the layby.'

'You could be right. I've just seen Aril walk into the trees, looks like he's seen something.'

'OK, let's give it another five minutes. If there's nothing there and nobody turns up, make your way here. I can try and stall them by making conversation until you reach us.'

'OK, thanks.'

Thomas and Lucy waited a few more minutes and the men stayed in the layby; the younger of the two was speaking on a mobile telephone.

'I think we should head back to the car,' Thomas suggested. Lucy agreed and stood up, glancing over at the men for the first time.

As they crossed the road, the young man ended his call and he and his companion hasted back towards their own car. By the time Thomas and Lucy reached the layby, they had pulled away quickly.

Thomas phoned Dale but the call diverted immediately to voicemail, so he tried Aril instead and got the same response. 'That's strange,' he said.

'Maybe they're on the phone to each other,' Lucy replied.

'True. We should wait here a while longer.'

It was all quiet for ten minutes. Thomas tried to phone Dale and Aril again but was directed to voicemail each time.

'I hope everything is alright. Dale said that Aril was heading into the trees,' Thomas said.

'Should we drive round there and see?' Lucy asked.

'They could be on their way here. Let's wait a little longer.'

After another five minutes, they decided to join Dale and Aril. Their route ran parallel to the main road, so they had to drive along until the roads converged then double back. A number of cars were pulling out of Cliff Road as they entered it. When they pulled in behind Dale's car there was nobody inside.

'Maybe he's joined Aril,' Lucy said.

They walked towards the meeting area and the cluster of trees Thomas looked into the trees, using his phone torch, and called out for Aril and Dale but there was no reply.

'What is going on?' Lucy was confused. By now it was quarter-to-eight.

'Well, they'll have to return to their car eventually. We should go back to ours and wait.'

***

Congressman Linden Keld paced up and down his office. His disciples were in the adjacent room on computers and phones. It might be Saturday but he wasn't going to give them time off while his daughter was still missing. His attorney, his advisers, his publicity staff – even his bankers – were all present.

Three hundred and fifty million dollars. Who on earth asks for that much money? He was livid but over a barrel. He had to pull every string he could to get the money. He wouldn't risk making a wrong move while Daisy was still captive.

Keld's office was dominated by a giant painting of Jesus and he had a wooden altar underneath for his own personal prayer space. The ornate carving on the wooden square bore his company logo, entwined with the sacred cross. This was his sanctuary. As he waited to hear from the FBI, he clasped his hands together and asked once again for Daisy's safety, the wisdom to know what to do and the power to exact vengeance on her captives and bring them to justice worthy of His might.

He looked out over Nashville. He was lucky. He owned this city, he had the power to call on any resource he needed.

He had allies in abundance. How would anybody *dare* to cross him and his family? This would be the biggest mistake of their lives; they would wish they'd never been born. He felt the anger rising again.

Shortly after lunch his secretary knocked. Special Agent Stirling Foxton was on the line. Linden Keld snatched up the phone. 'You took your time. What's the latest?'

'Sir, a man has been arrested in England and is waiting to be questioned. He had a number of items on him. I'm emailing a photo of them to you to see if any of them belong to your daughter.'

'Yes, send them to me now. MISS EASTON!'

'Yes sir,' his assistant replied.

'Open up my email, you'll find these things quicker than me. I don't get this new technology,'

Agent Foxton stayed on the line. The email was opened, there were a number of items including hair accessories, sunglasses, a shoelace and…

'That's Daisy's watch, I'm sure of it! What in God's name is that doing there?'

'Do you recognise anything else?'

'Not sure. It's possible. Edina is likely to know. I'll call her in.'

'Well, let me know as soon as you can and we'll get the police to question the suspect and find out what he knows.'

'Whoever you have there, you need to crucify him! FIND MY DAUGHTER!'

Linden hung up and returned to the office. He apologised to his saviour for his anger and frustration. Should he go to England? Daisy didn't have her passport with her. Could she have been smuggled out of the country on somebody else's ID?

Keld was suffused with rage. *Heads will roll, heads must roll!*

***

Thomas and Lucy returned to their car.

'I'm starting to get a bad feeling about this,' Lucy said. She could see in Thomas's eyes that he was feeling the same. She hoped it wasn't going to disturb him again. His episodes happened less frequently now but she was aware of the triggers. The fact that both Dale and Aril's phones were switched off was an indication that something wasn't right... Lucy put her hand on Thomas's.

'It's almost impossible to trust people these days, especially where money is involved,' Thomas replied.

'Maybe we should call the police if Aril and Dale don't return in the next half an hour.'

Ten minutes later a police van drove past and pulled over by the trees. Thomas and Lucy watched for a while in silence. Three uniformed officers were looking on the pavement and fence. They saw them head into the trees with torches.

'Oh no,' Thomas said.

Lucy knew this meant trouble. There was no reason that they would be there unless it was connected to the hunt. She felt her stomach tighten and hoped Aril and Dale had not been hurt.

'We need to find out,' she said, opening the door without waiting to hear Thomas's response. He joined her.

One of the officers remained on the outside of the wooded area; the other two were studying a tree.

'Are you looking for anything in particular?' Thomas asked the officer.

He didn't answer directly but looked at them both and asked if they lived locally.

'No. We're private investigators,' Thomas said, handing over his card. 'We're helping a client solve a geocaching treasure hunt. He and his father are now missing and we've been worried in case they are in danger.'

The officer called over his colleagues.

'Sir, madam, you need to come with us to the station. Your clients have been arrested.'

'Arrested?' Thomas said, shocked. 'There's not a criminal

bone in their bodies. What are they being held for?'
     'I think you need to come with us!'

– CHAPTER 20 –

I had never been inside a police station in my life, let alone a cell. No matter how many times I told the police officers it was a mistake, nobody replied. I was relieved Dad had been brought in with me – surely he could sort things out? But after a couple of hours I was still alone and terrified and tears had turned to sobs. What had I done? What had Clifton done? What was that message about?

There was little room in my cell. I paced three steps, turned back and paced again. A drunk in the adjacent cell was muttering to himself. I tried to block him out but I was aware of every sound. I wanted Dad to come in and tell me it was all a big mistake.

I had already had my fingerprints taken and my mouth swabbed. I was asked if I knew why I was there and I said I didn't.

Who had been kidnapped? My thoughts immediately turned to Unity. Had she left the house and her mum fabricated a vindictive story about me? Was she OK?

It was late when the duty officer collected me from my cell and took me into a room with a desk. In another room I saw Dad talking to two men, and at the end of the corridor Thomas and Lucy were talking to someone but I couldn't attract their attention. I was asked to wait. The clock on the wall said 11.20; I had been in that cell nearly four hours. I waited. I was thirsty, tired, shaky and nervous. I wanted to go home, go to bed.

Shortly after midnight a plain-clothed man entered the room. 'Aril, we need to question you under caution. Your father can't be present as you are seventeen and must be questioned as an adult. Do you understand?'

I could hardly talk, the fear rupturing my soul. I needed Dad. I hesitated before nodding.

'A solicitor can be present with you. Would you like to talk to our duty solicitor now or would you prefer your own?'

A solicitor? I'd never spoken to one but had seen them on television. No matter how hard I tried to speak, fear took a paralysing grip on my throat. All I could do was nod and the man's looked at me without expression until I whispered, 'Duty. Please.'

The solicitor introduced himself as Norris Southwell. He seemed friendly but professional, close to retirement age, and his hair had receded beyond hope, leaving the odd stray grey patch above the ear. His eyes told their own stories – they had a look of wisdom, the experience of injustice and the knowledge of pain.

'Aril, I've spoken with your father. He knows that he cannot be present when you're interviewed as you are seventeen and legally must be treated as an adult. He would also be a witness if you are prosecuted.'

'Prosecuted? How could I be? I haven't done anything wrong. Is this about Unity?'

'Unity?' he asked, looking confused.

'Why am I here?' I asked.

'I can't tell you, I must let the police explain that to you. Their questioning may appear severe, Aril, but you must understand that these people have a job to do and they need to know the truth.'

'What do I do?' I was terrified at the thought. I had seen on television how the police question people. I hadn't done anything wrong.

'You need to tell the truth. If what your father explained is true, they will need to understand what you know. Because at the moment they think you know more than you do.'

***

Detective Chief Inspector Newton Knock introduced himself and urged Mr Southwell to sit next to me. A woman followed with a folder and various evidence bags which she placed on the desk. She was introduced as DI Susan Moore. She whispered something to DCI Knock and I heard Thomas Riley's name mentioned. I noticed her give a brief shake of the head.

The interview was recorded and, after establishing that I was Aril Ousby, Knock began. He pushed two evidence bags in my direction across the table and I instantly recognised the contents. One had the gold watch; the other had my plectrum, the one I had left as a gift to Clifton.

'Do you recognise these, Aril?'

'Yes, I do.'

I was expecting another question but they all just stared at me. 'That's my plectrum and the watch I found in a cache at Little Eversden.' Still silence. 'Why am I here? What am I supposed to have done?'

'Do you watch the news, Aril?'

'Sometimes. Not much lately.'

'Are you aware that Congressman Linden Keld's daughter Daisy went missing in America last week?'

'No. Why?'

'She was lured away from her college, transferred to another vehicle and hasn't been seen since.'

'Oh. That's sad,' I said, confused. *What is this to do with me?*

'It is indeed. This plectrum,' he said, holding up the bag, 'was left in the abandoned car that she was last seen in.'

'What? How?'

DCI Knock held up the other evidence bag and continued, 'This is Daisy Keld's watch.'

I looked at my solicitor. Clifton had framed me. I felt sick.

What was all that about trust? I was angry but it wasn't my anger that was making me feel sick – it was disappointment. I had believed in Clifton. I had trusted him.

'I think you need to tell me everything. Linden Keld wants to crucify you – and he has the means to do so.'

I broke down. The fear and disappointment cut through me like a million needles. Nobody said a word. DI Moore offered me tissues and I tried desperately to compose myself.

I spent the next two hours telling them everything I could remember. They asked me about people who had seen me, or that I had told about the hunt. I explained about Summer, Denny, Henry and Unity, and how Dad had made contact with Thomas and Lucy Riley. My clues and notes were at home but they had already applied for a warrant to search the house. What would Dad say about that? I felt such a fool. But all the time the overriding feeling that was tearing me apart was disappointment in Clifton.

'I want to believe you, Aril, and I do. But there is evidence to implicate you directly. You're the only person to have had any contact with the kidnapper. And the kidnapper also thinks you know where she is and when to find her.'

'He what?'

'Aril, I think you know more than you realise you do. We are going to need to go through all the clues.'

'Thomas and Lucy Riley are here, I've seen them. They have every clue, they should be here.'

'We were waiting to question them after we had spoken to you. They've come forward voluntarily to give evidence. Normally we would deal with these things in the morning but we are under time pressure. There was a ransom demand, a large sum of money, which Linden Keld has paid. The kidnapper told us where to find you and said that you would know where and when we can find Daisy. Mr Keld is not a patient man. There are FBI agents on their way over to talk to you.'

'I'm the wrong person! I don't know if I can even help. I've no idea where she is. Clifton has let me down, he has hurt me badly. I don't want to do this any more.'

'Aril, you don't have any option.'

'I want to sleep, but I don't want to sleep in the cell. I can help you tomorrow. Right now, I can't think.'

Norris suggested we speak in the morning.

'Aril, this is a major case,' Knock said. 'The media are all over the story in America. We will try to keep this quiet for now. We need to keep you in custody so you will have to sleep in the cell overnight.'

'No. I just want to go home. I've done nothing wrong. It's a treasure hunt! This is a mistake!' More foolish tears fell. I wanted to die. Literally. I felt so betrayed, so alone. So tired.

'OK, we are nearly done for now, Aril. Can you recall seeing anything at all when you found these clues? Anybody acting suspiciously?'

'No. I missed someone though, at the Chelmsford clue. There was somebody by my bike. I saw the bike move and I saw a car but I can't remember much else. I was distracted by the clue.'

'Right, we will end this now and I will speak with Mr and Mrs Riley while you sleep.'

I was escorted back to my holding cell. It was noisy; there were several drunks nearby. Norris Southwell came with me and I spoke briefly with him. He tried to give me encouragement. I wanted to see my dad and make sure he was alright and not cross with me. Mr Southwell said he would make sure I could see him before I spoke to anybody else the next day.

***

Thomas and Lucy Riley arrived at their hotel at shortly before five in the morning. Lucy had booked online when it became obvious that they needed to stay locally overnight. It had been a night she would rather forget – and was about to get worse.

Thomas sat on the edge of the bed and put his head in

his hands.

'Are you OK?' she asked.

Thomas started shaking. First it looked as if his leg was twitching but then it was happening in both legs and his entire body shook. She had seen it before. She clasped his hands and looked him in the eye; sweat was forming on his brow. She laid him on the bed and opened the window. She put the kettle on; he would need sweet hot tea. She knew a case like this might trigger an episode even though he had them rarely now. He had learnt to recognise and control the flashbacks.

Post-Traumatic Stress Disorder took on many different symptoms for its victims. Thomas had locked away all his fear, anxiety and pain caused by the attack in Las Vegas five years ago, until his body's pressure valve finally gave way. It took a trigger to release it and it was something over which he had no control. His mind took over his body until he gained control again. Lucy had dealt with a dozen episodes or more, but this was the first in a long time.

Thomas curled up on the bed in a foetal position, trying to control the spasms. She had to stay calm; she couldn't show her own anxiety. She made the tea and tried to prop him up enough to drink it.

After twenty minutes Thomas was able to sit up. Lucy sat on the edge of the bed, gently massaging his leg with one hand.

'Are you feeling any better?'

'I think so. I don't know how you put up with me sometimes.'

'Don't be silly,' she said.

'I wish they would stop.'

'They will.' She leaned forward and kissed him on the forehead. They got ready for bed without talking about the case. It was going to be a busy day tomorrow. She hoped they could cope.

Poor Aril, she thought.

– CHAPTER 21 –

'A what? A treasure hunt? Are you kidding me?' Linden Keld was fuming.

'Apparently so. The boy knows nothing, I guarantee it,' Stirling Foxton replied. Linden thought Foxton should have gone to England himself, instead of sending his underlings.

'That's not good enough. Three hundred and fifty million for a wild-goose chase? This boy is good … but he doesn't know who he is messing with.'

'Sir...'

'Don't "sir" me, Foxton, I'll show no mercy on your soul, by Jesus. He knows. We need a warrant to extradite him. We have evidence. That amount of money should alert national security – it could be for arms. We need that warrant. Get it now!'

Linden hung up and retreated back to his sanctuary. He was seething.

***

I barely slept. It was noisy and uncomfortable and I was so scared that tiredness alone would not allow my mind and body to rest. Breakfast was brought to me at seven thirty. Not exactly *nouvelle cuisine,* but I would have eaten anything. I was told that I was to be questioned again at nine.

It was the first time I had been able to think about

Clifton. It all seemed wrong. I wanted to trust him but what was there to trust now? He had kidnapped some girl and implicated me. How could I make his dream come true and how the hell could he help my dream now?

There was obviously no treasure. The only treasure I had was Unity's friendship and even she might not trust me any more after this. She must have wondered why I hadn't called or texted. I wanted my phone back. Curse Clifton.

Norris Southwell was first to see me in the morning. I think he had been up all night.

'There are some men to see you from America, Aril. I've been trying to understand what happened and I've spoken with a number of people through the night. This is a troubling case because the evidence of your involvement is strong, but the only thing you can actually be charged with is being in receipt of stolen property.'

'Even though I didn't know it was stolen?'

'Yes. The problem is that the heavy mob is here. So I need to protect you. I've been explaining to your father that the missing girl's parents are pressing for you to be extradited to America so you can be charged there. It's unlikely that will be allowed but there's another problem. The ransom money was an extremely large figure, the sort of money that triggers international security in case it's used to buy arms. That means there's a different set of laws that come into place under the Prevention of Terrorism Act.'

'*What?* Terrorism? This can't be happening?'

'It is, Aril. This is serious. Now listen. It's obvious to everybody here that you are innocent. I want to ask for a deal where you are allowed to go home. The police or FBI can question you and you will assist the police voluntarily. You will be charged with possession of stolen property and released on police bail. If you attempt to do a runner, or you are found to be lying or withholding information, they will throw the book at you. Your dad is convinced you will cooperate.'

'I will. I'll help them find this girl, I just don't want to spend any more time here. I'm not a criminal. I'm devastated by this too.'

'I know. That's why I want all these powerful people to know that you are on their side.'

I thanked him as he left. As much as I was relieved, I was still frightened. I didn't even want to think about college on Monday and I was worried about what Dad would think. He was right from the start – but I hadn't done anything wrong. I had tried to be careful and didn't commit myself to anything. I had no way of knowing about Clifton's actions – even Thomas and Lucy hadn't. I wanted to see Dad desperately to get back some normality inside the chaos.

I didn't see Dad before my interrogation from the FBI. The morning became a blur. Same story, same explanations, same hostility, same accusations and the same threats. The nightmare continued but I didn't break down this time. The tears formed a river of ice behind my eyes as I tried to take my mind back to happier times: Unity's excited smile when she showed me her science experiment; my seventeenth birthday ride out; Unity's palm in mine…

What did *extradited* mean?

***

Dale Ousby greeted Lucy and Thomas at the police station next morning. They hadn't been able to speak the previous night. Dale looked as if he hadn't slept, Lucy thought. He was distraught and worried for Aril. He hadn't been allowed to talk with his son yet but his solicitor had. The solicitor told Dale that Aril was clearly distressed but had been cooperative. The FBI agents were with him at the moment; there were concerns that the ransom money could get into the hands of terrorists and now National Security was involved.

Lucy struggled to understand what had happened. They hadn't seen this coming. She and Thomas waited at the station for news. Dale and his solicitor wanted to ensure that

Aril was not extradited to America.

'I think we need to go back to each location and see if we missed something,' Lucy suggested. 'There might even be a landmark that was local to each area – maybe a windmill or a certain type of tree.'

'We do, though there's a lot of ground to cover,' Thomas replied.

'We could do it with Aril's help. He needs to talk us through each find.'

'I'm pretty sure we'll get help,' Thomas said, looking up at DCI Knock as he joined them.

Thomas explained their thinking to Knock. He clearly wasn't keen on this case landing on his doorstep, so was happy for any line of investigation to take the attention away from the south coast.

'How's Aril doing?' Dale asked.

'He is in shock,' Knock said. 'I don't think anybody believes he has any knowledge of this kidnap. I'm hoping these FBI guys will see that for themselves and relay it back. I interviewed Aril last night, I took the hard line with him too. He knows nothing. All he understands is how this Clifton guy's mind works. We need Aril to work with the criminal psychology team or GCHQ. He's a clever kid, but he isn't clever enough to run a multinational extortion racket.'

'GCHQ?' Thomas said.

'There has been talk of it,' DCI Knock replied. 'The Security Service was called in last night. They are letting us and the FBI talk to Aril first. GCHQ was their call. It depends what happens this morning. We don't know what timescale we are working to.'

'From what I can make out, we're looking at seven days,' Thomas said. 'I assume that is seven days from yesterday. Seven has been a recurring theme throughout this hunt.'

'Oh. Let me go and relay that to the others, in case it helps trigger Aril's memory, or thought processes.'

DCI Knock left. Dale looked subdued as he shook his head. 'What a mess,' he said.

'Aril's going to need extra TLC for a while,' Lucy said.

'I know. I'm not angry with him, I'm worried for him. I'm glad his friend Unity wasn't here for this.'

'She had a lucky escape. From what Aril was saying I think she was disappointed that she couldn't make it. She's probably wondering what's going on.'

'I don't have her number, otherwise I would have called her.'

It was nearing midday. Lucy wondered what Clifton was thinking. Why turn from hero to villain in such a major way? He seemed as if he was a man with good morals and respect for the world – a philanthropist with a respect for humanity and the species' role in the universe. Was it an act after all? She could empathise with Aril; the injustice was unbearable.

DCI Knock returned. 'The FBI is finishing up with Aril now. I don't think we can let him go without some charge, but it seems wrong. We need to bind him legally to cooperate for the sake of the FBI investigations. We won't be able to do anything until Monday, though.'

'No,' Dale and Thomas said in unison.

'He can't spend another night here,' Dale continued.

'I agree. He is cooperating as it is.' Thomas added.

'Leave it with me. I'll speak with my Super and Southwell when they finish up. The kid will be better off working with us all together, rather than like this. It's counter-productive.'

And so they waited.

– CHAPTER 22 –

I had never been so pleased to see familiar faces in my life. I can't remember hugging Dad so hard since I was about seven. The ice thawed on my tears and I thought I was drowning in them. I couldn't stop crying. I couldn't speak or acknowledge Thomas and Lucy, who stood awkwardly while I embraced Dad.

Norris Southwell was behind me. I eventually pulled myself away from Dad's arms and realised he had been crying too. My relief was overcome by guilt. He was hurting too. This was my fault.

DCI Knock told us all to come into his office. The FBI agents were still inside the building, on their phones. I heard them mentioning my name. I had done my best; I hoped they believed me.

'Aril, I've been talking with various people and the authorities all day to find out what to do for the best. There are options but I want to come up with one that will end up with us finding this missing girl and making sure that nobody is harmed as a result of the money her father has paid. Do you understand?'

'Yes. I'm willing to help. I just want to go home.'

'OK then, here's what we do. We release you without charge for now, but you are to cooperate with both the Security Service and the FBI. Thomas and Lucy have agreed to help. We need to go back to where each clue was found, so there will be a lot of travelling. We only have six days – we need to move fast.'

I nodded to Thomas and Lucy to acknowledge their help. 'We will, that's fine.'

'Aril, I must warn you. You must cooperate fully with us. If you don't, then you will be charged with receiving stolen property and conspiracy. Because of the nature of the case, the judge is unlikely to grant bail and you'll be held in custody for a long time. Do you understand?'

'Yes. I do. I don't have any reason not to cooperate.'

'Good. One more thing, Aril. This case is all over the news in America and reports are already leaking that there is a connection with the UK. If the money is likely to be used to form any sort of terrorist threat, there will be a media blackout. But until we get that authorisation, we need to control the amount of information that's released. It will protect your name too.'

'I won't say anything,' I said. Then I shuddered: *Unity*. I had to tell her. I looked over at Thomas. 'What about Unity? Does she know what's happened?'

'I'm not sure, I don't think so.'

'I need to say something to Unity,' I said to DCI Knock. 'She probably understands Clifton's thinking better than I do. She's helped with all the clues. She would be a help, though there's no way she could travel with us.'

'The problem is knowing how much you can trust her and any friend that she might tell. I don't think it's wise,' Knock said, shifting his eyes between Thomas and me.

'I don't know much about her,' Thomas said. 'But Aril is right: she is a potential asset and she was present during three of the finds. We've all spoken with her. She's certainly not the type of girl who craves drama or attention. Quite the opposite, in fact.'

'I'll speak only with her. You can monitor my conversations – or I could make them in the presence of somebody in authority.'

'OK, but only tell her as much as you feel she'll be

comfortable with. Bear in mind that her parents might also probe for information and they might not keep their mouths shut if the press offer money. It might not be wise to give her too much knowledge.'

He was right. I hadn't thought about that – but neither did I like the idea of holding back information. I nodded again, reluctantly accepting the wisdom of his words.

'It's likely that GCHQ will open an investigation room in Cheltenham. We'll need help from each police force where you found a clue and to get forensics into each location,' DCI Knock said. He looked at Thomas and Lucy. 'So you may have to base yourselves in Cheltenham for a few days.'

'That's fine,' Thomas replied. 'It's easier to have a central base to work from.'

***

I texted Unity as soon as my phone was returned. I had twenty missed calls in total, five from Unity, as well as countless texts. I told her:

> *Spent night in police cell, phone confiscated. Clifton set me up. On my way back, I will tell you on Skype. Glad you missed me, but I missed you more. Pleased you weren't down for this mess. x*

She texted back instantly, and my first smile of the day came from the relief that I could talk to her again.

Thomas drove us to Dad's car and we arranged to meet back at the house. Harvey must have been worried about us. I wondered how much he knew; he wasn't the best at keeping secrets.

I spoke to Dad on the way back. I was relieved that he wasn't mad at me but felt such a fool, and there were uncomfortable silences at times. I was hungry and tired but couldn't sleep or stop thinking "What if…?"

We finally arrived home around six. I knew I had a busy

week ahead and there was no way I could go to college. The Security Services would arrive at eight in the morning; it would take us at least two days to revisit all the locations of the clues.

Thomas and Lucy arrived shortly after we did. Harvey was pleased to see us. He had been eating snacks for twenty-four hours and empty packets and wrappers were strewn all over the lounge area. Dad wasn't happy.

Thomas, Lucy and I congregated in the kitchen with Dad while he made tea. Guilt got the better of Harvey and he offered to ride to the chippy to get us some food. There was one in the next village about five minutes' cycling time away. Dad gave him some money and I think Harvey was forgiven.

'Well Aril, little did you know this time yesterday that you'd be talking to the FBI, MI5 and be implicated in an international kidnap and possible terrorist plot,' Dad said. His tone was mocking to lighten the atmosphere, but I felt terrible. He had explained to me in the car what the police had said to him. I had explained how the disappointment in Clifton was worse than the reality of the trouble I was in.

The weirdest thing of all was that I still wanted to trust Clifton. I would have done if he hadn't left that last note. It was rude; it was as if I had proved my trust in him and he had turned it around as if to say 'Haha, Sucker!' I just didn't get it. Was it really his note? It was signed *T.M.* I explained my thinking to Thomas and Lucy.

'I agree with you, Aril,' Thomas said. 'I have a horrible feeling you were in the wrong place. Clifton knew you would be wrong too, because he led the police to you. That's why he left you that message. When we were dealing with an online treasure hunt a few years ago, the creator set up some pages that had the same tone to them when we read his clues wrongly. Things like *Nice Try, Try Again*. I can't help think that Clifton has studied that case.'

'Does that mean there's another container still out there?'

'We can't rule it out.'

'Did you check the area by the layby?'

'Yes. We went there first thing this morning and spent half an hour searching, even on the beach. We explained our thoughts to the police later. I think they are sending people out with metal detectors.'

'Where else can it be then? Have we been reading the line wrong? Has it been a red herring from the start?' I asked.

'I'm not sure. That's why we need to start from scratch and look again,' Thomas said.

'What do you make of "T.M."? Do you really think it was from Clifton?"

"We need to bear it in mind. It's hard to tell if it was Clifton's writing, but the star is too much of a coincidence for it to be unconnected. I think that's why GCHQ are involved.'

'What's GCHQ?'

'It's the Government Communication Headquarters. It's part of the three security services, along with MI5 and MI6. GCHQ deal with cyber-crime and anything involving technology. But the American National Security Agency – which is the US equivalent of MI5 – is involved because there are movement issues with the ransom money. It looks like Clifton has been very clever and engineered this delay to give himself time to access and distribute his money. I don't know how much is involved but it must be enough to worry national security.'

'I still can't believe this was about money,' I said. 'Clifton wants the money for his dream, especially if he is dying. Why kidnap someone, though? I hope the girl is safe.'

'I hope so too.'

Harvey returned with the fish and chips and we sat in the kitchen to eat. It was the best meal I had ever eaten. It felt good to be home; I never want to see the inside of a cell again.

I called Unity on Skype shortly afterwards. I explained that anything I told her had to be secret and it was up to her how much she wanted me to share. She was adamant that she wanted to know everything so I told her all that happened. Thomas and Lucy listened in. Unity handled it well, even offered to be a witness if she needed to be. She was relieved she hadn't come with us. Her mum would have probably killed her.

'Has it occurred to anybody that Clifton is in England right now, or has an accomplice if he isn't?' she asked.

In all the panic of the past twenty-four hours that simple fact had bypassed me. If Clifton left that note, he must be here. 'You're right,' I said.

'We told the police that we suspected he is in England. They were going to check flights out to the US,' Lucy said. 'Your thinking is good, Unity.'

There was that pride thing I felt again.

'When was the abduction?' Unity asked.

'Friday, November 9th,' Lucy replied. 'She's been gone over two weeks.'

'Poor girl. How old is she?'

'Fifteen. She's a child prodigy. She was already studying at university.'

'Wait,' Unity said, suddenly animated. 'We checked that W.C.G.C. golf marker before we knew what it was and found that the initials also related to a centre for gifted children. I'm not sure if it was on the line but I think it was, or close.'

I remembered that. I ran upstairs to get my notebook. 'Yes. The Westcliff Centre for Gifted Children.'

'I wonder if Clifton has an association with the place,' Lucy said.

'We need to investigate and mention it to the police tomorrow,' Thomas said.

'Do you think he could have a gifted child of his own?' Unity asked. 'Maybe in that Westcliff Centre?'

'Good thinking,' Lucy said, writing notes.

I realised at that moment how much the hunt had changed. Instead of feeling excitement at every new train of thought, I felt saddened – even sorry for myself. I was grateful for everybody's help. *We have a parallel trust; I trust you, Aril, and you must trust me.* Why, Clifton? I felt tortured inside, betrayed. It was the worst kind of heartbreak.

'Are you OK, Aril?' Unity asked.

I was scared to open my mouth in case I broke down. I nodded, looking down in case my eyes betrayed me. I don't think I fooled anybody.

'It's been a long day,' Lucy said. 'We could probably all do with some sleep.'

She and Thomas started gearing up to leave, offering idle talk and encouragement. I ended the call with Unity and promised to keep her updated during the week.

Dad came into my room as I was settling to bed. 'You handled yourself well today, Aril. This mess is not your fault, so don't blame yourself. I was proud of you, despite all the chaos. Switch off now, take your mind to a happier time and try to sleep.' He smiled and I nodded as he turned to leave. I couldn't speak.

– CHAPTER 23 –

Special Agent Stirling Foxton was taken to his temporary office in the GCHQ building in Cheltenham. He usually loved coming to England but was cursing this visit. He was missing Thanksgiving with his family back home, but time was pressing and Linden Keld's daughter had to be priority.

As soon as the police in the UK found the boy, Foxton sent two agents over to interview him but Linden was not happy with the outcome. He demanded that Foxton personally oversee the investigation in England. Linden's legal team were already like frenzied piranhas, feasting on the incompetence of the Federal Bureau.

The GCHQ staff filled him in on the latest developments. Aril Ousby would be arriving with two private investigators in an hour's time. They had been all over the UK retracing Aril's movements over the previous weeks.

The room at GCHQ was set up for the investigation. Two huge whiteboards detailed dates and locations and a map was pinned to the wall covered with lines and notes. Clifton's messages were scanned and placed in order on the desk. It was one giant puzzle, with the clock ticking relentlessly as a reminder that they had to think fast. It was Wednesday morning. They had four days to solve this. *Or else what?*

The British Security Services were monitoring the situation but were not yet directly involved. They were happy to let the FBI handle it with GCHQ and assess whether they needed to get involved as more information came to light.

Forensics had found traces of blood on the shoelace. DNA tests showed that it was not Daisy Keld's. They were cross-matching the criminal databases to see if it matched any known felons.

The gifts that formed the clues were the main focus of the investigation. Foxton could understand how Aril Ousby had been enticed in to the hunt; Clifton appeared to speak a language of hope, he had an altruistic outlook.

Foxton needed to see the kid for himself and assess whether he was smart enough to pull the wool over their eyes. He trusted his intuition.

***

My phone alarm woke me at 7:15. I had finally slept a full night. I had a hotel room in Cheltenham and Thomas and Lucy were next door. For the past two days we had revisited clue locations, together with the two American agents who had interviewed me on Sunday.

Clifton had removed all traces of the hunt: the sheared sticks, the red ink star on the rock, the ropes – even the barbed wire fence over at Hartside Pass had been fixed.

Luckily both Mum and Dad had been with me on a hunt, and Henry too. I was pleased that the FBI didn't question Unity. Henry was a star. It was good to see him again. He was given minimal information about the reasons behind the questioning but couldn't have praised me more or given a better account of his involvement in finding the two Scottish clues. I felt the pressure ease and the agents seemed to warm to me.

I arrived at the GCHQ building with Thomas and Lucy at nine o'clock. I was to meet a senior FBI agent and was nervous again. Thomas and Lucy were good to me. The more time I spent with them, the more I liked them. They told me about some of their own experiences; they'd experienced their own share of injustice, so their sympathy for me was genuine. They primed me for each round of questioning, which gave me confidence.

I was introduced to Special Agent Stirling Foxton. His intense countenance displayed a rainbow of emotions in an instant; you could tell he was a thinker. His hair was short, dark and swept from left to right, surfing the waves of his frown lines.

His voice was quiet yet spoke with authority. I could tell immediately that he was worried. 'I've spent the past two days studying this case and read the reports of your expedition with my FBI colleagues. You are obviously an intelligent young man. I don't want to know your story, you've had enough of telling that. I want to know what you think.'

I was caught off-guard. I had been trying to think all week but I had been living in the past, full of regret and disappointment. The thing that bugged me most was the last message. Clifton hurt me. I would have preferred to be arrested without the knowledge of that message, then I would still trust Clifton.

'All I've done is think and try to make sense of it, sir. I don't know to deal with the disappointment. That's tearing me up more than all this,' I confessed.

'Disappointment about being caught?'

'No. No not that!'

'In there being no treasure?'

'No. Not that either!' This was odd. Unexpected. 'Clifton. I'm disappointed in Clifton. I am disappointed that he didn't trust me.'

'You were working as a team?'

'Yes. I mean, no, not as a criminal team. It was an adventure.' I couldn't explain myself. 'I just liked his language, I liked his thinking and I liked the interaction with him. I believed he was a good man. I believed I was doing *good*. The treasure was a thrill but there was more to it than that. I wanted to help him. I thought he was dying and I wanted him to have his dream. I didn't think for one second his dream would involve kidnapping a girl.'

'What *did* you think, then?'

'I don't know,' I said quietly, looking down at the table. I really didn't know.

'OK then, Aril, where do you think you went wrong? Where did he lose his trust in you?'

Ouch. That hurt. I took a moment to compose myself. 'I don't know, sir. I trusted him and I thought he trusted me. He wanted me to think. He wanted me to help him. He was the person I wanted to be. Can you imagine how that feels now?' My voice broke. I looked over to Lucy; she was one jump ahead and handed me a tissue.

'I don't think this is fair questioning,' Thomas said.

'Mr Riley, what you think is of no importance to me or this case. Linden Keld will not rest until his daughter is safe and her abductors are brought to justice. The kidnapper traded Aril's knowledge for a huge ransom. His knowledge is now my property.'

'I am nobody's property! You can't buy my mind. I am here to help you of my own free will,' I said loudly, shocking myself with my vehemence.

'Aril, anything you know that is relevant to this case *is* my property,' Foxton said. 'Unless you want to spend the rest of your days in jail.'

Thomas motioned to Lucy. 'We are done here. So is Aril.'

I looked up, unsure of what to do.

'A word, in private, if you don't mind,' Foxton said to Thomas. They left the room and I stayed with Lucy. I felt a fool. I had been questioned hard before; I should have been used to it by now. Nobody seemed to understand the reason for my pain except Thomas and Lucy.

***

'We are here to help you, sir,' Thomas said quietly to Foxton in the corridor. 'Aril is not the type of kid who will be any use to you if he's under pressure. He is a positive person and responds to positive stimulation. He's hurting and scared and – above all – he's innocent.'

'I know, Mr Riley, but I had to see that for myself. Linden Keld is swarming all over the department. I need to be one hundred per cent sure of my facts before I report back to him or he will have me off this case and send in harder agents than me. Believe me, you want me here. What Aril thinks of Clifton is of vital importance because what he thinks is what Clifton *expects* him to think. I will go easier on him but I want to stay in control in there too. Get me?'

'Yes, I get that. I'll take your lead.'

'What do you make of all this, may I ask?'

'Clifton didn't know that it would be a kid who would take up the hunt. He didn't ask Aril for the guitar pick or any gifts. Aril volunteered his help out of trust. Clifton has improvised. I don't think this is as planned as it appears. Could these be the actions of a desperate man?'

'You're right. He can't be working alone, either. If he is ill, then how ill is he?'

'Could we coax Clifton out somehow? I think we were in the wrong place on Saturday. There could be another clue.'

'I'll see,' Foxton replied. 'We need some help from inside here, I think.'

'Do you mind if I ask how much money the ransom demand was?'

'Sorry, that's still classified, but it was beyond anything that you would normally expect, which is why it has to be taken as a serious threat.'

'Has it not been possible to chase the movement of the money?'

'It was complex and structured, involving cash, gold and money transfers. With Clifton's clever delays and warnings we are reluctant to openly pursue in case we place Daisy Keld in added danger. Though we *are* on the case.'

'I didn't think Clifton would be any sort of threat,' Thomas mused. 'I wasn't reading his "life on the line" comment deep enough. If he is dying, we should look for hospices that are located on the line.'

'Yes, I agree. You get back in there and put Aril's mind at ease and I'll go and see where I can delegate. Just remember, I want control.'

'Yes, I get you.'

***

I looked around the room at the whiteboards, maps and photographs. I used to watch crime programmes on television with Dad and follow cases like this. I used to think how good it would be to solve mysteries. Here I was, the centrepiece of the whole investigation, and I was useless.

Lucy was quiet. I suspected she was anxious because Thomas was outside talking to this *Special Agent*. I laughed: did those really exist? I expected Stirling Foxton to walk in any second with a neuralizer and that I'd wake up in bed at home with no knowledge of the past six weeks.

It hit me then. I was being selfish. This wasn't about me. This wasn't about my disappointment. This was about finding a girl. It was about distraught parents who had given up a huge amount of money, without care of the consequences, just to get back their daughter. I wasn't the victim here, I was the solution. I was the hope. I was no longer Clifton's hope, I was Daisy Keld's hope. A wave of energy rushed through me.

Lucy looked at me.

'I'm a fool,' I said. 'Get them back in here.'

She didn't have to. Thomas opened the door that moment.

'I'm OK,' I said. 'You don't have to go, I want to stay and help. This isn't about me. He had a right to ask me.'

Thomas looked shocked; he glanced at Lucy and she smiled and shrugged.

'It's OK,' Thomas said. 'I understand why Special Agent Foxton took the hard line with the questioning. He had to. Listen to him and answer the best you can. He knows you're innocent and he knows you are disappointed in Clifton – but he really does need to know what you think and why you think it. If you were wrong with the location, then Clifton knew you were going to be wrong. We need to work out *how* he knew.'

After Foxton returned we went through Clifton's messages in order. I tried to explain my own thinking at every stage. I was doing most of the talking, the only person not taking notes. We were trying to work out why Clifton would ask about the circle and square and Paris to Milan when Foxton had his own epiphany.

'Daisy Keld was abducted from her university in McKenzie, Tennessee.' He went to the computer and showed it to us on the map. The road that ran through it had the town of Milan to the west and Paris to the east. They were about thirty-five miles apart; forty-five minutes by car.

'Woah!' the three of us said, in unison.

'He was telling us all along. He said that even a name is relative,' I continued. *'Look outside the hunt, look to the world for the bigger picture.'*

This opened up an entirely new train of thought.

I hadn't been paying enough attention.

– CHAPTER 24 –

Linden Keld was at home with his wife. It was the first time in weeks that he had sat down. He had hardly spoken to Edina; she was too quiet and he was too busy looking for their daughter. He was not used to being powerless – it was an alien concept. He wielded his power as a God-given right, but now he was at the mercy of technology and communication to help find his daughter.

Another thing that was alien to him was *guilt*. Why did he feel this way? He had to block it out. He was a good person; these feelings of anger and hate were justified.

'Stay home with me tomorrow,' Edina said, breaking his train of thought.

'You might be able to stay here and do nothing but wait, but I can't. I need to find her. The Lord won't let me rest until I do.'

How could he stay at home? There would be no Thanksgiving – there was nothing to be thankful for. Jesus would understand. Keld was not feeling thankful. He wanted justice; he wanted that English punk within range of his wrath. He wanted…

'Please. Linden. I don't want to be alone. I've been alone most of the week. I don't want to be alone tomorrow.'

'How can you expect me to ask my staff to come in on Thanksgiving if I stay home with you?'

'They have families, Linden. They go in because they are

too afraid not to.'

'Rubbish. They come in because they care. They care about our daughter, *your* daughter. Everybody is trying to find her.'

'Yes. They care. But they don't want to come in. They want to thank the Lord that they have their lives, that they're not in the same position as you. They go in because they feel too guilty not to, too afraid to undermine you or look as if they don't care. You give them money, Linden, but you don't give them respect. Give them a break. Let the professionals do their job and stay home with me.'

Linden took a deep breath. Not only did he have no power over his daughter's captors, his own wife was wielding an axe of guilt. Even his own staff didn't respect him. He was furious. He wanted the rage to go away. No. He wanted to *use* this rage. He wanted to turn this rage into a source of power to find his daughter. To eliminate her captor. To…

'Please…'

Then, like a sledgehammer, the power of his wrath crashed down on him with the weight of the entire world.

***

During the day, Special Agent Foxton was called out of the room on numerous occasions and reappeared with new information. GCHQ staff had been allocated to assist us but were yet to come up with anything new. Kent Police had failed to find a canister on the beach even with metal detectors. Apparently the shoelace had traces of blood on it, but the blood didn't match the kidnap victims or anybody on their criminal database.

I helped as much as I could but recapturing my thoughts about Clifton was painful. There was this hook constantly pulling at me, saying *Trust me, Trust me*. Why was trust so important?

'Just a thought,' Lucy said. 'If we have to think outside the hunt and look to the world in order to see the bigger picture, could the gifts be from seven different people? Do we need to look at other news stories? Even stories in Milan and Paris?'

'Good thinking,' Thomas said. 'It doesn't have to be an abduction report; it could be a missing person.'

'I'll relay that. It could be a nightmare if that's the case,' Foxton replied.

'If there are traces of blood, then it doesn't bode well,' Lucy added.

Foxton shook his head in acknowledgement before leaving the room. I was hungry; it had been a long day. We had been drinking coffee and snacking but not eaten a meal. My mind was drifting to Unity too. I hadn't texted her all day, it had been hard to stay in touch during the week. I took the opportunity:

> *Hey, I'm still in meeting. It's been hard work, catch you up later. Out of curiosity, what are your own thoughts on Clifton now? I keep being asked that question. Do you think he lost trust in me? I hope you are OK x*

I texted Dad too, though Lucy had phoned him earlier to give him a brief update. I missed him. He had joined me to revisit the clues but I had come to Cheltenham with Thomas and Lucy. Dad wanted to stay locally but I knew he had to work so I managed to convince him I'd be OK. I missed my bike too. I wondered what the people at college must be thinking. I felt bad for Po as well; I had let him down on Saturday and been out of touch all week. He had phoned and texted several times and I hadn't replied.

Unity texted back:

> *Rather you than me. Right now, I hate Clifton because of what he's put you through. I liked him before. His words were wise and inspirational. He brought excitement to us both and I believed in him. I trusted him too. He wanted to be trusted. So I'm clinging on to some hope that good can come from all this. What is the price of trust if we still trust*

him? I don't think you lost his trust. He needed you there. He knew you would be x

We both felt the same way and she was right: Clifton did bring out the excitement in us both. Part of me still hoped he would trust me.

I felt restless and paced up and down the room thinking, chewing at my fist.

'Unity asked what is the price of trust if we still trust Clifton now?' I said to Thomas and Lucy.

They paused and looked at each other. Lucy spoke. 'That might be the question we should be asking.'

'What could Clifton want from me personally?' I asked.

'Daisy Keld had already been abducted before you received the Hartside clue, let alone the Little Eversden one. Maybe this was planned long in advance after all?'

'Am I to lead Daisy to safety and take a cut of the ransom money as treasure? Surely Clifton wouldn't think that would work, especially if he knew I was going to be arrested and probably charged. What good could I do from a prison cell?'

'He needed you to be arrested,' Thomas said. 'If his intentions are bad, there would be no reason for him to ask you to trust him.'

'Exactly. Maybe he felt I betrayed his trust by bringing Dad in on that Cambridgeshire clue. That last note upset me more than getting arrested.'

Special Agent Foxton returned. Thomas filled him in on our thoughts. He said that the trust issue was what the GCHQ team was having the biggest problem with. The existential messages were powerful wise words. Clifton said that his dream was taken from him. If Congressman Linden Keld's greed took that dream, there were going to be a lot of awkward investigations. Keld was a political doorstop for new ideas, especially in relation to science innovation, and it was obvious that Clifton was a scientist.

'Any luck with hospices on the line?' Lucy asked.

'Nothing as yet. The more we pry, the more questions are

asked.'

'I bet. Are they going to name Clifton to the public?'

'Not yet. As much as it might give us leads, it could also seal Daisy's fate. We want to collect as much on him as possible and strike quickly when we know where she is.'

At last food was suggested. Foxton was tired, having flown in on the early flight, so he suggested calling it a day. We were to meet again at nine o'clock next morning.

We ate at the hotel and headed to our rooms shortly afterwards. Thomas and Lucy praised me, which was awkward, but I definitely felt better being part of an investigative team than being a suspect.

I phoned Dad and told him about my day. He offered again to come and stay nearby. I knew he was worried but I was OK and there wasn't much he could do and I knew he was also busy at work now that Eva was back from her travels. I told him I was coping and how good Thomas and Lucy had been. Eventually he accepted and again praised me, which made me relieved as opposed to awkward.

I got into bed and called Unity on Skype. I spoke to her whilst lying on my side and she mimicked me by trying to talk to me sideways. It was good to see her face. I told her about my day. The conversation got quieter as we both relaxed.

'I miss the innocence of the hunt. I hope not all the good things have to end,' I said, again, thinking aloud as the conversation was ending.

'Not all the good things,' she replied softly with a smile.

'I hope not. Night, Nutty.'

– CHAPTER 25 –

Thomas Riley was up first and showered, having slept well. Lucy joined him in the bathroom as he was shaving; she was bleary-eyed and half-awake. Her hair was zigzagging over her face. He smiled.

'Morning beautiful,' he said.

'Shush, I know I'm a state,' she replied and poked him in the ribs.

'Careful!' He pulled the razor away from his neck in time. He liked her morning face. 'I take it you didn't sleep as well as me?'

'No, my mind was too active. I could sleep now, though. I need coffee!'

'What were you thinking?'

'I was thinking what the FBI or the Tennessee Police Department know. Daisy Keld's abduction was organised and she went willingly. She was a clever girl. How come they have no leads at all? I don't think Clifton is the guy's real name either. Has anybody followed through on the T.M. signoff on his last clue? It may not have been from Clifton after all.'

'We need to find out from Foxton. You're probably right about the name. I think we should take our laptops in today. As much as I can help the investigation through discussion, I'm much better with the internet at hand. It helps us rule out misdirection of thought more quickly.'

Thomas watched as Lucy got ready. He cringed when he thought about his PTSD attack at the weekend. Lucy accepted him unconditionally; he was a lucky man – lucky to be alive, lucky to have this stunning, caring and intelligent woman as his wife and partner. He enjoyed every moment in her company. Lucy had her own trauma to deal with; she had witnessed his ordeal in Las Vegas. She hid her emotional scars with grace and optimism while he was still learning.

'And quit staring!'

Thomas smiled and left her to get ready. He sat on the edge of the bed to put on his shoes. It was always a major effort these days but he was lucky to be able to walk and have use of his legs.

He felt that they had wasted yesterday. They had spent the whole day thinking about where to find Clifton and what he knew about Aril. They should have been thinking about where to find Daisy. They were looking at this upside down – Daisy was the treasure. They should be looking for the next clue, the next canister. Aril had sussed out all seven of the other clues because he wasn't thinking about himself, he was thinking about how to solve the puzzle. He didn't care about the expense or how awkward the distance might be; he wanted to help Clifton's dream.

'We need to get hold of a map of Tennessee. We need internet access,' Thomas said as Lucy entered the room.

'We can ask. You don't think she could have been smuggled to England on a phoney passport?'

'It's possible, I suppose. In which case she could be in Hythe.'

'Would the most southerly house on the line be in that cul-de-sac?'

Thomas recognised a familiar wave of excitement. He phoned Stirling Foxton. If they were right, Clifton could have been watching the whole thing from his window with Daisy in the house. It was highly unlikely he would still be there but Daisy might be. It was an avenue they had to pursue.

We arrived at GCHQ shortly after nine. Special Agent Foxton was on the phone to Hythe Police. I thought about DCI Knock; he probably wasn't too happy right now.

We noticed there was another road called Ferguson Close, between Cliff Road and the canal. The police certainly didn't want to go in with sirens blazing so Foxton suggested that a couple of local patrol officers made door-to-door investigations for something routine, targeting all the houses on the block to divert attention from their primary targets. The officers could report their observations so they could assess how to move in properly. They might also be able to get some local gossip about the activities of their neighbours. That might flag up anything out of the ordinary.

I didn't think Clifton was still likely to be there and if Daisy was, she was unlikely to answer the door. I don't know what they expected, but I hoped they would find her and I could go home.

When the phone call finished, Thomas asked if he and Lucy could access the internet from their computers. While they were waiting for the servers to sync, Thomas asked Foxton about Daisy. 'How was she lured away so easily?'

'She was going to enter a competition for gifted children, which was being televised. The TV company had approached her online and everything seemed genuine. Her parents knew all about it. The filming was supposed to take place the following week but Daisy received a call on the Friday and asked if she could be excused classes. She signed out of school, everything looked completely genuine. Then the car she was travelling in was found abandoned a few miles away. Her cell phone was inside, together with Aril's guitar pick.'

'Couldn't the FBI trace the correspondence?' Thomas asked.

'Oh yes, and it all seemed genuine. We've since discovered the production company website was registered to NASA space headquarters. The device used for correspondence used proxy IPs and many were routed through government offices. The car was hired locally using stolen ID.'

'Very well planned then.'

'Must have been planned for months. The TV production company made contact with Daisy back in early August.'

'They must have known about her and that she was starting university young.'

'Yes. We've questioned every person that we know who approached her in the past year or so, but we can't make a connection. Linden has his staff working round the clock on the search. He's often steps ahead of us.'

'So she was definitely targeted. There's nothing at all random about this?' Lucy asked.

'No, I don't think so. Even the British side of the hunt is difficult. We're trying to collect CCTV from the dates of the clues but all the areas are remote, far from main roads. We're searching for a raindrop in a puddle.'

'Clifton went to all this trouble, then relied on luck with me – and got lucky,' I said, bewildered by the background story. 'Was it a coincidence or was I chosen too?'

They were silent for a while. I directed my gaze at Foxton.

'He didn't half get lucky,' he said, looking down at his notes.

A possible truth hit me then but I didn't want to make the obvious connection. I wanted to be wrong.

Let's hope they found Daisy in Hythe.

***

Linden Keld sat with his wife over dinner. In case of a miracle, a place was set for Daisy. Edina had made more than enough food. Usually they would have all the family over at Thanksgiving but Linden had cancelled the party. The phone had been ringing relentlessly but they had kept conversations short in case there were developments. He was still waiting to hear back from Stirling Foxton. The FBI hadn't ruled out Daisy being in England.

'Two days, Edina. We have two days. Then what? I should be out there, searching.'

'Daisy is a clever girl. I'm not losing faith but I'm never going to let myself feel like this again. She is young, she should be home with us. Just because she's gifted doesn't mean she has to grow up so fast.'

'Don't turn this on me, Edina. She wanted to go to university. You wanted it, too.'

'I wanted her to be able to use her gifts, yes, but only when she was ready. She is too young, Linden.'

'You say this now. You never said it before.'

'You don't listen Linden. You talk, you draw your own conclusions and you decide, but you don't listen.'

'I listen to the voice within, the voice of our Lord, the voice of opportunity.'

'And yet you fail to hear the voice of your wife, the voice of your own daughter. She went to university to make you proud, because she knows nothing else except to obey you. We… You've pushed her since she was old enough to remember.'

'What are you saying? Did she not want to go? She never said.'

'You wanted her to go to Cambridge. She had to plead to stay in Tennessee. She saw it as a victory but it wasn't a personal choice. She is gifted, yes, and she's proud of her gifts. She will come through this stronger than we will, but she must be allowed to be the child she still is.'

'School was corrupting her. She needed strong moral principles, not the recklessness of youth. Not the science of the devils and the misery of poverty. She was a star that shone brighter than every…'

'*Is* Linden, *is*…'

Linden stopped, furious at the damning indiscretion of his words. Had he given up inside? The pain was unbearable.

***

The day dragged. There was so much action but no sense that we were nearer finding Daisy Keld. Thomas, Lucy, Foxton and I were joined by several members of the GCHQ team. There was not much they could help with other than data checking and referencing the clues. They even had a Latin scholar reading *Nova philosophiae planetarum et artis Criticae Systemata Adumbrata.*

There were no Cliftons registered to any of the hospices within the line. GCHQ had been in touch with the Westcliff Centre for Gifted Children and run a search on all registered children. They had contacted MENSA to see if any of its members was referenced under that name but with no success. The conclusion was that Clifton was not his real name. There were places called Clifton and one of these was on the line. Local police had been contacted and were trying to make a connection. There were space observatories close to the line, including Brayebrook, where Dad worked. Attention turned to the *T.M.* sign off for the last clue, though we still referred to him as Clifton for now.

Kent police investigated the properties in Hythe. The southernmost one was a large house with outbuildings but the people who lived there were well known in the community and there had been no strange activity in the area. DCI Knock wasn't convinced and wanted access to the outbuildings but he had no reason to ask, and a warrant was hard to obtain on the basis of a hunch. The buildings backed on to the canal so Knock stationed surveillance officers the other side of the property to monitor it.

I tried to put myself in Clifton's shoes, to understand what he wanted from me. Did he want me to sacrifice myself – my innocence, for his guilt – in return for my own dream? What good would that be if I was in jail? If he was genuine and as altruistic as he claimed, what did he expect me to do for him?

Then Lucy had a brainwave that stopped us all dead in our tracks. 'What if Clifton is a victim? What if he isn't actually controlling this but is also a victim, being played by the real villains? He said Aril had to find him. What if Clifton has Daisy, and Clifton's life and death is on the line *because* of all this?'

I felt guilty. It hadn't crossed my mind that Clifton could be a victim. If this was the case, not only did I forgive him, I owed him. It added up. *His death on the line, his dreams taken from him by the greed of the few, trust.*

'If the last note was written by his captors, we need to think about *T.M.* Is there an organisation or a group of political activists using this acronym?' Lucy said.

'What if,' I interrupted, again thinking aloud, 'Clifton is here in the UK, acting on orders from America? Maybe the watch was posted over here. You don't think he is doing this to protect his own gifted child do you, and that we have two missing children?'

'I hope not,' Lucy said, shaking her head at the thought.

'Let's go back to trusting Clifton and see what there is in front of us,' Thomas said.

Foxton acknowledged the conversation without speaking. He wrote notes, relayed messages and left the room occasionally to update his colleagues in America. The story wasn't hitting the main news over there as regularly as it had been, but there were reports that the investigation now involved European police.

Having spent two full days in the room at GCHQ, I was feeling claustrophobic. I wanted my own thinking space. I resorted to pacing the room but I needed to expel energy – exercise, walk, run; anything to be alone and think. If we were right, there may well be another clue, another canister. Was the *unlucky for some* message for me personally after all? It would have been visible to anybody curious enough to look; it wasn't hidden.

Po must have been cursing me, he would have finished band practice by now. I had left my phone off all day as I knew he would try to phone. I would do anything for normality again. I had a lot of college work to catch up on too. I could see myself spending the entire Christmas holidays working and revising.

I began to wonder if I was really needed. As much as I wanted to think about Clifton, rescue the girl and live happily ever after, I was still a seventeen-year-old boy living in a seventeen-year-old's world. These professionals were better than me. If I could lead them to Daisy, I would have done so by now. I had nothing more to add.

'Am I needed now?' I was developing an unhealthy habit of thinking aloud.

'I don't know,' Foxton replied. 'I still believe that you have something to add to the search for Daisy.' He looked up at me, holding his pen against the side of his lips. 'It's possible that it wasn't your thoughts about Clifton, or the knowledge you had, rather the experiences you've had with him that Daisy's kidnappers were talking about when they claimed you could lead us to her.'

'I agree,' Thomas said. 'Aril has college and it's obvious that he doesn't know any more than he's given us. I think we can do this collectively without Aril being here. He can make himself available if for some reason we do need him.' Thomas smiled at me. I felt relief and excitement at the idea of being home and sleeping in my own bed.

'I'm going to have to discuss it with the team back home,' Foxton said. He left the room.

I thanked Thomas. 'I need thinking space,' I admitted. 'I think better when I'm walking or riding or even lying in bed. My brain shuts down after a while when I am with people all the time. It makes me feel drained.'

'It's called introversion,' Lucy said. 'Some people like to have others around them constantly to feed off ideas, and they gain energy from it. Others, like you, need space and quiet time to think and recharge.'

'I suppose so. I still want to help. I probably do have more to offer but I can do that better from my comfort zone. I'm worried about college too; this is a critical time for my studies.'

When Foxton returned, he ushered the other staff out of

the room so that he could talk to me. 'I have a dilemma, Aril. My boss wants me to keep you here until we find Daisy Keld, or at least until after the seven days are up and the investigation moves to a new phase. I know you've cooperated and you're unlikely to add anything new to the enquiry. I think we should call it a day now so that you can have a break. Stay overnight at the hotel and we'll meet here early tomorrow, say 8am, and we'll assess things then.' I nodded as he spoke. 'The staff here are checking missing persons in Europe and America and looking for a connection with T.M. I think we can leave them to it for now.'

I returned to the hotel with Thomas and Lucy and we sat downstairs for a while, drinking coffee.

'I hope that Daisy is alright,' I said. I hoped Clifton was too. 'I wonder what will happen to her if we don't find her in seven days.'

'That's the worry,' Lucy replied.

'Nothing makes sense. The hunt was cryptic but I never lost a sense of direction with it, only motive.'

'You've done your best. You're clever and your mind is older than your years. I'm sorry that it's all gone so wrong for you. I'm grateful that your father called us in so that you had witnesses – it would have been much harder for you if you'd done the entire hunt solo. I think Daisy's captors were relying on that fact to divert attention away from themselves for a while. I know time is running out, but we're several steps closer than Daisy's captors think we are.'

'I guess.'

'I think the bigger worry for Foxton is that if this money is being used for terrorist purposes and we don't find Daisy by Saturday, there could be an attack. That's why they are reluctant to let you go home. You may have no use here now, but you still need to be nearby. It's not impossible that Daisy's captors will demand to talk to you.'

This really *was* serious. Norris was right.

– CHAPTER 26 –

It wasn't the alarm that woke Thomas at 6.45am, it was his phone. His eyes couldn't focus on the display to identify the caller. His thumb found the answer button.

'Sorry if I woke you, Thomas,' Foxton said. 'I've been speaking with my colleagues. We can let Aril go home if he agrees to be accessible at all times.'

'I'm sure he will. What about us? Would you like me to come in and Lucy take Aril back and return later?'

'I was going to ask if you could still help with our investigations. I'm returning to Hythe this morning; they've arranged a helicopter. I'll probably be back here mid-afternoon so that should give you enough time to get Aril home and return.'

'Yes, that's fine. Are there developments in Hythe?'

'Possibly, I need to go and see for myself. We've been tracking the missing person reports and there was an abduction earlier this month near Fargo in North Dakota. There's been no ransom demand but the victim was a businessman's daughter, like Daisy. We're unsure if it's connected but we can't rule it out. We've requested DNA to see if it matches the blood on the lace.'

'Let's hope not, for Daisy's sake.'

'I agree. Let's keep in touch by phone and meet back here later.'

Thomas updated Lucy, who was awake watching him.

'Another road trip, wonderful,' she said with jovial sarcasm, stretching a yawn. Thomas smiled.

***

Dad was home when I arrived shortly before noon. It was a relief to see him and I gave him a hug. I was grateful to Thomas and Lucy for bringing me back. Dad made us all lunch. Eva was also here; they had decided to work from home so that I wouldn't have to be alone.

Eva was nice. I didn't know how much Dad had explained to her so I was careful with my conversation and could tell that Thomas noticed my tact. Dad had informed college that I was ill to explain my absence; they were going to send my missed work notes through by email so that I could catch up.

After Thomas and Lucy left I went upstairs to my room, leaving Dad and Eva to continue their work. I lay on the bed looking up at my ceiling; the day too bright for the constellation above to reveal itself, just like the stars in the day sky. They are always there, of course but we can't see them with our eyes, only our imagination. The comfort and familiarity of the room was an overwhelming relief. I wanted to listen to music, talk to Unity, hell I even wanted to go to band practice – even if it was out of guilt!

I looked out of the window; the sky was grey. Dad often reminds me that it's always a nice day above the clouds, especially when I'm disillusioned with the weather or have had a bad day.

What must Daisy Keld be thinking? I hoped we would find her while there was still daylight.

***

Lucy drove back to Cheltenham. Thomas found it hard driving long distances: his knees seized up if he sat still for too long. It was easier for him to drive in towns than on motorways. There was a comfortable silence in the car and

Lucy tried not to think too hard about the search for Daisy Keld. Her mind drifted to Christmas; she hadn't started buying presents yet. Her family were going to stay with her and Thomas this year.

'You know what I think?' Thomas said. Lucy shifted her brain back into gear. 'I think this search was meant for Dale Ousby. Aril was right, Clifton got lucky. I'm sure Aril knows it too and that's why he was keen to get home.'

'You could be right. He did say that Dale's observatory has just acquired funding. We need to quietly investigate his new investors.'

'Hmm, that was my thinking too.'

Lucy was shattered by the time she reached GCHQ. Special Agent Foxton had not yet returned from Hythe so they waited for him in the canteen lounge, drinking coffee. The canteen had the TV news channels on screens on the wall; they were watching the headlines so were caught off-guard when Foxton arrived at their table.

'It's been a long day. Let's go through and I'll update you on the latest,' he said.

Lucy explained about their latest theories and the background checks they needed to do on Dale Ousby's new investors as they walked.

'Yes, we must get on to that. Time is pressing,' Foxton said.

They entered the investigation room, which was a hive of activity. The staff had just confirmed that the blood on the shoelace matched that of Alexandria Fernwood who was missing from Fargo in North Dakota. The daughter of a businessman, her car was abandoned near Jamestown and drops of blood were found at the scene.

Foxton phoned Jamestown Police Department to find out more information about the missing girl. Lucy shuddered. There wasn't much they could do right now but the worry was that this was an abduction that went wrong – and the reason there was no ransom demand was because Alexandria had been killed. As much as it boded well for the chances of finding Daisy alive, this was now potentially a murder investigation. It would be hard to keep the press away from making the connection to England. Lucy worried that the stress could set off another PTSD episode in Thomas. She had to tread carefully.

'Right, this changes things,' Foxton said, ending his call. 'Linden Keld is not going to like the news. Alexandria's father is a successful businessman, he has a large textile business in Fargo. He is a multimillionaire but not in the same league as Keld. Her abductors have made no contact so we can't rule out the possibility of finding a body. We need to study the area and look for a possible link to Clifton's clues.'

'I'll do that now,' Thomas said. 'Were there any developments in Hythe?'

'DCI Knock put surveillance on the outbuilding at the back of the last house on Ferguson Drive. Some kid, a girl, was seen scaling the wall. Knock sent a DI down there to talk to the householders and they refused permission for them to check the outbuildings. The police needed clout to get a warrant, which is why I went down. I went with Knock to assess if we needed forensics. Turns out the building was being used as a love nest by the house owner's son and his girlfriend. They are kids, Aril's age.'

'OK, dead end then,' Thomas said.

'That was. But this…' Foxton pulled out an evidence bag. Inside was a silver container lid. It was bent at the rim but the top was engraved with a seven-point red star with an ellipse around it.

Lucy looked at Thomas. 'We need to MMS it to Aril, see if he recognises it. It fits the description of the containers in the hunt. Where did you find it?'

'In the grass at the base of the wall the girl was scaling,' Foxton replied. Knock has spoken to the son. He denied any knowledge of it.'

'And the girl?'

'He won't give her name and his parents don't know it. If this canister turns out to be connected, we'll bring him in and check his phone records. We wanted to be sure first. We can't risk an MMS in case Aril puts it in the public domain. It's evidence.'

'How about Skype, if Dale is present?'

'Yes, speak to his father first.'

***

I must have drifted to sleep. My brain certainly switched off for a few minutes before I heard the house phone go.

It felt good to be in my bedroom. I had an urge to go out on my bike but daylight was about to disappear. I thought about giving Po a call to tell him that I'll join the rehearsals tomorrow. It would be some semblance of normality. How the hell could I miss Po's banter? I chuckled to myself.

Dad knocked on my door and I told him to come in. 'That was Thomas on the phone, he wants to show you something but he will need to Skype you,' he said. I reached for my laptop and switched it on while he continued. 'I am to witness your conversation in case you make a screen capture. They can't risk you sharing possible evidence.'

'OK. I'm intrigued,' I said.

I opened Skype and saw Thomas's invitation to contact and accepted. Unity started talking to me immediately so I sent a quick message explaining that I was back home, Thomas wanted to speak to me on Skype and I'd bring her up to date shortly.

Thomas opened the call. He was seated in a busy room and I could see Lucy to his left. 'Aril, can you describe the container lid again,' Thomas said.

'It was silver chrome and had a red star engraved on it with an ellipse orbiting it,' I said.

'Like this?'

Thomas held up a clear freezer bag. The glare of the computer made it hard to focus at first but then I recognised the lid. There was no doubt about it.

'Yes. Yes, that's it! Where did you find it?'

'Hythe, behind the canal. The container is missing, it's just the lid. The police are going to try and find the rest of it. It might have been found innocently by a passer-by.'

'Oh. Wow.'

I was shocked. I wondered what was inside this time. I was excited by the idea that there could be another note. Maybe the note on the tree was not connected directly with Clifton. I was also confused, as any clue inside would have been the eighth clue – which didn't tally with our theory of *seven* being the linking factor. But then, there were only *six* gifts.

Thomas said they had identified the shoelace as belonging to another woman who had been abducted the week before Daisy. She was also the daughter of a successful businessman but her abductors hadn't made any ransom demands. She had been kidnapped a thousand miles away from where Daisy was taken. I hoped that this woman hadn't been hurt. Thomas told me to keep thinking; he would remain online in case I had any ideas.

Dad asked if I was alright after I ended my call. I was shocked but I told him I was fine and would talk to Unity, so he left the room and went to make something to eat.

I opened up the call with Unity and gave her a full update. She was concerned too. Neither of us could make any sense of the new canister. If it had contained a vital clue to Daisy's whereabouts, it might have been lost forever.

'Are you OK?' I asked. Unity looked troubled. Her smiles weren't reaching her eyes and I felt guilty that I'd been doing all the talking.

'Yeah, I'm fine. I'm looking forward to spending Christmas in Scotland with my grandparents.'

'That will be cool. Is it the same-old, same-old at home? Or has it got worse?'

'It's not been the best of weeks, but I'm OK. It's nice to talk with you, even if we are trying to solve international crimes now instead of looking for treasure,' she laughed.

She was right; how things had changed in a week. It would have been nice to share the treasure with her so that she could pursue her own dreams.

'Whether or not Clifton turns out to be a criminal, what he says is right. We mustn't give up on our dreams or take time for granted. I want to believe that there's always a reason to hope,' I said. She needed some encouragement, I didn't want her to give up.

'You sound like Clifton,' she said. 'No, don't worry, I'm above it all. I store hope in jars that I bank in the cellar of my mind. I have enough in reserve to cope with anything fate throws my way.'

'And dreams?'

'Yes. And dreams. Maybe one day I'll even share them with you.' She laughed again and the smile reached her eyes. She was back in control and I felt relieved about that.

***

Thomas looked to Foxton for guidance. They were against the clock now, which was rapidly moving towards the seventh day. If there was a clue in that canister, they needed to find it quickly. It was hard to set wheels in motion without drawing attention to themselves but he needed DCI Knock and his colleagues to coordinate a search immediately. Thomas searched the Fargo district on the online maps to see if there was any connection to link Clifton's words with the area, while Foxton spoke with Knock.

Lucy found a recent article about the expansion of Brayebrook Observatory, which had received funding from the West European Space Initiative. It was a joint venture with the European Space Agency and a private American space research company. She looked for the directors' names and online news articles in case a Clifton was mentioned.

'That was hard work,' Foxton said, as he ended his call. 'Kent Police are setting up an incident unit. They will bring in the house owner's kid for questioning and find the girl. They've had backup from the Security Service. The worry is not only about finding Daisy Keld within the seven days but, until they rule out terrorist involvement, they're worried about triggering an attack.'

'It's a concern now,' Thomas said.

'We are investigating the movement of Keld's ransom payment but the kidnappers have been damned clever with it, considering the amount involved. There's no way that this is a single-man operation. They've used sophisticated IT and they've been able to create government accounts. The chances are that by the time we identify the kidnappers, they'll be long gone, leaving a trail of havoc.'

Three hours later, the room was buzzing but they were no closer to piecing together Clifton's puzzle. No container had been found; there was a team sweeping the canal, but it was dark so they set up temporary floodlights. The girlfriend of the boy on Ferguson Drive had been found and was being questioned. Police made door-to-door calls to ask if anyone recognised the canister and they investigated neighbouring outbuildings. The Latin book from Eusebio Amort had been scanned but no solid connection was made to link Clifton's messages. They were now looking into the Bavarian philosopher's background. Thomas looked into the area around Fargo and Jamestown, North Dakota, but it was rural and largely unpopulated.

The incident had alerted local media attention and police liaison officers were delicate with their explanations. Thankfully, nobody had made a connection to America.

Lucy investigated the heptagonal red star to see if it was a recognised company or organisation logo. 'It's hard to know if we have to look for Clifton, Daisy or an entire network,' she said. 'I doubt there was anything in that canister, unless Clifton was there and he destroyed it after Aril was arrested.'

Thomas thought Lucy could be right. Maybe Clifton was in the area and had needed a local observation point. Maybe, when Aril had got it wrong, he gave up.

'I think he's been watching Aril,' Lucy said. 'I wonder if Aril had turned up on his own at Little Eversden, Clifton might have approached him? Maybe Clifton saw Dale and

Unity with him and drove away.'

'It's possible. In which case, he probably felt that Aril had betrayed his trust. That's why he set him up.'

'Do you think Clifton is a teacher? He said his lessons will be *told by others*. If he's not a teacher then does he intend to teach some people a lesson?'

'Yes. You could be right.' Thomas shuddered.

The workload was piling up and time was running out. Thomas explained Lucy's thinking to Foxton.

'It's not impossible that Clifton is a teacher,' Foxton said. 'We should investigate but I'm dubious about his real name. If he is teaching people a lesson, let's hope he means they will *literally* tell his story and not posthumously.'

Thomas nodded; they were on the same wavelength.

– CHAPTER 27 –

I upset Unity. I didn't mean to. I care, and I don't know if it's a primal instinct for a guy to want to protect people they care about, but she mistook my compassion for authority and that's the opposite of what I intended. Before settling for the night, I asked again if she was alright. I hadn't seen anybody in the house with her and was concerned, especially when she told me that she hadn't had the best of weeks.

'I don't need sympathy, Aril. I need a friend. It's been this way for years. I'm tough and I'm confident in myself. I'm not weak or unhappy and I like my own company. You're undermining my strength. The more you question me, the more I end up questioning myself. I'm fine, Aril.'

'I know. I'm sorry and you are strong, I know that – a damned sight stronger than me. It doesn't alter the fact that it's wrong and you shouldn't be in this position. You shouldn't have to put a wall of armour around yourself at sixteen. You shouldn't have to be thinking beyond your years in order to have the courage to look to the future.'

She was quiet and looked away. I was shaking; I didn't want to upset her. I genuinely cared.

'You know me well,' she said, offering a brief, nervous smile.

'I care as a friend,' I said. 'Regardless of my gender, regardless of my age and regardless of *knowing you well*. Even as a stranger looking at your situation, it's still wrong. You're the nicest person I've ever met. There's nothing bitchy about you, there's nothing false, there's no ulterior motive or attention seeking, and considering the life you have, that's a frigging miracle. You deserve a better life... And you know what?' She looked up. 'I have no doubt that you *will* carve a better life for yourself, I have faith in you. You'll never be like your mum. You've already made damned sure that will never happen.'

There I was again, thinking aloud, although my voice was gentle. I was nervous and my stomach was gripped by a strange pain but I needed to let her know.

'Sometimes you can change what's wrong and sometimes you have to accept it and learn from it,' Unity said. 'I've learned from my mother's mistakes. I'm lucky. I haven't had to drag myself that low. I'll never be like her. I love her, she's my mum and she probably loves me, but I'm better than her. I love what I make of my life, I'm happy to do it on my own.'

'I hope Clifton gets to meet you. I hope we can still trust him. I think he would fall in love with you and your spirit. He may even be inspired by it.'

She laughed. 'I don't know about that. It's easy for me, I don't try. I don't think I have a spirit, I just do what I do and build on the foundation of what I am, as a human being.'

Every time she spoke I felt proud. I would never tell her because she would consider it patronising but my awe was fuelled by pride. It shouldn't be me telling Clifton's story, it should be Unity.

'You inspire me, Unity. I'm glad we've shared this adventure together and that I've got to know you. You're my faith in humanity.'

She smiled again. I thought I should change the topic but she beat me to it. 'So, does this mean you're going to make peace with Po tomorrow, now you're back?'

'I think I better. The guilt has been nagging me all week.'

'You should do the gig too.'

'Man, you're as bad as he is,' I laughed.

'I want to come and watch,' she said.

I cringed. I was bound to mess up, out of sheer nerves.

'If I do it, I think you should come. Maybe you should drag your mum down for a night out. Tell her it's her Christmas present!'

She laughed, loudly. 'Perish the thought!'

***

It seemed likely that Special Agent Foxton would be sleeping in the investigation room. He showed no sign of stopping. Lucy was shattered and it was past midnight. There were more than fifty people working on the case in the UK and scores in America. Lucy overheard the conversations between Foxton and Linden Keld and knew the pressure was adding to Foxton's frustration. There were many lines of enquiry but little progress.

The hunt for the container was abandoned, to resume again in daylight. Spokesmen told the US media that the two abductions were linked and it made headline news again. There was speculation about a ransom payment and that the FBI was cooperating with international police. The FBI sought to control the flow of news by imposing restrictions until a terrorist threat had been ruled out.

Foxton could see that Lucy was weary. 'You two should try and get some sleep for a few hours,' he said.

'I'll probably be able to think clearer after a rest,' Lucy admitted. The room was loud and airless and she had a thick head.

She and Thomas gathered their things and then left for the hotel.

'I don't miss the chaos of the investigation rooms,' Thomas said, as they entered their hotel room.

Lucy remembered her days as a detective sergeant. 'I prefer it when you and I work together. I don't feel I'm contributing as much as I'm capable of. I think my mind was more focussed when we were working with Aril and Unity.'

'I agree. There's so much going on with this case. Foxton has a team here now. Do you think we should head back up to Cambridge?'

'Yes. I was going to suggest it, but couldn't find the opportunity.'

'Let's get some sleep and phone Foxton in the morning.'

***

When Mum and Dad were still together and we were living as a family we used to have a dog, a clumsy black Labrador named Eldridge. Harvey and I would get home from school and Eldridge would be over-excited and relentlessly jump up, displaying his pleasure to see us. I recognised that familiar greeting from Po the moment I walked into the Fox and Hare with my guitar case on my back.

'Oh. Oh wow, you didn't let us down!' He came bounding over and I didn't think he would decelerate in time to avoid a collision. He high-fived me, then grabbed my sleeve to guide me to their wondrous corner-space rehearsal area.

'Yeah, I know it's nothing special, but we can use their PA.'

I liked it, in truth. It felt real, compared to the rehearsals at college. I could imagine the punters, watching us like ghosts. The sound was tighter as the acoustics were better, so the guitar had a warmer sound and Po's drums were less overpowering. I caught a nod of approval from the manager. I kept half an eye on my phone in case I was needed. The only text I received was from Unity, hoping I hadn't slept in. For two hours, I felt seventeen again.

'I think you're an eight now,' Po said as we started packing up.

'You've got some catching up to do then,' I replied with a smirk.

'Cheeky git! You are gonna do this gig, aren't you? You've got to now we're this close.'

It was hard to commit with so much uncertainty; my scrunched-paper existence made planning difficult.

'I can't promise, but I plan to. There's a lot happening with my family and I could find myself in Carlisle. I'll try.'

'Ah man, you have to, even if I pay for your train fare up north on the Sunday.'

I shrugged.

I mounted my bike and set off home. It was noon and I hadn't heard any news. I wondered how the investigation was going. This was Day Seven and I reckoned we had until 7pm – the time on Daisy's watch – to find her. I couldn't bring myself to think of the consequences of failure.

When I pulled in to the drive, I recognised Thomas and Lucy's car. Nerves hit me like a cold tidal-wave of reality – this could be bad news.

***

Speculation was rife. As the FBI looked for connections between the two abductions, investigations uncovered a smorgasbord of tenuous correlations between past cases, serial killers and corporate manipulation. Congressman Linden Keld wasn't popular. His business practices were often questioned and his open objection to science exploration was accredited to his Christian beliefs, which were seen as extreme by his peers. He didn't care; his conscience was clean, he had earned his success and his power and he had a right to use them. And right now, he wanted to find his daughter and bring her captors to justice. Not *any* justice but a justice worthy of diffusing his imperious wrath.

How could a team of more than a hundred people fail to find his daughter? He had done his part, he had met the ransom demands. This street-punk English guy was what he'd bought with his three-fifty, but the kid was useless; they were no closer to finding his daughter than they were before he paid the ransom. What use was all this technology? Instead of being able to find his daughter it was being used to hide her and distribute his money.

Keld couldn't sleep. This was Day Seven. It was an ungodly hour in Nashville but in England it was mid-morning. He had to get up and crack the whip.

***

I entered the room nervously, expecting to hear bad news. Thomas and Lucy had their laptop computers open. Dad was with them.

'Hey,' I said. 'Any news?'

'No. We felt it would be easier to work independently of Foxton's team so we asked Dale if we could work with you from here. We also wanted to double check that there wasn't a connection with the observatory's new investors that we've overlooked,' Thomas said.

That was a relief. I had been looking for an opportunity to speak with Dad myself about that, but it was difficult the previous night with Eva here. 'What do you think?'

'Well, we still can't rule it out but I understand that this is a project that Dale has been working on for nearly two years.' Dad nodded. 'There appears to be no obvious connection on the evidence so far, but I wonder if Clifton's hunt was meant for Dale initially.'

'Oh, right. Did anybody find the rest of the canister or a clue?'

'No. Hythe Police have the metal detectors out again and are checking the canal. There was a girl spotted on Thursday night, scaling the wall to the property. Police questioned her but she denies any knowledge of it. DCI Knock believes her.'

'Damn. I was hoping there might be a final clue.'

'It's still our best chance. Time is running out; there's a major police operation there.'

'Is there any good news at all?'

'Possibly. We've worked out why you were in the wrong place. We were focussing on the golf courses. In the nursery rhyme clue, if we'd made that connection with Paris to Milan in America, we would have realised that there's a Norwich in America famous for its university. Norwich University in Vermont is a major military college. The canal is the Royal Military Canal. We were close – a few hundred yards out.'

'Damn, that sucks!'

'He knew you were going to be wrong. The golf marker was a red-herring. Why, I don't know. We need to find out what was in that canister.'

'Clifton was probably there. He probably witnessed it all.'

'It's possible. Police are appealing for witnesses locally but it's hard to do so without explaining why. As soon as the media make the connection, they could make things awkward.'

'True. It still seems a weak link to Norwich, but we probably would have sussed it out if we had followed that train of thought.'

I took off my leathers and collected my laptop to join them. I asked if I could call Unity. I texted her first; she was home, so joined us online. I updated her with our news and set her on the table as we had previously.

'Déjà vu,' she said. 'Though it was more exciting when we thought we were searching for treasure.'

– CHAPTER 28 –

Time was no longer an ally. Like a runaway train, the clock careered towards the seventh evening hour of the seventh day as we frantically tried to make connections. Special Agent Foxton kept Thomas and Lucy updated. People were questioned, witnesses sought and CCTV examined but there were no leads to where Daisy Keld was being held. The canister base had still not been found. By mid-afternoon, Linden Keld had made a statement to the press admitting he was desperate and offered a million-dollar reward.

At 5.07pm we made a discovery; it was so obvious that we had missed it. So had GCHQ – and Foxton was livid. The map of Britain was open on the table, together with maps of Tennessee and North Dakota. Unity added up the grid-reference numbers of the first two locations and realised they were the same. At first we thought it was hardly surprising, being a straight line, but when we altered the direction we found that a line drawn from any other point changed the numbers of each location. We looked at all seven clues and the aggregate number was the same for each one: 52.1775. It was following a specific geographical line.

'The number has to have some relevance,' Lucy said, typing it into her internet search engine. 'There are 52.1775 weeks in a year.'

For the first time, the pieces of Clifton's jigsaw started to fit. The perspective of time came down to numbers:

Everything in the universe is just numbers, as Clifton had said. 52.1775 weeks in a year; 7 days a week – he was counting down: weeks, days and now we were left with hours, maybe minutes.

It was as if somebody had ignited fireworks in our minds. Lucy studied the display of notes, clues and scans in front of her and she honed in on 1775: Bavarian philosopher, Eusebio Amort died 5th February 1775 – 5-2-1775.

'The clues are all here,' Thomas said. 'We've not looked at them the right way.' He phoned Foxton. The FBI linked the two abductions in America but the numbers didn't tally in the same way. However, we concentrated on a line between the two regardless.

Thomas's phone rang relentlessly. I could hear my name mentioned a few times and he looked alarmed. I stared nervously while he was talking with Foxton. He scribbled notes which I couldn't decipher. It was 6.30 when the call ended.

'Is everything OK?' I asked.

'Linden Keld is going frantic, as you can imagine. He keeps telling Foxton he wants to speak with you directly, but he's in no state to be gentle with his words. Foxton thinks Linden wants to shock you or scare you into giving information that we all know you don't have.'

'If it will put his mind at ease I'll talk to him,' I said nervously, hoping he would decline my offer.

'Foxton doesn't think it's a good idea. However, Keld is making all manner of threats.'

'What can he do?'

'In America, money is power; he can make things uncomfortable for you. In the end, he just wants his daughter back. I'd be the same if I was in his position.'

'Tell him I'll talk,' I said. I didn't know where my bravery was coming from but my conscience was clear; I figured I couldn't make things any worse.

'Are you sure?'

'No. But I think I should, even though I don't want to.'

***

Linden Keld was in his office with Edina and two senior FBI agents. The seven o'clock deadline was approaching in UK time. He paced up and down, mumbling to himself as if he was alone. His frustration and anger burdened him more than his fear; he was even angry at his Lord. He didn't need this lesson in weakness.

When his cell phone rang, it was Foxton.

'This better be good,' Keld snapped.

'The boy wants to speak to you…'

'Good, put him on.'

'Sir, he is not here, he's helping from another location. Can you access a computer? He will talk to you on Skype.'

'Skype? I don't want to see this punk's face, I want to ask him where my daughter is!'

'Sir, I think it will help. I think you'll see for yourself that Aril is volunteering his own time to help you. He has been set up too. He is also a victim.'

Linden Keld avoided Foxton's words as if he was dodging the arrows of truth. One of the FBI agents brought a computer into the room. Linden didn't know his own email address so the agent made a temporary account and Foxton talked him through until they connected.

When Linden saw the frightened dark eyes of the kid before him and could hear other voices, he felt a power surge.

'Where's my daughter?' he said, before Aril could speak.

'I'm trying to find her, sir.'

'Not good enough. Where's my daughter? Don't tell me you don't know. I know you know. Where is she?'

Aril turned the computer to the table. There were maps and photographs and scribbles everywhere. Two men and a woman were with him, also using computers. 'We're all trying to find her,' he said.

Linden turned his computer towards Edina's tired face. 'That's my wife. She's beside herself and has been for weeks.'

He turned the laptop towards the FBI agents. 'These are two of a team of more than a hundred, who all think you know where my daughter is.' He turned towards his attorney, who had just entered the room. 'This is my lawyer and he will be the one who crucifies you if anything happens to my daughter. Hell will seem like paradise for you. Now quit playing around and tell me where my daughter is!'

'Can I ask you a question?' Aril said. He looked unphased.

Linden was shocked. 'Only when you answer mine: where is my daughter?'

'All of the notes I found have clues. What exactly did your daughter's kidnapper say? I mean word for word.'

Linden threw up his hands and looked at the FBI agents but they just nodded. Once again he felt powerless. Nothing he could say or do, no matter how forceful he tried to be, could make any difference. Never in his life had he felt so weak.

'Dear Lord help me. After the ransom exchange, the kidnapper phoned to say that a young man would be searching for red stars and gave me the names of two streets in England. He said the boy would know when and where to find Daisy. He told me I had to trust him as Daisy had to trust that I wouldn't interfere with the money exchange.'

'A parallel trust,' he heard Aril say quietly to one of his companions.

'What did you say?'

'A parallel trust. Did he say that to you?'

'How do you know? Yes he did. I remembered then as you said the words. He said my daughter and I have a *parallel trust*. You *do* know, punk. WHERE IS MY DAUGHTER?'

'Sir, think. It's you who knows, not me. Think of exactly what he said, no matter how trivial you think it is. We should have had this conversation last week.'

Linden was confused. The kid was too damned smart and completely unintimidated by him. He wasn't used to this. Nobody undermined his authority. Nobody.

He thought back to the conversation but there wasn't

much else said.

'Did he make a threat?' Aril asked. 'Did he say Daisy's life was on the line?'

'Oh, by Jesus, he did. That's exactly what he said. Where is this leading to?'

'I don't know, sir, but you've helped. He used similar phrasing with the notes he left for me. I think she's alive and I don't think her life is on the line in a literal sense. I think she's safe.'

'She better be. For your sake.'

Linden walked out of the room. He needed space. The FBI agents ended the call and Edina said, 'Thank you'.

***

Dad put his arm around me immediately after the call and Lucy reached for my hand. 'Well done,' she said. 'One day he will see how brave that conversation was.'

I was sweating, my back was wringing wet. As much as I was twisted with nerves, I was also relieved. I also felt that I still had a connection to Clifton, something I could hold on to. 'I need a shower; it might help me think.'

'I think Daisy is still alive too. We need a bigger map of America,' Thomas said.

'If Daisy is alive, Alexandria might be too. If Clifton knew we were likely to make the connection from the clues, he wouldn't have spoken about trust if one of his victims was already dead,' I said.

'You're probably right. Go and shower and I'll update Foxton. You did well, Aril.'

I smiled, embarrassed, and left for the bathroom. Unity had missed it where I had to end her call to speak with Linden. I really wanted to see her. If we found Daisy, I thought I'd treat myself to a ride out to Manchester.

– CHAPTER 29 –

There was an eerie silence as the clock hands moved past seven. Behind the scenes, the terror alert was critical and would remain so for the rest of the day. Dad put the live news channel on turned low. The mood around the table changed; I felt disappointment in the air. My hair was still wet, but I felt better for my shower and less shaky. I called Unity and explained about the conversation with Linden Keld. She had made the same conclusions that we had.

Eva turned up shortly after seven and Dad left to speak with her in the kitchen.

Foxton phoned and spoke to Thomas. They had drawn a line from McKenzie to Jamestown and extended it, looking at the main towns and cities close by. They found another missing person who might have been abducted. The previous month, a woman had disappeared after a house viewing in Georgia. Her father was a businessman too, so it might have been connected to the other kidnaps. The FBI was looking into it. Again, there had been no ransom demand.

I kept thinking about Linden Keld. I could see why he was a powerful man. It had only occurred to me as we were speaking that he might know more than he realised, which could have been a reason why Clifton had connected us. There was no doubt the kidnapper had used Clifton's language – maybe he wasn't a victim after all. I shut that thought out of my mind.

'Things are starting to piece together now,' Lucy said. 'We need to look at the things that don't add up and find the connection.'

'The biggest question of all is, *why*,' Unity said. 'Why go to all this trouble? Why not just kidnap Daisy, get the money and run? Why did he have to cause all this hurt?'

'It seems possible that he wanted to convince himself he was doing the right thing, to justify his actions,' Lucy said. 'Clifton said that *some people may believe I do wrong but my motives are the opposite.* Maybe he doesn't see wrong in what he has done or there's a bigger picture we don't see as yet.'

'He seems fascinated by the evolution of science and yet comes across so spiritual.' Unity continued the conversation. I listened, trying not to let my pride show. 'Could he need the money for a science experiment? Maybe something the congressman would hate or wouldn't allow funding for? He said his dreams were taken from him. Maybe he wants a name, maybe he wants to be remembered for a scientific achievement.'

'You could be on to something there.'

Thomas phoned Foxton again. I gave Unity a thumbs-up and a wink. She looked deep in thought, troubled.

***

Edina Keld hugged Linden from behind. He sat in his chair like a deflated balloon. The deadline had passed and even though nothing had changed, the mood was subdued and he was defeated. For the first time in his life he had to concede that he had no control.

'I don't know what's making me more miserable: not finding her or not having the ability to find her,' he admitted solemnly.

'Daisy. You never say her name. You refer to her as your daughter – a possession of yours – and you're angry because somebody has taken your possession away. She is our daughter but she is Daisy Keld – fifteen years old, intelligent, gifted and beautiful.'

Edina's words were gentle but cut like the sharpest blade. He was too weak to fight, he sank further into his chair and squeezed his wife's hand gently. 'I don't know what to do and I'm afraid.'

'I know. So don't be ashamed of that fear. People care, everybody cares, even that poor boy caught up in the middle of it all, four thousand miles away. We must respect that.'

'When did you get to be so strong? Look at me. I'm weak. I should be the motivator.'

'I'm honest with myself and honest with my faith, that's all. There's no rule that says a man should be strong. We are human, we all hurt sometimes. Money can't always buy power and power can't buy God's immunity from evil. What we do have is hope, we have faith and we have hundreds of people who care enough to help us find Daisy.'

'Foxton thinks this guy might want to teach me a lesson.'

'Well then, my love, pay attention.'

***

I lost count of the lines of investigation the FBI were following but this new information needed even more staff. Foxton had to delegate in America to investigate major science funding that had been blocked or cut, and explore any unorthodox projects that had come to light. It was going to be yet another major drain on resources.

As the evening went on, we ran out of ideas. We discussed and dismissed numerous trains of thought and as the new day approached in England, time ticked towards the seventh hour in Tennessee. The American team was less optimistic than me that Daisy would still be alive. They took her life to literally be *on the line* and we could tell that the language of hope was fading. As the seventh hour passed, that eerie silence returned. Was it now too late?

I felt the guilt bubble inside me. I had failed. Was Clifton dead? Were mine and Daisy's lives now on the line too?

Unity was thinking the same thing.

'You've done your best,' she said with a compassionate smile. 'I don't think it's over yet. There are hundreds of people working on this, all with the same information you have.'

'Yeah, I know. It doesn't stop me feeling like I've let everybody down. I hope nobody gets hurt.'

Security remained high and we were glued to the news. I refreshed Twitter regularly to see if there was breaking news of an attack but after an hour, nothing happened.

'I think you were right, Unity,' Thomas said to her. 'I don't think this is about terrorism, it's about science. I think Daisy is alive but maybe we've lost Clifton. It's now a matter of finding Daisy fast in case she has no access to food or drink.'

'I agree. But I think we're all tired now, we should try and sleep then resume again tomorrow,' Lucy said.

Thomas called Foxton, who was also struggling to stay awake as he had been up the previous night. We left the table as it was. After Thomas and Lucy left, I took the laptop upstairs. Unity stayed online. She was on her own but I chose not to mention it.

'I feel numb,' I said.

'It's been a hard week for you.'

'I'm so tired, I could sleep for England. I was hoping to take a ride out to see you tomorrow. I don't think that's going to happen.'

'That would be cool.' She made a deliberate sad face. I laughed. 'Maybe next weekend,' she added, her smile returning.

'I will,' I said waving. 'Night, Nutty.'

I turned the light off and looked at my ceiling. The glow stars seemed extra bright. My conscience was troubled. If Clifton's story was over, how could I tell? Did any remaining trust simply come down to finding Daisy alive? I was convinced this was not the story he wanted me to tell but now I might never know.

Sleep took hold and cradled me and my misplaced conscience into the new day.

– CHAPTER 30 –

Thomas Riley awoke to the sound of the phone again. It was nine o'clock. He fumbled to answer, focussing quickly. Lucy sat up, rubbing her eyes and yawning.

'Sorry to wake you, Thomas,' Foxton said. 'It seems you were right, that abduction in Georgia is connected. The hairpin has been identified as belonging to the missing woman. Her name is Triana Perry and she's an estate agent for her father's business in Columbus, Georgia. I think we could be looking at seven abductions on a new line. We're looking into it now.'

'Right, we'll head to Aril's in the next hour. There must be a pattern.'

Thomas finished the call.

'*A parallel trust.* So there are two lines, probably parallel. One has Aril's life on it and all of his dreams, and the other has Clifton's death on it. In which case Clifton could be American,' Lucy said, while getting dressed. 'How did he set up the clues over here? He must have travelled regularly or had somebody working for him.'

'True. He probably has people working for him. This is well organised, especially with the use of technology in moving the money. I don't think there is an extremist motive, I think it's scientific. What's worrying me is why he has abducted these women.'

'You're right. I dread to think of the worst-case scenario.'

I heard the doorbell go but couldn't find the energy to move. I knew it would be Thomas and Lucy. I dreaded the thought of any more bad news but knew that the investigation was entering a new phase. I stayed in bed, drifting in and out of sleep until Dad came in with a coffee.

'Thomas and Lucy are here. Did you sleep?'

'Eventually, but not enough. I want this nightmare to end.'

'Yeah, I know, Aril. Don't lose faith. Regardless of what turns out to be the truth, what Clifton said is right. Come on, finish your drink and join us. Eva's here, she's going to cook us all a Sunday roast.'

I sat in bed drinking my coffee, contemplating the day. A Sunday roast was almost enough motivation to venture downstairs. Sleep must have emptied my mind; I couldn't seem to focus my thoughts. My brain had been active for so many weeks; now it felt like it had shut down overnight and there was comfort in my empty thoughts.

Half an hour later I was downstairs with my laptop, ready to join the hunt once more. Thomas and Lucy sat at the table with a large map of America and Harvey was on the sofa gaming, seemingly unperturbed by our guests or the seriousness of our rescue mission. The smell from the kitchen excited my taste buds, I felt like Pavlov's Dog.

'Morning,' Lucy said as I joined them.

'Hey, any news?'

'Yes, Foxton confirmed an abduction in Georgia in October. An estate agent, the daughter of an influential businessman. The hairpin belonged to her.'

'Oh no.' This was bad news. There may have been seven abductions after all. 'Is this far from the others?'

'It is but there does seem to be a line of sorts.'

I looked at the map. The line Lucy had drawn between the three abductions was almost straight and ran in the same direction as the UK line.

'Parallel lines – *a parallel trust*,' I said.

'It seems so. Foxton's team are looking through the missing persons' register anywhere close to the line.'

I called Unity on Skype and we updated her on the latest news.

'This is bad,' she said, solemnly. 'Was there a ransom demand for this one?'

'No, there wasn't,' Thomas replied.

There was silence for a few moments, as if all our thoughts were synchronised. I was trying not to speculate but I worried that my failure to see the bigger picture might have condemned these women. I should have realised the connection earlier. The guilt became a burden, like the weight of the world crushing my shoulders.

***

Linden Keld awoke early on Sunday morning, leaving Edina to sleep for a while. He needed fresh air. The grounds of his home were expansive and ornate and the garden flourished even in winter. For the first time in his life he didn't want to go to church. The idea of having people around him was unappealing. These unfamiliar feelings plagued him, forcing him to think about things he would normally fight. Soul-searching was weakness. Jesus was the only judge worthy of his care and his conscience was solely at His mercy. But this was different.

Was his quest for justice greater than his quest to find Daisy? This kid in England, barely older than Daisy, was the key to finding her. Should he trust him? Had the passing of the seventh day had a consequence on Daisy's life? There were now other fathers looking for their daughters. Instead of hope for Daisy being diluted by these other missing women, their fathers should unite as a force.

Linden returned to the house and made breakfast for his wife. 'Go to church without me today, Edina. Ask the Lord's forgiveness for me.'

'Are you sure?'

'I have to confront my own demons.'

***

We cleared the table for lunch and sat together. We spoke about Christmas, news and sporting events rather than the case, as it wasn't for Eva's ears. She made one of the nicest meals I've ever eaten at home and everyone enjoyed it. For half an hour, there was release.

'How come you ended up an astrophysicist, Eva? If you don't mind me asking,' Lucy said.

'It was my father's passion,' she replied instantly, smiling as if she was pleased with the question. 'I was in awe of my father's work. He used to take me out with him on expeditions to observe the night sky.'

'Ah, it's in the blood. You grew up with it then.'

'Well, we moved away when I was seven. His work was based in the States and my mother wasn't keen on staying but the excitement of those times remained with me. It seemed the right career path.'

'He must be proud of you now.'

'I guess. I try.'

Eva was motivated in a similar way to me. I'm lucky that I still live with my dad. I love my mum but I could never see me growing up with the same passions or the encouragement that I have from Dad if I'd stayed with her. It seemed as if Eva's motivation was still her father. I suppose astronomy and cosmology are considered part of a man's world – or was that me being sexist? Either way, she was doing well for herself and I liked her and the positive effect she was having on Dad.

We helped clear up and returned to the table. I called Unity again; she seemed animated.

'Guys, I've been looking at online maps and extended the American line. It's not as easy as the UK but I might have found something.' She sent a screen shot of an area close to Des Moines in Iowa. She circled in red *Willow Creek Golf*

Course. 'If you go online, their logo seems familiar,' she added.

It *was* familiar. Thomas reached for the photo of the golf marker and held it to the screen for comparison. It was exactly the same.

'Excellent work, Unity. I'll call Foxton now.' Thomas said.

I smiled and put a thumb up to Unity. I used the computer to check the area; it did seem as if it should be on the line but my excitement was countered by the realisation that there could be another abduction. More worried parents.

Lucy stared at the wall, her head tilted to the side.

'Are you OK?' I asked.

'Yes. There are seven clues and only six items. If each of these items corresponds to an abduction, does this mean there were six abductions or seven?'

'Maybe there was something in that last container after all.'

'Possibly. Unless Clifton was the seventh himself, and that's what he meant about finding him.'

She could be right.

'I always thought the red star was a metaphor for a star nearing the end of its life. Could the crushed red star also have some symbolic meaning? Crushed dreams or hope?'

I nodded but hoped she was wrong. I felt guilty. The consequences of my failure to work out Clifton's clues or look to the bigger picture might have destroyed everybody.

Thomas returned in time to stop my conscience imploding.

'Foxton's on to it now. He will see if there's an abduction reported in the area. They will narrow the line a little too. Linden Keld has been more cooperative since your chat with him.'

'That's something, at least.'

We tried making sense of the line. It was hard to be specific without precise locations and we only had the names of the towns where each abduction took place, but it was too much of a coincidence for it not to be a parallel line. Both lines appeared to run north-west to south-east.

It was late in the day when Foxton phoned back. Thomas

took the call and we watched him as he spoke, anticipating the news.

'No abductions have been reported,' he said as soon as he ended the call. 'There are missing persons and these are being investigated. There is, however, a Clifton registered to the Willow Creek golf course. Des Moines Police Department are on to it now.'

'Oh wow,' Unity and I said in unison.

We waited.

CHAPTER 31

Linden Keld listened for once but he wasn't sure if he liked what he heard. The FBI explained about the new missing woman and the fathers of both Triana Perry and Alexandria Fernwood agreed to talk to him. He was advised not to mention the ransom demand. He didn't like Ashton Perry. There was no doubt the man was concerned for his daughter but he seemed morally corrupt. He spent as much time bragging about his business exploits and how he was benefiting from the *fracking boom* as he did talking about his daughter's whereabouts. Linden was frustrated. He felt strongly that Ashton was hitting him for future networking.

Douglas Fernwood was no better.

'Sorry to hear about Alexandria. Is there any more news?' Linden asked, after introducing himself.

'No. The police say there was a struggle. They think it's connected to your daughter's disappearance.'

'It could be. I pray constantly that Daisy is safe and will have the wisdom to know what to do. Alexandria is in our prayers too, sir.'

'Yeah, well, praying has its limitations. There's some sick bastards out there. The timing couldn't be worse. We've been worked off our feet ready for Christmas. If it wasn't for foreign labour, fuck knows what we would do right now.'

Once again, Linden was stunned. Is this what it all came down to? 'How are you able to carry on, knowing Alexandria's missing, possibly harmed?'

'I'm delegating. I'm on Jamestown PD's back every day, helping as much as I can. What else can I do? I prepare for the worst and hope she is alive and safe. I don't have a faith, Congressman, I'm a practical man. If she has been harmed then I'll fight for justice, relentlessly.'

Linden didn't know to respond. He couldn't imagine for one moment how anybody couldn't have a faith, especially under such extreme circumstances. How could a person be so cold, so unempathetic? He hoped he wasn't seen in this way. Edina's lectures echoed in his thoughts and he dismissed the niggling worry in his head ... *were these girls hand-picked because of their fathers?*

'Then I shall pray for you both, Mr Fernwood.' He hung up.

***

As another day ended in England, the FBI continued their work in the States. I was tired; the day had been exhausting and I had to attempt college tomorrow. I was falling behind and knew if I didn't catch up I would have to abandon it and resit my twelfth year.

Foxton updated Thomas regularly on events in Des Moines. There was hopeful anticipation – even excitement – when we heard they had traced Clifton, the golf course member, and had him in custody. For a few hours the conversation drifted away from the hunt and we talked about the imminent launch mission to the moon. As the day went on, it became clear that the man in custody was unconnected to the hunt.

Willow Creek Golf Course confirmed that the golf marker was theirs but it was not a custom marker, it was one used by all players. There were historic missing persons' cases in Des Moines and serial runaways, all of which were being investigated. The only strange case was of a man who had abandoned his car near the golf course and had been out of touch for about a month, but his family believed he was in Europe. The FBI was still tracing his movements.

Thomas and Lucy left about 10.30, followed shortly afterwards by Eva. I took the laptop upstairs and talked to Unity for a while.

'Do you think there was anything in that container after all?' I asked.

'I think there must have been. It makes sense to have seven items,' she said. 'I do think Lucy might be right about the red star metaphor, mind.'

'Yeah, it's possible. It's so hard to work out if Clifton is a good guy or bad guy. His actions are bad but his words are good.'

'People are judged on their actions in the end. Words can lie.'

'We can't trust his actions, unless he is a victim too.'

This was a strange conundrum. I thought about how we are all victims. There's no life without injustice. Unity was a victim of her parent's lack of care; I was a victim of my ignorance; Eva was a victim of her parent's decisions. All three of us were motivated by injustice. Being a victim wasn't a weakness, it defined our strengths. Clifton's dreams were taken from him by the greed of the few, so were his motives now inspired by injustice or justice?

'You know what?' Unity asked, halting my philosophical journey.

'I'm sure I do, but humour me.'

'You think too much,' she smiled. 'You need a break.'

'Not much chance of that, plus I have college tomorrow. I need a ride out to see you soon.'

'That will be nice, though you're probably sick of people right now.'

'I am. But I'll make an exception for you,' I winked.

'Thanks, I'm honoured,' she said, poking her tongue out.

'You should come here for Dad's lunar evening on Friday. We're watching the space launch with Eva and some colleagues. I think Thomas and Lucy will be here too, depending on what happens.'

'Yeah, Mum will love that!'

'She probably won't notice you've gone.'

She looked distant. 'You could be right, maybe I should talk to Grandad as a backup.'

'Yes. Yes, do,' I said, excited at the prospect.

'I'll think on it. No promises.'

'Think hard! Night, Nutty.' I waved and she rolled her eyes before waving back, smiling.

I settled for bed and gazed at the glow stars on the ceiling as I drifted into sleep. What a week.

*****

Lucy and Thomas returned to their hotel. It was hard to switch off long enough for any conversation outside of the case. Christmas was approaching and Lucy needed time to prepare but it was impossible to plan.

'I don't think we can contribute much more,' Lucy said.

'It's a different case to the one we took on. We certainly can't charge Aril now. He's done well to keep it all together in truth.'

'He has. It's more detective work than a treasure hunt now, but I can't see how we can sign off it.'

Lucy joined Thomas in the bed. He opened up the paper to attempt the crossword. She chuckled to herself: *does he ever switch off his mind?*

'I don't think we can sign it off. I keep thinking there's still more we can offer. We still have to find Daisy and possibly six others, not to mention Clifton.'

Lucy sighed but Thomas was right. She snuggled on to her pillow facing Thomas, who was concentrating deeply on the crossword. She always liked his arms; they were perfectly shaped with muscle lines and shadows that were an artist's dream and yet compact and modest, perfect for hugging.

'You're checking me out again,' he said, without looking away from his paper. She felt the blood rush to her cheeks.

She smiled and closed her eyes. Ten seconds later, Thomas abandoned his newspaper and placed a perfect arm around her.

***

After the stress and turmoil of the last week, college seemed an anti-climax but I respected the normality. It was surreal, looking at life going on around me, rather than feeling that I was embedded in it. Trivial lives, trivial problems and trivial gossip, with no idea of the adult world that awaited all these students. I wanted to join them, regress to an innocent age when it was safe to wonder.

But then again, there was Po. The moment I stepped into the lunch hall he jumped on my back. 'You'll never guess what?' he said.

I tried to keep my balance. Why does everybody think I'm psychic all of a sudden? 'Oi, get off!'

He jumped down and spun me round to face him. 'We can rehearse here on Friday night after college for the next two weeks.' He didn't hesitate, to prevent me denying him. 'You can't say no. Whatever plans you have, scrap them.' He looked at me sternly.

'I can't it's the lunar launch, Dad's having a...'

'Party? Dale is having a party?'

'Erm not that type of...'

'Awesome! You can come to practice and we can all head to yours after...'

'No!' God, I wish I could think quicker. I didn't want him to come and I couldn't tell him who was likely to be there. I certainly didn't want him quizzing Thomas and Lucy. 'It's his work colleagues, it's no major party.'

'Great! Then he won't miss you while you rehearse. We can have the hall for two hours, dude, we can run through the full set twice.'

'I can't. I'm sorry, I really have to be there and help out. I'll come on Saturday as normal.' I hated having to stand up to him, he was as demanding as a starving kitten.

'Man. You're such a pain in the arse. You can't prioritise your old man's party over your future.'

'My future?'

'Yes, Aril, you're future. The road to success is paved in golden G-strings. You'll have fame, fortune … girls. Your guitar will be a magnet for hottest chicks in the land. One touch and their clothes will drop…'

'Jeez, you're full of it!' I laughed.

'Come on. It's two hours. Not a lot to ask of your best mate,' he pulled a sad face.

'No promises,' I said. Unity's words resonated in my mind. I needed an escape plan if she was coming.

It was enough for Po. 'Thanks, dude. You won't regret it.'

***

When I got home after college, the house was quiet. I expected Thomas and Lucy to be there but even Harvey was out. I went to the kitchen and found a note from Dad by the kettle. *Make yourself tea, Thomas and Lucy arriving at 7pm. I won't be back until after 10 x*

I had two hours of peace. It was the first time I'd been alone in the house for weeks so I paced up and down, enjoying the space. I made my food, played loud guitar for a while and fantasised about discovering life on a distant exoplanet. I'd call it *Unity*. She was never far from my thoughts.

The doorbell sounded.

'Hey,' I said, letting Thomas and Lucy into the house. 'Any news?'

'Nothing concrete as yet, but developments,' Thomas said, as we made space on the table. I asked if I could Skype Unity. She was waiting and I felt guilty that I hadn't called her earlier.

Thomas told us, 'The FBI have been trying to trace monies and looking for spikes in receivers but Daisy's abductors have been very careful. They certainly haven't been using electronic communications unless they've been talking in code.'

'How does the FBI know?' Unity asked.

'The NSA and GCHQ have their ways,' Thomas replied with a smile. 'The thinking now is that there were two separate hunts – one on each line. Messages could have been left using geocodes on the American line as well as the UK one.'

'I suppose that makes sense, especially since they sent me the first clue on a memory drive.'

'That line's not straight though,' Unity said.

'So it seems, but the deviation is only about fifteen miles. The FBI has been targeting twenty miles either side of the mean, so there's a forty-mile band of investigation.'

Lucy opened the American map. She had highlighted a thick line from North Dakota down to Florida. There were many towns on her map so there would be hundreds, if not thousands, on the online maps.

I had a thought. 'Could there be more clues to places within the random incidental lines in Clifton's messages – like that comment about cordwainers?'

'It's possible,' Lucy replied. 'We looked into cordwainers and they are an exclusive guild of shoemakers from London that used a particular brand of goatskin leather to make soft leather shoes.'

'Oh right. Dad thought it was a posh word for shoemakers,' I said.

'So did we at first,' Lucy admitted.

Unity offered to write out the names of towns and villages on the American line. Lucy drew up a timeline to see if there was any obvious correlation between the events but with only three abductions, there wasn't much to go on. Speculative guesses were all we could offer right now.

Sterling Foxton rang and spoke with Thomas. With attention returning to America, Foxton felt it would be wise to return home to oversee the investigation there. GCHQ would continue its investigations and he asked if Thomas and Lucy could base themselves in Cheltenham again. They could mediate any links with myself and individual forces, as necessary. Thomas agreed.

I was on kettle duty but found myself pacing the room in my own world. Not that my thoughts had any clarity but I was excited again – there was no reason other than a feeling.

Lucy offered a penny for my thoughts.

'What is the price of trust? In fact what *is* trust? How is it defined?' I asked.

Thomas looked at his notes and replied instantly – he had obviously been thinking the same thing. 'Firm belief in the truth, reliability or ability of something or someone,' he said.

'So trust is a form of faith, like belief is faith,' I said. I didn't know where I was going with this.

'I guess,'

'So why demand money from a guy who has faith in abundance and not the other fathers?'

'I see where you're coming from,' Thomas said. 'The kidnappers said to Linden about trust; they want a parallel trust too.'

As much as this became another piece of the puzzle there was a part of me that felt some weight lifting from my shoulders. I wasn't bearing this burden alone.

When Dad returned, he looked exhausted. Thomas and Lucy briefed him on the latest news and explained about going to Cheltenham. I was partly relieved but also felt a twinge of guilt. I liked Thomas and Lucy but desperately needed my own time. Once again, I hadn't done any homework so the idea of freeing up my evenings was a blessing. They agreed to come back Friday night to watch the lunar launch.

After Thomas and Lucy left, I went upstairs. I wanted to sleep but some of the homework was urgent.

I kept Unity online. 'Have you had any thoughts about Friday?'

'I haven't spoken to my mother yet but I want to, if it's alright with Dale.'

'It is. You can sleep in the observatory. It's nice up there.'

'I'll phone Grandad on Wednesday, if I don't get to talk to my mother before then.'

I crossed my fingers and smiled and she did likewise. 'Beat you to it,' she laughed.

– CHAPTER 32 –

I spent the next two days lost in college work. It seemed a fruitless task and it was harder to catch up with maths than it was the sciences. I spend lunchtimes in the maths block. *Everything in the universe is just numbers.* Yeah, right.

There was little progress in the hunt for Daisy. Thomas and Lucy phoned a number of times in the evenings but there were few developments. They had found vague lines of investigation from Unity's notes and looked further into the towns in the areas. The FBI had looked for more gifted children and local police forces looked for missing persons.

It was late on Wednesday night, as I was settling to bed that we got the breakthrough. Unity was still online when I got the call from Thomas.

'Just had a call from Foxton. They are linking the disappearance of this golfer to the missing girls,' he said.

'How come?'

'He never left the country. His phone and bank account haven't been touched since he disappeared – which was exactly a week between the disappearance of Triana Perry and Alexandria Fernwood.'

'Wow. There really must be seven abductions then.'

'Oh there's more. This golfer, Martin Wildwood, his car was abandoned on the road south of the golf course. The exact co-ordinates were 41.5210 degrees north, 93.6985 west. The aggregate is minus 52.1775.'

'No way!' I couldn't believe what I was hearing.

'When they checked the other cases, Alexandria's car was also on this line – as was Triana Perry's. And the abandoned car used in Daisy's kidnap was found on the Austin Peay Memorial Highway, which was on this line.'

'So there's no doubt about it then, it's a direct line. At least we can narrow down the search,' I said.

'The FBI is on to it now. I believe Martin Wildwood is also the son of a rich family and worked for the family firm.'

'So Clifton could be teaching these people a lesson. There has to be some link to the parents of these victims, surely?'

'You're thinking like a proper detective,' Thomas laughed. I didn't know if I should be flattered but I liked the praise. 'Yes, that's what I was discussing with Foxton before I phoned you. They are on to it now.'

I updated Unity after the call; she had heard my side of the conversation and was intrigued. I might think like a *proper detective* but she thought like a proper treasure hunter.

'There's no way you could have pieced these clues together in the weeks you were hunting. It would have been impossible to make those connections. He must have known you'd piece it all together afterwards,' she said. 'We need to think like treasure hunters again and let the FBI and police do the detective work.'

'You're right, Nutty. You're spot on. We need a brainstorming session. I don't suppose you've spoken to your mum about Friday?'

'Nah, but I'm planning to come anyway, I'll explain to Grandad. I can leave school early as it's Friday.'

'Ah brilliant,' I said. 'Let me know when you work out the train times. Dad's already said we can pick you up from Cambridge.' For the first time in ages, I felt that old excitement return, as if the hunt was fresh and Unity part of it. I couldn't wait.

'He's a star.'

'Yeah, we all need a life-saver every now and then.' I smiled and she squinted up her eyes and laughed.

***

Thursday was chaos at college. My phone was on silent but I noticed that Thomas had left a message to call him. I found a quiet space at lunch break and phoned.

'There was a possible abduction a week before Triana, near St Louis, Missouri. A man named Dean Hatfield. His car was abandoned on the highway and again the GPS was exactly on the line. There must have been one the week before, and may well have been another a week after Daisy. The FBI thinks the sunglasses belonged to Dean.'

'That means the moonstone pendant is probably another woman then. That's the only other item we have,' I said.

'Foxton's team is on the case. They may lift the news blackout in light of this, I'm not sure how much evidence they will release but I hope they limit the UK information.'

I knew what he was saying. The thought was scary and I didn't like the idea of media focus being on me. 'OK, let me know if I should be worried. Unity is joining us tomorrow night. She wants us to think like treasure hunters again. I think she's right.'

'She is right. Lucy said this same thing this morning. It would be good to get our heads together, though it might be difficult with Dale's guests.'

'True. We'll see how it goes.'

No sooner had I ended the call when Unity texted me with her train details. I had to pick her up at Cambridge at half-past four, which was perfect – or so I thought. I had forgotten about Po. The moment I walked into physics, my memory kicked in: I had agreed to band practice on Friday. I spent the lesson oblivious to my teacher, thinking about how I could let Po down. I knew we had our usual Thursday rehearsal immediately after the lesson so I had to give him heaps of attention today, to lessen the blow for tomorrow.

I acted like a prat. I matched Po's ego beat for beat. We acted out the whole eighties' *Glam-Rock* shenanigans and I must admit my guitar playing was impressive even by my own high standards. We had the rest of the band in stitches. Most of the time, Po couldn't play for laughing. I got carried away and led the stage as we pitched our punked-up 'Stop the Cavalry' to the embarrassed cleaner, who chose the wrong moment to walk through the hall. I pogoed on stage to the beat, as if I'd been given enough glucose to waken the dead.

I was breathless at the end. We packed up our stuff and Po patted me on the back. 'You're a ten, dude. That was awesome. We'll shake the Fox and Hare to the ground.'

I high-fived him and smiled to myself. 'Yeah, well, I had to make the effort today because I really have to let you down tomorrow. I've got to go to Cambridge straight after college with Dad.' I shrugged. Po's face was a picture. I thought I should seize control of the moment and reverse the roles for once. 'Hey, we'll knock them dead – you're a nine now.' I grabbed his shoulders and shook him. 'You need to practise, Po, practise.' The band laughed.

'You bastard!' he said. I smirked. Eventually he laughed, though not before smacking both of my ears with his drumsticks.

'You're on for Saturday, aren't you?'

'Yeah. Barring a disaster,' I said, knowing full well it was unlikely. I didn't know when Unity would have to get back.

***

When I got home, Dad was out again. Harvey stuck a pizza in the oven to share and I sat downstairs for half an hour with him, catching up with news. I felt for him sometimes. He didn't appear to have any ambition or drive. He worked minimum wage, without fuss, came home and played games. His social life was limited to multi-player MMO strategy gaming. He was envious of my recent attention but couldn't bring himself out of his comfort zone enough to join me.

'Unity is coming tomorrow,' I said. I knew this time I couldn't hide her, though he had seen her when she came here as we were leaving and over Skype.

'You're lucky, she's pretty.'

'Well, we're not together in that sense. She's helping me solve these clues.'

'Hmmm. Maybe for now, but you like her, don't you?'

'She's a nice girl. I respect her, she has a difficult life.' He stared me out with one eyebrow raised. 'What?'

He laughed. 'Admit it, you like her. There's nothing about her not to like.'

'Oh so you like her then?' I said, trying to divert the awkward conversation.

He threw a cushion at me, then finished his pizza. 'If you don't ask her out, someone else will,' he said, returning to his game.

I left to do my homework but Harvey's closing comment had reached my stomach. Were these butterflies excitement or fear? Was it the thought of asking her out or the fear that rejection could ruin our friendship? The prospect of not having her in my life was infinitely worse than the acceptance of not being her lover. But could I honestly cope with her hand being taken by another guy?

My quantum mechanics homework was far easier on my brain than Harvey's emotional torture. *Why is everything in life so damned hard?*

I was wondering how things were going in America when Thomas phoned. 'We are struggling to find any more missing people on the line but there does appear to be a chronological pattern,' he said.

'Chronological?'

'Yes, the pattern of you going north and south for clues seems to correlate with the order of abductions. We don't know where the first clue would be but the assumption is to use your house as the starting point where you were sent the flash drive. We are trying to assess where that would be in relation to the American line.'

'What's the southern point?'

'Well, there's not much happening at the south end of the

line in Florida. There's a complex of island strips and the mainland point is by Chain of Lakes Park near Titusville. The FBI is checking nearby towns and cities in case there are reports of missing people.'

I was multitasking, entering the location on the online maps. I could see what he meant; Orlando wasn't too far. I searched the history of the city in case I could find a clue. 'It's a major tourist location, could it have been a tourist?'

'Possible, but unlikely. It looks like the victims were targeted specifically because of their parents, so it would be difficult to improvise.'

'But a victim could have been led down there, offered a free holiday or something, and been abducted without their family realising they were missing. Daisy was lured in that manner.'

'We can't rule it out. I suppose, you're right.'

I wondered what was in the missing container and how important any note would have been. It may have contained the coordinates to find Daisy and the other missing people.

I called Unity on Skype after Thomas's call and updated her. She had a giggling fit when I told her about my rehearsals with Po. She bugged me to let her watch the pub rehearsal on Saturday. Thankfully my excuse was practical: I could only get her there by bike and it wouldn't be fair to ask Dad, when he also had to take us to Cambridge.

'I feel so bad for Po,' she said.

'I wouldn't, trust me.'

'You're prioritising me over your best mate and he needs you.'

'No, he doesn't. He needs a guitarist. Honestly, he only loves me for my strings.' She laughed. 'You're far better company, plus I see him every day, and me and you have work to do, people to rescue and treasure to find.'

'You owe Po big time. I must find a way of coming to see you play. Grandad is supposed to be picking me up that weekend; I'm staying with him for Christmas.'

'Maybe he can come too and take you up north on the

Sunday?'

'Maybe. God knows what he would make of it!' She laughed.

'It will be nice to see you tomorrow. I'm looking forward to seeing the launch too. Dad's got a second screen in so we can also watch the live stream from the space centre control room.'

'Yeah, it will be nice. I've told Grandad but not my mother. I'm leaving her a note.'

'She's going to hate me,' I said. My conscience jabbed me; I would hate to get Unity into trouble.

'It will be fine. I have to do it; I need a life of my own. I was so miserable when I missed out on Hythe the other week. It's another personal landmark for me in this fight. Plus, I don't think she will notice. She didn't come home last Friday. I'll keep my phone with me. What's the worst she can do?'

'I guess. Though, it's a blessing in disguise that you didn't come to Hythe in the end.'

'Yes, I think my mother might have lost it completely!'

– CHAPTER 33 –

The cameras flashed and clicked as Congressman Linden
Keld entered the makeshift press room in Nashville
with Edina. The press lockdown was lifted and this was a
public appeal to Daisy's captors. Linden's faith was being
crucified by the fear that it might be too late to save Daisy.

It was Edina who had asked for this appeal. In the previous
appeal two weeks before, Linden had offered a million-dollar
reward and had shown strength and determination, through
his faith, that they would find Daisy and bring her captors
to justice. Somehow that hope was dissolving and Edina's
courage was the only faith insoluble.

All eyes were on Linden and there was an audible
shuffle as the gaze diverted to Edina when she stood up
to the microphone. She was quiet and timid, yet there was
anticipation of something profound.

'Twenty-eight days ago, our daughter, Daisy was lured
from her college and hasn't been seen since. It now seems she
is not the only child who's gone missing – there may be as
many as seven. Whoever has Daisy will be watching this, so
please listen. You wanted to teach us a lesson. Well, we have
searched our souls more in the past twenty-eight days than
the previous twenty-eight years. You win. We were wrong.
The change in us can only be proven by our actions and
that will take time. And as days turn to weeks and months
and years, you will see that we have learned our lesson. Our

children should not have to suffer for our mistakes. Please. Let her go… Let our children go and give us a chance to prove to you that our change of heart is genuine.

Money has no use other than for security; the rest is just numbers. I could have a dollar for every star in the universe and it won't mean as much as a single moment with my child. Please … whoever you are, I trust you and I believe you have compassion. You speak the truth and your actions are a desperate message of change needed in our lives. We who are privileged have a responsibility to steer mankind to righteousness. Let us start this today. Please… Give us our children back.'

The cameras were silent. Edina's words were absorbed by every person in the building.

Edina took Linden's hand. Her graceful to nod to the press was returned by a wave of respectful gestures. In all of his days in politics, Linden had not once witnessed such reverence.

***

I couldn't believe how busy it was at the station. The weekend commuters congregated at the station in packs. Dad had to park some distance from the entrance so he remained in the car while I waited for Unity's train. I was already tired, I hadn't slept much and the day had been intense at college. Po had one last shot at trying to convince me to go to practice and lectured me about standing up to my dad, stating that I had to stop him running my life. If only he knew.

Unity's train arrived fifteen minutes late but my eyes caught her as she left the train. She had a small rucksack that matched her Galaxy messenger bag. Even if I wanted to hug her I couldn't because people were everywhere. We resorted to shouting our greetings and making small-talk as we left the station.

She thanked Dad as we got into the car and I filled her in on the news.

'Thomas called, they're on their way up,' I said.

'It's good they can come. Is there any more news?'

'Apparently the Kelds made another television appeal for Daisy.'

'They must be going through hell. Did they find any more abductions on the line?'

'Thomas said they are narrowing the search area to correlate with where our house would be on the American line. That seems the logical starting point but there's been nothing reported recently.'

'Unless that's not the starting point and one of the clues points to something else. Maybe to do with moonstone, or Monday because of the pendant.'

'True. They mustn't rule it out.'

'Are you looking forward to the launch tonight, Dale?'

'I am indeed,' Dad said. 'The conditions seem right so hopefully there won't be any delays.'

'What time is it?'

'It's 7.20pm our time. Eastern Daylight Time is five hours behind so it will be mid-afternoon at the launch site. I'm surprised they hadn't made the launch on the hour. They must have their reasons.'

'Probably TV rights and advertising,' I said.

'You could be right, Aril. This mission is privately funded and has been fraught with financial problems from the start. It's possible they have fallen in with advertising demands.'

I remembered the documentary I'd seen about it in physics. It was a miracle this launch could go ahead.

'What will they do when they get there?' Unity asked.

'It's part of a long-term project to test conditions for life in space. Moon temperatures are extreme, ranging from around 120 degrees to minus 150 degrees Centigrade. The space crew will experiment with controlled biological extremophiles to see if life could exist, even in plant form. They have created a self-sustaining ecosystem that they plan to monitor up there.'

'Oh wow,' Unity's face lit up as Dad spoke.

'Because it's a vacuum and there's no atmosphere or atmospheric pressure, there are other experiments they can try. They can also create conditions for testing new drugs. They even have some lab mice that they want to put to sleep then leave to test the rate of decomposition, if any. All these experiments are essential if one day the human race is to look for other planets to inhabit. Our future depends on it.'

'It would be awesome to live on another planet.'

'There will be some exoplanets out there capable of supporting human life.'

'Just imagine hopping on board a passing asteroid and hitching a lift to a different part of the galaxy? "*Bye folks see you again in forty years!*"'

Dad laughed. 'That's not as crazy as it sounds.'

Eva and Harvey were preparing food in the kitchen when we got back. I introduced Unity then showed her upstairs to the observatory. I had already pulled out the sofa bed and made it up ready for her. She took off her coat and I noticed she wore an elegant black dress with sequined stars on the shoulders.

'This is amazing,' she said, looking at the giant telescope and dome ceiling.

'Hopefully the skies will clear later and you'll be able to see.'

'It feels like we're inside a giant crystal ball.'

'The telescope where Dad works is twenty times more powerful than this and the new one will be better still.'

'How could you not look to the universe with wonder?'

'Exactly. I told the FBI agent that Clifton got lucky with me.'

We went downstairs to help out. Eva had made some sandwiches and snacks. We took them into the main room while Harvey sorted out drinks. Thomas and Lucy arrived before Dad's work colleagues. We spoke briefly in the hall before joining the others; I was pleased Unity could finally meet them. There wasn't much news but Thomas was waiting for an update from Foxton. Everybody was hoping that the

Kelds' latest appeal might resonate with Daisy's captor.

At seven o'clock we were joined by three of Dad's colleagues. As well as the television on the wall, Dad set up the computer monitor with a live stream. This wasn't the first astronomical get-together Dad had held – he often held them during shuttle launches – but it was the most important. It was forty years to the day since the last manned mission, Apollo 17, set off to the moon.

Unity and I were engrossed with the images. It was a glorious day in Florida, though I suppose winter never bites there.

Shortly before the launch I went to the kitchen to pour out a drink. Eva was in there alone and for a moment I thought I caught a tear in her eye. 'Hey, are you OK?' I asked – then regretted it in case I had embarrassed her.

'I'm fine. I was deep in thought. It's a strange day for me today. I was wondering how my father was doing.'

'I would imagine he will be watching.'

'Oh he won't miss this for the world, I know.' She smiled and filled my glass with her moonshine punch.

'What's in this? It tastes great!'

'Faith, hope and a dash of vodka,' she joked. 'So go easy, no getting too drunk, especially your guest,' she winked.

'Yeah, I'll go easy.'

We returned to the front room as final preparations for the launch were underway. Thomas sat to my right with Lucy to his right. He looked distant. 'What's the date today?' I heard him ask Lucy.

'Seventh of December,' she replied.

We continued watching the television as the countdown started in earnest. 'T minus ten,' the control room announced to the cockpit. I'd been exceptionally tuned in to the number seven in recent weeks. I wondered what Thomas was thinking.

– CHAPTER 34 –

Ten minutes doesn't seem long but when you are waiting, it is an eternity. Listening to the last-minute checks by Commander Leslie Peterson and his crew you got a sense of the amount of organisation needed for everything to work precisely. There was no room for error. It must have been challenging for the crew to focus when the eyes of the world were watching. I felt nervous for them; we were all transfixed by the television screens. All except Thomas.

Nine pairs of eyes flicked between the television monitors but Thomas looked at his phone. He seemed agitated. I wondered if Foxton had sent a message or if there was any more news. I glanced down and saw he was looking at a calendar app. My attention to the launch was derailed as I tried to synchronise my thoughts with Thomas's. Clifton's words kept haunting me: *trust me, trust me.*

Eight drops of moonshine punch landed on my foot and broke my concentration. Unity laughed. Embarrassed, I took a paper napkin to soak up the splashes. I looked up as the cameras panned an aerial shot of Cape Canaveral around the launch site. In the distance there was a crowd of thousands. The Banana River separated the mainland from the inlet. A geographical anomaly ran down the Florida coastline as a tiny strip of built-up land, stretching as far as the camera could see, disappearing into the horizon. It must be more than fifty miles. I wondered how far this was from the USA line.

'Seven clues,' Thomas said quietly to Lucy.

'Six items though and…'

'Five missing people. Yes,' Thomas interrupted her. 'I still think seven is the key though. We need to find a bit of space to ourselves after the launch. I have a theory.'

Four minutes to launch and I could sense conflicting emotions in the room. There was excitement and anticipation, deep thinking from Thomas and Lucy – and I was somewhere between the two while savouring Unity's company beside me. She looked over and smiled then asked if I was OK. I nodded and returned the smile, reaching my little finger out to briefly stroke the top of hers. The moonshine punch might have affected me but I felt calm.

Three times I looked over at Thomas's phone. He was looking through maps and I wondered if he was pondering the same thoughts as me. I had a strong feeling I was finally in sync with him. Lucy also watched him and pulled his wrist towards her so she could see clearly. Thomas tapped his phone twice, sat back and exhaled.

Two seconds later, he looked over to me and Unity. We both caught his gaze: he looked shocked. It was impossible to leave the room or talk so he raised one finger and shifted his eyes in the direction of the kitchen. Unity and I nodded. We turned to the monitors as the final sequence for the launch started. I desperately tried to predict Thomas's thinking and felt a knot in my stomach.

One overwhelming thought consumed me at the moment of ignition: *Clifton was on that flight.*

'*We have lift off!*' The rocket launched to a round of cheers and raised glasses in the room.

Thomas, Lucy, Unity and I stared at the screen, our mouths open.

***

A few minutes later Thomas motioned us to the kitchen.

'He's on that flight,' I said.

'He told us,' Thomas said, rushing to the table. 'He told us and we didn't listen. Clifton said that when he was younger he wanted to be an astronaut and earlier he said he had always been a dreamer and followed every dream. Look.' He showed us the map with Cape Canaveral on his phone. 'The line runs through the Space Complex close to Kennedy Space Centre at the south. We had figured the southernmost tip to be on the mainland area.'

'It wasn't seven days, it was the seventh,' Lucy said.

I had a thought but before I could voice it, Unity beat me to it. 'That last note was from Clifton after all. *Unlucky for some* wasn't an insult – it was a clue. It meant thirteen. It was thirteen days until the launch on the seventh,' she said.

'Trust me,' I added. 'TM must have meant, "Trust me".'

'What does this mean now?' Lucy asked.

Where was Daisy Keld? We might have found Clifton but this didn't tell us where Daisy or the others were.

'I need to phone Foxton,' Thomas said. 'We don't know if we're right but it makes sense. If we *are* right, we sure as hell know what the money was for.'

Thomas made the call and I offered coffee. Eva came through and gently squeezed my shoulder as I was filling the kettle. 'Is everything OK?' she asked.

'We're treasure hunting again, can't you tell?' I said with flick of the head in the direction of the table.

'Knowing your luck it's in that spacecraft,' she said, nudging my arm.

'Many a true word spoken in jest. You could be right, though.'

'Well, I sure hope not. You'd need a space-bike.' She laughed and returned to the front room with our guest's punch.

I brought our drinks to the table then ran upstairs to collect my laptop. Sure enough, we could see the line in detail running through Cape Canaveral. It was a narrow inlet strip like a peninsular, running up from the south of the state.

Thomas ended his phone call. 'Foxton's on to it now. He's of the same opinion; they will look into the background of the crew and try to retrace their steps in recent days.'

'It's like every sentence has some relevance,' Lucy said. She had a file open with photocopies of the notes and scanned photographs of the clues. 'If the southernmost part of the line led to Clifton, where are Daisy or the others?'

'Could it be that the she's at the starting point of the line? We don't know where that is yet,' Unity said.

'The FBI considered a correlation with this house, since the initial clue was sent here,' Thomas said.

We used online maps to try and work out where this would be. It certainly wouldn't be too far north from where Daisy was abducted near McKenzie, because my house wasn't too far north of Little Eversden where Daisy's watch was found. There were no major built-up areas but the small city of Fulton was about thirty-five miles away from McKenzie. It was famously labelled the 'Banana Capital of the World'; it had and old ice house that provided the ice blocks used in storage carts for transporting bananas across the country. We were unsure, but the banana connection might have some relation to the Banana River in Florida.

We were about to investigate Commander Peterson when Dad entered the kitchen with a colleague. He was in good spirits, relieved that the launch had gone well, and I didn't feel it right to mention our possible discovery.

'How long until they land on the moon?' Thomas asked.

'It will take about five days. There are two moonwalks, or EVAs as they are known, scheduled about thirty-six hours apart. Then they will return in ten days.'

'Amazing. I suppose technology is far superior to forty years ago,' Thomas said.

'Absolutely. The lunar module is fully computerised, there's very little manual involvement, even in the landing and ascent. It could practically land itself. Hopefully the crew will be able to set up their experiments and complete the mission without complications.'

I deliberately avoided eye contact with my fellow hunters. I felt uncomfortable because this meant a lot to Dad. He was too young to remember the original lunar landings and space was his life. We were going to have to break the news gently to him if we were right. We continued talking until Thomas's phone rang. He excused himself and took the call in the hallway.

Dad and his colleague returned to the sitting room. When Thomas returned from his call, you could sense his urgency. 'Commander Leslie Peterson was born Clifton Leslie. He was given his father's name,' Thomas said.

Unity and I looked at each other. What did this mean?

'Well, the FBI know that he's going nowhere right now and to intervene with the mission might put the crew in danger. They're planning to make a move directly after they land. Meanwhile, they are going to look into his movements over the past few months and try to find these missing people.'

'I have a bad feeling about this,' I said.

'I agree. This adventure doesn't draw a parallel with the tone in his messages,' Lucy said. 'Is he simply in the latter part of his life or is he about to die?'

'He wouldn't endanger his crew,' Thomas said.

'Dad said they are expected back in ten days. I suppose that gives us that time to work out what happened and hopefully find Daisy.'

'What's the press situation?' Lucy asked.

'On hold for now,' Thomas said. 'Foxton wants the investigation made as discreetly as possible at this stage.'

We joined the others in the main room. It was hard keeping up the pretence that everything was OK and harder still to distance our conversations from the thoughts in our heads. We knew we had a secret that was about to rock the world.

– CHAPTER 35 –

It was past midnight before people started to leave. The live feed continued in the background and the conversations in the room were fascinating. Thomas and Lucy were last to go; I wondered if they would mention our revelation to Dad but they didn't. They thanked him for the evening and told me that they would be in touch the next day. I didn't know if they were leaving the responsibility of talking to Dad about our discovery to me but I wasn't brave enough right now.

After they left, Unity and I helped Dad tidy up. I could see the moon from the kitchen window and felt mixed feelings about Clifton: proud that he was likely to follow his dream and that he would look on to the world after all, but angry at what he had done to achieve it. The cost could mean his freedom as opposed to his life. Maybe that's what he meant all along: he had to do wrong in order to achieve his dream and the price he would pay would be to die in jail. His *price* of trust.

'The sky's clear,' I said to Unity. 'Come on, let's see the night as it's supposed to be seen.' I looked to Dad and he nodded.

The sky seemed extra magnificent tonight, as if it were putting on a show for our entertainment. Unity's excitement was infectious. Her creative mind took over, making up stories of travels between stars with characters hopping from planet to planet. She was in her own world. It was two hours of magic, as if the real world had been left light years behind us and we were sharing these adventures together. I sat on the sofa bed and eventually she joined me and laid back, hands behind her head. The room only had a soft wall light but the sequins still sparkled on her dress.

'I don't blame him you know,' she said.

'Clifton?'

'Hmmm. If you had a chance to walk on the moon, something you dreamed of all your life, then somebody stole that from you at the last moment, wouldn't you do everything in your power to make it happen?'

'I'm not sure I'd go as far as kidnap and extortion.'

'He was wrong there but, I dunno, Aril.' She turned to face me and I reached to remove a strand of hair from over her cheek. 'I still want to trust him.'

'Yeah. I do too. I'm kind of envious of him right now.'

'You'd make an excellent Clifton,' she joked. 'You're like two peas in a pod.'

'Maybe,' I said with a smile. I couldn't help but like him but I enjoyed being with Unity more.

She let out a yawn, then apologised. 'I suppose we better get some sleep,' I said, giving her hand a gentle squeeze.

'Yeah, I know. I've enjoyed tonight. Feels good, doing my own thing.' She looked at her phone. 'Mum hasn't even called or texted. I don't think she came home.'

'I'm glad you came.' I stood up slowly and asked if she needed anything else.

'I'll be OK, thanks,' she said softly.

I raised my hand to wave. 'Night, Nutty. Sleep well. See you in the morning.'

She waved back and smiled.

For once I didn't have that empty space inside. Not that I slept, I couldn't stop thinking about her.

***

Lucy was tired when they returned to the hotel. The evening's events signalled a massive shift and a fresh approach to the whole case was needed. She knew Thomas was troubled and she rubbed his leg for a while as they talked. Tiredness often caused his right leg to seize up.

'What age do astronauts retire?' she asked.

'That's what I was thinking. Clifton is at the end of his career. He has to be early fifties, I'd say. He must still be extremely fit. The strain on the body will be phenomenal.'

'True. Maybe he was burning the candle of his career instead of life, with his talk of being the opposite end of life to Aril?'

'Not sure, Lucy. He said his death is on the line.'

'You're right. I sure hope we're not too late to find these missing people.'

'Well, at least we have new hope. I would be less confident if seven days was the cut-off after all.'

'I dread to think what Linden Keld will make of this latest news. I wonder if Foxton still needs us, in light of this.'

'I can't see what more we could do. I'm assuming that keeping us on board keeps us close in case Aril does have information, or turns out to be an accessory. It's unlikely Clifton will make fresh contact with Aril now.'

Lucy climbed into bed. Thomas wiped a strand of hair from her cheek and kissed her forehead then pulled her to him. They drifted to sleep in each other's arms.

***

'You *have* to be kidding me!' the voice on the phone said, the moment I picked it up and mumbled *hello* into the receiver. I don't think I had slept more than a couple of hours and I was still half asleep. 'Please say you're on your way?'

Ah damn, I forgot about band practice. 'Sorry, Po. I just woke,' I confessed.

'Not good enough. Get your arse here now!'

'I can't. I've got take Unity back to...' I stopped myself too late. Thinking with my mouth is going to be the death of me. Why the hell did I mention her? I came to my senses in a flash.

'Woah. Stop. Rewind. You're doing what? Is she there? Put her on the phone.'

'No. She's upstairs and no we didn't, before you ask or insinuate.'

'You said you'd do this today after you bailed last night. You didn't mention the girl, you sly bastard.'

'It was a last-minute thing. Long story,' I lied.

'Bring her with you. She can watch her stud wield his axe like you did the other day.'

I cringed. 'I'm not even up, none of us are so there's no way I can get there, mate. I'm sorry. Dad would have to bring us and I'd be lucky to get him out of bed.' I was doing a mental calculation of the time: we would barely have thirty minutes to rehearse.

'Well, this is just great,' Po said. 'I don't care how you get here, just get here.' He hung up.

I let out a moan and wrapped the pillow around my head, resisting the urge to scream. Then my senses sharpened. I could hear voices downstairs and … I could smell bacon!

I got up and went downstairs to investigate. Dad was making breakfast and Unity was at the table, cradling a steaming cup of coffee with both hands. 'Morning,' she said with a smile.

'Hey. Did you sleep OK?'

'Out like a light. It's so quiet here compared to home. It reminds me of Scotland.'

'You slept better than me then. I was rudely awoken by Po. I think he's pissed at me.'

'Aril! Yes, you're supposed to be at practice. I feel terrible.' Dad laughed loudly.

'He'll get over it, don't worry. What time do you need to be at the station?'

'I've no plans, I can fit in with you – I was just telling your dad.'

'It's too late for band practice now, so there's no rush.'

Dad dished up our fry-up and the three of us sat at the table. Harvey stayed in bed; he must have drunk most of the moonshine punch last night so would probably be suffering. After breakfast I went upstairs with Unity while she packed up her clothes.

'I didn't mention Clifton to your dad. I didn't know if he knew,' she said.

'No he doesn't yet. Thanks. It's something I need to ask Thomas and Lucy about. Dad will take it badly, I know.' I watched her fold her dress away and pack it neatly. 'You looked stunning in that dress last night,' I admitted. Thankfully, she smiled.

'I thought I should make the effort. I've been looking for an excuse to wear it for months. I bought it for an end-of-school celebration that never happened because my mother tripped and ended up in A&E after drinking all day.'

'Bummer.'

'Yeah, it's happened a few times, usually when I plan something for myself. I've learned not to look forward to anything so I don't get disappointed. The up side is that when something does happen, it's twice as special. I needed last night.'

'Any time. You'll always be welcome.' I meant it.

'Thanks. I like your family, you do normal.'

I laughed. 'If you call normal being indicted in a multi-million-dollar kidnap and extortion racket, then yeah, we're pretty normal.'

She laughed and rolled her eyes. I knew what she meant, though.

'Well, apart from that minor side line. I'm fine though, I can cope with home life. It's just nice when something goes right for once. I don't take anything for granted.' She pointed at the ceiling, a motion to Clifton. 'He must have been pretty desperate.'

'I guess. Desperate, but stupid.'

We returned downstairs, and I detoured to my room to collect my phone. Five missed calls from Po, with two abusive texts, and one missed call from Thomas. I put the kettle on then phoned him.

'I don't think Foxton slept all night,' he said. 'He's still up now. Peterson did travel to England briefly in October but most of the time he's been in Florida. The FBI has been feeling their way in rather that going all-out. They've been trying to gain information from a distance. Peterson doesn't have much of a family left. His father died when he was young and his mother died last year. He hasn't seen his ex-wife in over twenty years. She lives in Geneva and he has a daughter, Ellerslie, who probably lives in Geneva too. Nobody is aware of any contact between them. The FBI has applied for Clifton's medical records but it's assumed that he is healthy if he can make it into space.'

'There's no way he could have managed this alone, surely?'

'No, there must be more people involved. The FBI has the NSA retracing his online movements as they assumed Daisy's captors had re-routed IPs from NASA and government buildings, but they might have been genuine. Then again, there's no way they can seize computer equipment from NASA during this mission so there's an operation to investigate them after the crew return.'

'Oh right. Scary.'

'Even I'm going to be kept in the dark on that for now but this leaves the search for Daisy and the others as priority in the meantime.'

'OK. I'll keep my thinking cap on. It's hard though with college, I have so much catching up to do.'

'No, don't worry. That must be your priority. But it's good that we've identified Clifton. The FBI is in a better position to work things out.'

That was a relief because it eased the pressure. I had stopped thinking of the hunt as a personal treasure hunt long ago – I was little more than a thinking canister – but I still believed I was the last remaining hope for finding Daisy Keld. More weight lifted from my shoulders. I ended the call and returned to the main room.

'Dad, what do you know about Commander Leslie Peterson?' I asked.

'He's a very clever and committed man. I'm pleased for him this mission has finally taken off.'

'Have you ever met him?'

Dad laughed. 'No, unfortunately. I'd like to one day. He's a good man. He's worked relentlessly to help our understanding of space and science. He is a genuine inspiration.'

Unity had her head down, she knew what was coming.

'Dad, we found out Commander Peterson's first name is Clifton. He never uses it, it was his father's name. We think he's the one.' I spoke gently but I could see Dad's face drain. I didn't look at Unity; she was probably cursing me but I hoped she would understand my timing.

'Wow,' Dad said quietly. 'I can't believe for one moment that he would harm anybody. I take it the FBI knows?'

'They plan to arrest the whole team after they return. It would be wrong to seize any computer equipment now. There's a news block on the case so technically I shouldn't even be telling you.'

'Did you work this out yourselves?'

'Yes, literally as the rocket took off. The FBI confirmed it shortly afterwards. There was no way I could tell you last night.'

Unity offered to make another coffee. She must have felt awkward and I didn't know exactly how to respond.

'Please. If you stick the kettle on I'll come through in a second.'

She smiled and winked at me. I asked Dad if he was OK. 'I was dreading telling you, but I didn't want you to find out later and realise I already knew who Clifton is.'

'No, no, I'm fine. Just shocked. I should've seen it but I didn't put the pieces together.'

'Nobody did, not even the FBI when IP addresses linked to NASA. They thought they had been re-routed.'

'I knew he was clever, not this clever. Why you, though? Why here?'

'I think the clues were for you. Maybe the fact you lived in this house made you the perfect target, I don't know. No doubt we'll find out.'

I joined Unity in the kitchen, leaving Dad alone with his thoughts. I squeezed her shoulders from behind and thanked her. 'Sorry about that, it had to be then. I think he's OK,' I said.

'Yeah, you did well. It took guts. There was me thinking I was brave for leaving my mother a note.'

'No that *was* brave,' I said laughing.

'No, Aril. I was a coward. I hate confrontation and live my life trying to avoid it. You've confronted all these injustices head on. Not just your dad but Linden Keld, questioning by the FBI and the police – even dealing with Po.' She laughed but the sincerity in her voice touched me deeply. 'I've been proud of myself just for being able to rise above my own circumstances and keep looking forward. I thought I was strong.'

'You are, you do well and you're an inspiration.'

'It's trivial compared to your strength. My strength is internal and it stays there. Yours can be seen by everyone.'

I turned her round to face me. She looked down, so I hugged her briefly. 'I wouldn't have got through this without you. You're brave every day; I've been brave for two weeks.' I let her go but reached for her hands and gave them a squeeze.

'God, you're annoying.' She laughed and poked me lightly in the chest. 'I keep waiting for you to turn into an arsehole like every other guy I know. You're stubborn!'

'Sorry to disappoint you,' I said, embarrassed by her confession.

'No. It's good. Makes a change to know I can let my guard down a little.'

We made coffees and returned to Dad in the main room. I don't think he had moved a muscle.

*****

We crossed paths with Thomas and Lucy's car as we were about half a mile from the station and waved. I wondered what their plans would be and whether they would go back to London.

The station was busy again and Unity's train was running late so we waited in the coffee shop while Dad stayed in the car. There was still no call or message from Unity's mum. It was nice for her to have been away with no drama for once.

'You'll have to come down for the gig if you can,' I said.

'I'll bend my granddad's arm. You need to make peace with Po; he might sack you beforehand and you'll be gutted to be kicked out the band.'

We heard the Tannoy announce her train so left for the platform. I hugged her then watched her settle before the train left the platform. That butterfly feeling returned immediately but there was also a strange warmth and calm. I could still smell Unity's perfume.

– CHAPTER 36 –

The River Thames is majestic at night and even more so as Christmas approaches. Thomas and Lucy looked out from their office window over the lights of London. It was nearly three weeks since they had been in and their secretary had been keeping on top of general admin and phone calls but there was a lot to catch up on.

They had watched the updates on the lunar mission on television; everybody was in good spirits and the mission was going to plan. It was Sunday evening and there was little news breaking from America but intense work was going on behind the scenes.

Thomas's phone rang; it was Foxton. 'Hey, any developments?' Thomas asked.

'We might have. We've been tracking money movement in relation to the launch. It's unlikely that NASA is directly involved; Peterson's company paid to use their staff and facilities for the launch and technical design. There have been deals made for TV rights and documentaries, which are ongoing and will continue after the mission. There's certainly nothing in the NASA employees' movements to suggest any involvement but Peterson employed more than fifty staff and has a research facility near Atlanta.'

'That's not far from the first known abduction.'

'That's right. We've held back on going in until we know that a raid won't endanger the mission, but we're likely to enter the facility in the next twelve hours. It does seem the most likely place the victims could be held. We're also looking into Petersen's staff but as yet their movements and money transactions don't flag up any involvement.'

'It could be that he has hired some people who are not on the official payroll.'

'Yes, that's our thinking, which makes me wonder how much his staff know. It's going to be awkward. We're taking the line that because his name is Clifton, it's inevitable that he's a suspect, since he has a money motive. So we're going easy, as if it's an avenue that we have to explore in order to eliminate him from our investigation.'

'It's the truth really. We still don't know for sure.'

'We don't but I hope we find the kidnap victims safe and it's not too late.'

'Let's hope. We're back in London now but keeping in touch with Aril. He wants this resolved quickly too.'

'I can't clear him yet. Let's see how things go in twenty-four hours.'

***

I don't know if Po thought giving me the silent treatment would make me feel remorseful or more likely to become their permanent guitarist but he was failing. I enjoyed the quiet and spent lunchtime Monday working in the library. He reminded me of a disgruntled four-year-old brat, nose in the air and dismissive of my presence. Shame, because I had some good news for him. I let him stew for a while. I knew him well; he would crack eventually. He lasted until physics on Tuesday morning.

The news from America was eerily quiet and the news from space was encouraging. The mission was going to plan and any technical hitches were minor. I hadn't switched off from the hunt for Daisy but I couldn't think how I could be any more help.

Po sat next to me and smacked his head three times on

the table.

'Dude, you're losing it,' I said, laughing.

'Arghhh, you're such an arsehole,' he said.

'Apparently I'm not. But that's another story.'

'Eleven days until our big gig and you've missed two practices. It's useless practising without an effing guitarist. We're a rock band not a poncey popshite band.' He banged his head again on the table.

'Good job Dad's let us set up in the garage Saturday afternoon then, isn't it?'

Po's head had just reached the table again when he stopped, gave me a sideways glance, then lit up like a beacon. 'You're not kidding me, are you?'

'Nope. Only Saturday though. Our neighbours like their tranquil Sundays.'

'YES!' He banged his fist on the table as the teacher walked in.

'I love you, Aril.'

'Calm down,' I laughed. I feared he might kiss me.

***

On Tuesday evening I found myself thinking about Clifton again. Eva was home and the live television feed was broadcasting from the NASA control room while we were eating. Mission Control commented that EVA, which I understood meant *Extra Vehicular Activity*, was in thirty hours.

'Were you named after a moonwalk?' I asked Eva.

She laughed. 'I was,' she said. 'My father was still at university when I was born, studying astrophysics, but my mother wasn't keen on the name so agreed to compromise if I was born on a Monday.'

'I guess she lost?'

'I held out until 7.20pm.'

'So all this time she's hated your name?'

'No, she likes it really. The number one song when I

was born was Michael Jackson's "Billie Jean" which had his famous moonwalk dance in the video.'

'It was destiny then?'

'That's what my father believed. I'm eternally grateful I wasn't called Billie.'

After eating, I went upstairs and spoke to Unity on Skype while doing my homework. It had become a familiar routine to have Skype on in the background while we did our own thing. We didn't need to talk constantly. Every now and then one of us would speak out loud and a mini-conversation would ensue. Friday had gone well; Unity's mum hadn't even noticed she had gone, so Unity had removed her note and asked Henry not to mention it.

It was just after nine when Thomas rang.

'The FBI is still no closer to finding Daisy. They raided Commander Peterson's research facility, and detained and questioned the staff that remained there. Most of his technical staff are in Florida. Even though all the pieces point towards him, there's nothing as yet to actually link him.'

'So they are having doubts?'

'They strongly suspect he is involved but there's nothing they can hook onto. So they need to intensify their search for Daisy and hopefully find the others too.'

I didn't know what to feel. I didn't know if I wanted Clifton to be hours from walking on the moon or not. Was I still an integral part of the puzzle?

After the call I updated Unity then looked on the online maps to get a clearer picture of the line. I scrolled screen by screen from Jamestown all the way south, past Des Moines, McKenzie, St Louis and Columbus and into Cape Canaveral. The complexity of the geography in Florida was fascinating; I had to zoom in and out to navigate. There were many inlets, harbours and basins and I struggled to find the exact point where the line reached the land. Unity joined me in our investigation and looked into the history of the area.

'The main island north of Port Canaveral is government owned. There's a naval port that intersects the island. It looks like the line crosses government-owned sections of Merritt Island too,' she said. 'The mainland area north of Titusville is the first non-government-owned land the line hits, I think.' I followed her directions and saw what she meant.

How would Clifton have got away with using government land and buildings unnoticed? Thomas said the area around the Titusville lakes had been thoroughly investigated. My only conclusion was to return to the area in Tennessee or Kentucky that might correlate with my house.

'Aril, you need to read this,' Unity said as I was making my way back up the line. She sent me a link. The article explained about bomb testing that took place on Cape Canaveral more than a hundred years ago. There were military bunkers with observation points from Jetty Park. It wasn't known what happened to these bunkers but there were underground tunnels and passageways which extended under the ocean. The main building had been used as a private school in recent years. I looked on the map and the line just scraped the area.

'Abandoned military bunkers on the southernmost tip of the line?' I said.

'It might be something, I suppose.'

I called Thomas on Skype and talked him through our discovery. He was convinced enough to call Foxton. I could hear his side of the conversation and sensed that Foxton was keen to investigate.

'Good work, Aril. They'll look into this now. Try and get some sleep, it's late,' Thomas said.

I looked at the clock; it was approaching midnight. I agreed but called Unity again. 'The FBI is looking into it,' I said. 'Thomas said good work.'

She smiled.

We said our goodnights and I settled for the night, looking up at my ceiling constellation, willing Clifton to make contact, willing myself to trust him.

$$- \text{ CHAPTER 37 } -$$

Linden Keld spent his seventh day at home. He had rarely spent so much time away from his office and sanctuary. He wasn't ready to face people yet or to see his Lord's towering body above his personal altar. All this information – seven days, thirteen days – all came to nothing; this was day seventeen since the English kid was arrested. Had Daisy been abandoned and left to starve to death? Keld had more faith in Edina's hope than he had faith in his saviour.

He had been told about the latest developments but he didn't have the energy to be angry. Nor did he believe Daisy's kidnap was anything to do with NASA. If it was Commander Peterson, surely he wouldn't have harmed anybody. Keld's staff kept him up to date but it all meant nothing. They were no closer to finding their daughter; even Edina's pleas to the public had failed to touch the conscience of Daisy's captor.

The phone rang as he was about to settle for an early night. He recognised Foxton's number on the display and grimaced in preparation for the next round of nothing before reaching to answer.

'Dad! Dad, I'm here. I'm OK! Daddy, I'm coming home!"

***

Thomas Riley should have been used to Agent Foxton's wakeup calls, but after a restless night he was disorientated and knocked the phone to the ground. Lucy moaned. It wasn't even six in the morning. Eventually Thomas answered before the voicemail kicked in.

'Got them!' Foxton said. 'Got them all, they are safe. You were right.'

Thomas sat bolt upright and grabbed Lucy's hand. 'Wait, you've got them all?'

'They were in the bunkers. The main building has been used as a private school for gifted children but at the end of the grounds there's a sealed door leading to the old military bunkers. Over the years there's been a tunnel built into the school itself. It's a separate area. The students in the main school are separated, they knew nothing about it.'

'Do we know who is behind it?'

'They are being questioned now. They were lured and threatened initially but apparently once they arrived they were treated well.'

'Oh, thank God! That's a relief. Were there seven victims?'

'No. Just the five.'

Foxton had to go so the call ended. Thomas updated Lucy. The relief brought a tidal wave of emotion. They held each other briefly.

'You need to tell Aril,' Lucy said. 'I don't think he will mind a call this early.'

***

I don't think I'll ever be a morning person. I have this hatred of my phone's alarm and I don't think I ever get the sleep I need. I reached out to hit the screen to make the noise go away, but then it dawned on me that it wasn't my alarm tone. The phone was ringing; it was Thomas and he was about to make my morning.

'Bingo, Aril, you did it! They found Daisy safe.'

I sat up and reached for my bedside light. 'At Jetty Park?'

'Yes, the others were there too. Foxton's not sure about the story yet but they're all safe. Well done, Aril. I didn't think you'd mind the wakeup call for once.'

'Oh my God.' I burst into tears. I'd never felt such a rush of relief.

'Get yourself a coffee and treat yourself to a chocolate breakfast. I'll let you know more later. You did it though, Aril. Well done.'

I spluttered a thank you before hanging up and buried my face in my pillow to compose myself. I must have woken Dad because he knocked on my door to check on me. I jumped up and hugged him, tears still preventing speech.

'What's happened?'

'It's … it's OK... they … they've found them … they are OK.'

Dad hugged me tighter. It was awkward but I didn't care, the relief was overwhelming and uncontrollable. If I felt like this, what must Linden Keld be feeling?

'Thank God,' Dad said, quietly. He released me. 'Come on, I'll put the kettle on.'

It took me ten minutes to compose myself enough to venture downstairs. I needed to tell Unity. I texted her to ask me to let her know when she was awake, thinking it was considerate, but felt a fool when she replied, 'I am now!' I phoned her and my voice started breaking immediately. It took all my concentration to keep it together.

'Oh my God!' she let out a scream and then I heard her say 'Sorry, mother!' and giggle. 'You did it. You found the treasure,' she said.

'*We* did it,' I corrected her.

***

Congressman Linden Keld had never felt such a release. He had thought he would never hear Daisy's voice again. She was safe. He found Edina upstairs, preparing herself for bed.

'She's coming, my love, Daisy's coming home!'

Edina collapsed into his arms in tears and he hugged her tightly. 'Did you speak to her?' Edina asked.

'I did. She sounded well and bright. I can't tell you how good it felt to hear her voice. I had given up inside, Edina.'

They sat on the edge of the bed and Linden cradled Edina's head onto his shoulder. 'I know. But Daisy doesn't have to,' Edina said softly.

'I just thank the stars above that she's safe. I'm not sure if I could have lived with myself if she was gone forever.' The tears began again.

Edina squeezed his hand. 'The only thing more fragile than life is the living we take for granted.'

– CHAPTER 38 –

News had been breaking all day and a press conference was scheduled at four o' clock British time. Thomas and Lucy had been following the news but hadn't heard from Foxton.

'I wonder what will happen now,' Lucy said.

'This is where the fun begins. The entire nation will want justice.'

'That's what worries me.'

They sat in their office watching the river below. Thomas was convinced Peterson must have been behind it all, but couldn't work out how. Some things still didn't add up.

Lucy was on his wavelength. 'Only five victims in the end. It's like there's still pieces of the puzzle missing,' she said.

'Even if Clifton himself was the sixth, you would have expected a seventh.'

'The first gift, the moonstone pendant, do you think that was Clifton's?'

'I think we can assume it was. It would make sense – especially if Clifton does turn out to be Commander Peterson.'

'It has to be him, surely.'

The press crews waited in the conference room in Titusville. Thomas and Lucy recognised Foxton as a team of agents filed out to the microphones, though it wasn't Foxton who spoke. The chief of police explained that they had found the missing kidnap victims following a raid in a property at Jetty Park the previous evening.

'We can confirm that they are all safe and unharmed. Their families are here. They will help all of us with our investigations over the days ahead so we will release more information during this time. From what we gather so far, the victims have all had extensive schooling while they have been imprisoned. The school is owned by the American Research Institute of Science and Technology and is primarily a school for gifted children. However, both the management and existing students were unaware of the presence of the victims because part of the building leading to the military bunkers is sealed off. We are currently tracking down the school's owners. The school will be closed until the January term.'

He thanked everybody involved and mentioned the joint operation with police and 'valuable sources' in England.

'So Clifton was speaking literally when he said about his lessons being *told by others*.' Lucy said.

'It's curious. We are piecing the puzzle but still can't make out the picture.'

After the press conference, Thomas and Lucy took a walk along the river. It was dark and the air was chilly.

'It's ironic that the news of the release is overshadowing what should be the main news. The first moon landing is later tonight. Only a handful of people know that the stories could be linked,' Lucy said as they strolled, holding hands. They both looked up to the skies in search of the moon.

'Yes, it is,' Thomas said. 'At least they've been found safe. I wonder how long they would have been there, if we hadn't worked this out?'

'I have a feeling Clifton took his chances and trusted that Aril would find them.'

***

I was hyper all day in college and couldn't explain why. I

held secrets so big that I don't think anybody would have believed me if I told them. I blamed it on the excitement of the first moonwalk in forty years. My physics tutor fed off my enthusiasm and explained to us the difficulties the astronauts would encounter and the conditions up there. It was imperative they timed the walk right so that they could make as much use of the lunar dawn as possible before the temperatures rose too high. It was fascinating. I always got the impression that he aimed much of the space talk in my direction, knowing my father's work and my own ambitions.

I kept an eye on the other news stories on my phone. For once I felt proud. I knew I had to keep it under control and I didn't care that there wasn't a treasure of value to me personally, because I might have saved the lives of five people. How many people can claim that at the age of seventeen?

I couldn't shake the smile off my face even on the cold ride home after college. Dad wasn't having another party tonight as the moonwalk would be so late but we were going to stay up, at least to see the initial walk on the moon. *Was it really our Clifton?*

After tea I skyped Unity. She had also kept an eye on the news in America and mentioned how heavily our secret bore down on her. I got the impression that she regarded her friends with the same caution that I did mine. She stayed up to watch the moon landing with us; EVA was scheduled for one-thirty our time. As it approached, I could feel the excitement in everybody – even on television. It was like a wave of positivity, all this good news for once. I was convinced that Commander Peterson was Clifton; even if it turned out not to be the case, he was already Clifton to me.

There were cheers all round when the lunar module landed successfully. There was a delay while we waited for the news camera feed to connect. There were cameras embedded into the module itself, the same as in the landings back in the sixties, only these were far more sophisticated with sharper images. The feed was beamed live via satellites and broadcast virtually live – there was only a thirty-second delay. I watched Dad's face as we waited for the pictures; he had a child-like excitement.

The hatch opened and the ladder descended. The television cut to the control room and panned to the faces of the staff who displayed the same wonder I was seeing in Dad.

Commander Peterson began his descent to the moon's surface; his lunar module pilot was to follow shortly after. As his feet touched ground, there was a huge roar of celebration from the control centre. It was hard not to get sucked into the emotion; my eyes started to well even though I was smiling. A quick glance around suggested I wasn't the only one. I gave a thumb-up to Unity on Skype and she smiled. If this was Clifton, he had done it.

'Hello Earth,' we heard Commander Peterson say. *'We live ... on a true miracle of a planet. It's a scientific wonder. We must work together ... to keep it this way. We need to imprint these images into our minds ... and remind ourselves every day how lucky we are. We are human beings ... not nations. We should let history be what it is... and make the history we want our grandchildren to see.'*

There was silence. Commander Peterson turned the camera towards Earth and the feed caught up. We looked back at our planet, half in darkness, the other half a blue and white splendour of hope.

'We've been granted the gift of life ... from the tiniest microbes to the giant redwoods ... whether by science or God is irrelevant... We owe it to ourselves ... to the planet and to the universe ... to cherish this precious gift. Burn this picture onto your memory ... and visit it every day.'

There was no doubt about it – this was Clifton's language. Clifton Leslie Peterson was looking down on the world and he *was* making a difference. He kept the camera still and there was silence, even in the control room; it was as if the world stopped still in order for its picture to be taken.

The astronauts began their work and after twenty minutes the television began interviews with scientists while the live feed became a corner feature. We headed upstairs to bed knowing we would all be tired tomorrow. There was a second EVA scheduled for Friday morning.

I took my laptop upstairs. I was still online to Unity. She was in her bedroom and tucked under the covers, her head on the pillow. 'It really is Clifton,' she said.

'It has to be. I can't help but feel proud. I'm glad Daisy and the others are safe.'

'I only wish I understood why he did it all like this.'

'He was wrong, he caused a lot of hurt for a lot of people. Maybe he considered the temporary damage to be a small price for the overall good he could achieve.'

'The price of trust.'

Unity smiled. It had been a good day for both of us; a good day for the world. My own head hit the pillow and we were sideways on, lying next to each other, in kissing distance of our screens and yet over a hundred miles apart. We had watched and heard Clifton talk from a quarter of a million miles in space.

'It's almost like you're here,' I said softly.

'I am. In my head.'

'Night Nutty.'

– CHAPTER 39 –

The breaking news was relentless. Thomas and Lucy stayed at home, hoping that Foxton might be able to straighten the truth from the media's crumpled lies. There were many theories and journalists' investigations had uncovered spurious nonsense, but there was some accuracy and some had linked Commander Peterson to the released victims. Witnesses said that Peterson was often seen in the Jetty Park area and had given talks in the school. There seemed a novelty in linking the two main stories.

It was late afternoon when Foxton finally called. 'We have something for Aril. It's with our forensics but we'll need to speak with him later,' he said.

'From Clifton, I presume?' Thomas said. Lucy watched him intently as he spoke.

'Yes. I think we have the canister base, it had a letter inside with a hand-drawn red star and ARIL written on it.'

'Where was it?'

'Inside the bunker complex on a high shelf. We're drip-feeding information to the news teams for now. We now know for sure that Commander Peterson is Clifton. The victims have identified him, though they didn't know who he was at the time. We have to tread carefully because we're unsure if his actions could endanger the rest of the crew or if he has committed himself to spend a long time in jail.'

'Yes, you need to.'

'The victims' stories are very strange. We know Peterson owns the school, or rather he runs the company that owns the school and they own the land – even though the bunkers are government owned. He's turned them into self-contained living quarters. The victims were living like reality TV stars without the cameras. Most days Peterson would see them, sometimes for an hour, sometimes for much of the day, for lessons in science, humanity and ecology. They've all become very close.'

'Only Peterson?'

'Apart from the days when they were abducted, yes. They built up a trust in him over time. They have nothing but good things to say about him. Daisy had a necklace that was like a mini version of the canisters. Inside he left a folded up note for Linden Keld and that's why we need to tread carefully.'

'That's very strange. Has the note been read?'

'Yes. Peterson says that he's written to his legal team to assign all the revenue from broadcast rights to Linden Keld and he's handed over his own share in the space company as well as the school and research facility, which he owns outright. He asked Linden to listen to Daisy and embrace all the good that science can do, telling him that he now owns a piece of history that humankind will treasure for millennia. Peterson's urged Keld to carry on the voyage of exploration and discovery.'

'He will love that.'

'I think Peterson's had more faith in Keld than we have. Keld's been soft on him so far but then again, he has his daughter back. He probably can't think beyond that right now.'

'No, I can imagine. What about the struggle and the blood on the shoelace from Alex Fernwood?'

'Nosebleed apparently. Brought on by the trauma but she claims she was treated well.'

'I see.' As Thomas thought about Peterson's note to Linden, his unease grew, 'It does sound as if Clifton's giving up on material things now he's achieved his personal ambition.'

'I think you're right, Thomas. It's worrying. These victims love him. There's something in his language that seems to resonate with these people. All five came out hand in hand with a unified voice. If they've been brainwashed, it's of a positive kind.'

'It's easy to see why. He seems to have touched everybody's sense of wonder. Aril and his friend, Unity, were prepared to trust him in spite of everything happening behind the scenes. It shows the power of that wonder if you can tap into people's imagination and compassion.'

'I think the American public will be less forgiving.'

***

I was still hyped up on Thursday in college and put on a show for Po again in rehearsals after lessons. I was dreading Saturday and entertaining the gang at my house but Po was full of it. I believe Po thinks we are going to have overnight international stardom after one gig at the Fox and Hare.

I phoned Thomas when I got home. He had left me a message to call him.

'I've spoken with Foxton. Clifton left a note for you in the bunkers,' he said.

'For me?'

'Yes. Aril, Foxton confirmed Peterson is Clifton. He is keeping it from the news right now. The victims identified him but they are going easy on the media until Clifton gets back.'

'Oh. Well, we had thought as much, I suppose.'

In some ways I was relieved. Although there were still unanswered questions, at least this puzzle was solved and the victims had been found safe. I was pleased for Clifton that he had fulfilled his dream and curious about the note. Thomas explained about the canister and his conversations with Foxton. I suggested a Skype call later so Thomas said he would call Foxton to arrange it.

I finished updating Unity as Thomas interrupted to tell me Stirling Foxton was coming online.

'Hello again, Aril,' Agent Foxton said. I was nervous. 'Clifton left you a letter. It was on a high shelf in a metal canister with no lid.' He held it up and showed me the envelope. 'Our forensics team opened it as it is evidence.'

'Can I see it?'

'I'll need to get clearance in order to send you a digital copy but I can read it to you.'

'Please.'

Agent Foxton unfolded the letter and began.

Aril,

I knew you would have figured things out by now. I didn't want to bow out with a villain's monologue. I want to leave a legacy of love and hope for humanity. At the risk that my words would be muted by my actions, I needed somebody to tell my story. I got lucky with you, Aril. You remind me of me. I achieved my goals by following a path that was wrong and yet justified by my conscience when I considered the bigger picture.

Children should never have to suffer for their parents' mistakes. Not as individuals, not as generations and not as a species in this vast cosmos. We have a responsibility to our children and to our future generations. We must not live as slaves, led by the unbending arm of corporate economics, nor create that for our children. We risk our water supplies to mine geological history for our temporary consumption. We put ourselves at the mercy of seed imperialism for our food supply. We create change faster than we can adapt to it. Our physical evolution could never catch up.

Yet we are the wonders of this universe. Each life tells a story and our experiences are handed down through each generation. We need to act now and admit our mistakes and work together as one Earth-nation to provide for our children's children, a legacy of continued hope and love.

Peace costs nothing and there lies the problem. We live in a world where the people who profit most from chaos have the power to maintain it. It's your generation, Aril, that has the loudest voice and the ability to make change happen.

When I was seven, our teacher took us outside just before close of school. It was getting dark and we were living in a small rural town in Kentucky so the skies were clear. He told us that humans were about to walk on the moon for the first time and that one day we could too. All we needed to do was to want to – to follow that dream and it would happen.

I've made mistakes too, and I've seen my child suffer because I couldn't give the gift I wanted to. What a child needs, as much as love and security, is encouragement.

I bought the trust of good strangers to help me achieve my dream. None of my staff know, nobody at NASA knows. It's taken three years' work behind the scenes and enough trust to build an entire religion. People had faith and belief in me and I hope, as future generations look on to this historic moment, that I have repaid that with interest.

Tell my story, Aril. With the money you make, live your dream and share your journey with people you love and who love you. My motives were not contrived under an illusion of hope, Aril. There is hope — it's with your generation. Learn from your parents' mistakes and never let your own children suffer for yours.

Keep my mother's moonstone pendant until you figure out what to do with it.

Thank you for trusting in me, Aril. I believe in you.

Keep dreaming, Commander,

Clifton Leslie Peterson.

Inexpressible emotion filled the void of silence that followed. Both of us struggled to contain it. With it came a fear that Clifton's surrender would impact on his crew. The story was too big for me to remain in the shadows of anonymity. It was as if had Clifton laid a path for me that I was committed to for the rest of my life. He believed in me, he trusted me to honour it. The reality was terrifying; the thought of him 'bowing out' even more so. I needed him.

– CHAPTER 40 –

I set the alarm for six but I couldn't sleep. I decided not to go in to college. The final moonwalk was in an hour, the astronauts were to finalise the platform for their ecology experiments. Scientists planned to monitor the eco-station remotely and learn about how the conditions on the moon affected the potential for life and how ecological systems could form on other remote planets. At least for now, there was *life* on the moon.

Stirling Foxton had explained to me what to expect from the media when the full story came to light. Journalists and publishers had already approached Clifton's victims for their stories but for now they were still talking to the FBI and spending time with their families and loved ones. The truth was yet to break.

I had talked to Dad until the early hours of the morning. I got the impression that he was not happy with the burden Clifton had landed on me and didn't want me to abandon my career. He explained that I had no obligation to tell Clifton's story, but I wanted to. I needed to.

I ventured downstairs as Eva arrived with a McDonalds breakfast for us. Harvey and I sat in our dressing gowns; it was too early to care that we had company. I watched Clifton descend the ladder one more time. He was there, treading the rocky ground of the moon, as his teacher had promised when he was seven. He was a hero now but he knew that when he returned his accomplishment would be overshadowed by the path he took to get there. I was overwhelmed by pride and pity.

We were all emotional. I could tell Dad was thinking like me and I noticed Eva's eyes welling with tears too. I understood why Clifton couldn't tell his story in the way I could – a profound monologue would be muted by his actions when the truth came out. We watched in awe. The control room in the corner of the screen was buzzing with activity and we could hear the discussions between the astronauts and scientists.

The news channel kept a red button option for viewing the astronauts throughout the morning so, after an hour or so, I went back upstairs, had a shower and dressed then joined Dad and Eva downstairs with my laptop. If I had to tell Clifton's story, I needed to know more about him. I knew two details: he grew up in a small town in Kentucky and he had a child.

Wikipedia ran a detailed analysis of his career but there was little about his younger life. He was born May 2nd 1962 in Mayfield, Kentucky, son of Clifton and Gale. The article mentioned his father was an astronomer who worked with Lyman Spitzer on the first space telescope. Clifton spent much of his youth in Europe and went to university in Cambridge, England. That made sense: he had to have knowledge of the area. He met his wife, Heydon while studying and married her after university. He moved back to America and got a position with NASA in 1990, when he was twenty-eight. Over time, he worked with the Hubble telescope and even had a stint on the International Space Station. He had split with his wife and she moved back to England with their daughter, Ellerslie.

I searched many sites, making notes while keeping half an eye on the television. Eva caught me writing and asked what I was up to. For once I stopped my mouth from speaking my thoughts; I couldn't tell her the truth.

'I'm just fascinated by Commander Peterson. I wondered

what it took for him to get there and what you have to do to be an astronaut.'

'Hard work and a lot of passion, I would think,' she said, softly. 'Are you interested now?'

'Maybe.'

We were aware that the control room was urging the astronauts back in the lunar module. It was nearly time for the mission to end. I was pleased it had gone well but I couldn't stop feeling nervous – I couldn't tell if it was about Clifton, or the attention that was about to be thrust upon me. The astronauts headed towards the module and the cameras caught Commander Peterson behind his companion. He had stopped to look up to the Earth. I thought I knew what he was thinking. 'Come on Clifton,' I thought. 'You've made that difference, I'll help make it happen for you.'

Clifton stayed still, like a statue. His companion reached the ladder and looked behind. 'The Earth is beautiful. I've thought about this moment all my life,' we heard Clifton say. The control room staff urged him back.

'Go ahead now, I want to stay…'

I looked over at Dad and gasped. The sound feed was cut and a few seconds later the picture feed was cut too. A *technical error* page showed so we flicked back to the main news channel, which was showing a weather update. Something was wrong.

'Oh no,' Dad said. Eva sat on the sofa staring at the screen, barely blinking. I tried the NASA online stream but that was also down.

After thirty minutes, there was still no news. Not a single mention. Had we heard Commander Peterson right? Thomas phoned, he had been watching it too with Lucy and they thought the same thing. I grew more worried by the minute and feared in case the crew couldn't get back without Clifton. I refreshed the NASA web page every few seconds. Nothing.

Linden Keld listened. For two full days he had been with Daisy as she was questioned by the FBI and the picture was becoming increasingly clear. He would never forgive Commander Peterson for what he put the family through but he couldn't deny the positive influence Clifton had had on Daisy. She had been lured by trickery rather than by force; at no time did she feel in danger but neither did she know the truth. Daisy thought that everybody back home was aware of where she was and she had no knowledge of the ransom demand. She thought that the entire thing was part of a reality TV show for select people whose fathers' actions were harming mankind. She knew the others had been abducted but they had all been convinced that they weren't in any danger and that their teachings and 'Breakfast Club' style discussions were being televised.

Linden listened as Daisy explained their daily routines and how they learned about the dangers of continuing to sacrifice the long-term stability of the planet for short-term profits, and how ignorance and greed lead to a selfish and paranoid existence. Clifton had explained in detail how money controlled every political decision and how greed trickled down to an individual level with the brand-shaming tactics of advertising to sell goods that were needed purely for status. Linden was fascinated as much as embarrassed because he had never been forced to think this way before – he had considered it left-wing *hoodoonomics*. He was angry at Clifton but proud of Daisy for delivering such reasoning, even when she was challenged.

Daisy explained in detail how the inertia of our decisions to tap into fossil fuels was likely to exceed tipping point. To mine twenty per cent of the known reserve of fossil fuels would raise the planet's temperature to a level where methane under the polar ice would escape into our ozone layer and destroy it – even if mankind stopped all carbon emissions. Daisy explained how we would have to spend more than our global defence budget just to defend our towns and cities against nature. That would happen in her generation's lifetime.

Linden listened as Daisy explained about global equality and that the money owned by the super-rich could vastly improve and save the lives of billions. Yet hundreds of millions of dollars were spent in legal expenses and lobbying governments by the super-rich to maintain their super-rich status. She explained, using graphs she must have memorised, how the current economic system could not be sustained in the long run and how it would inevitably break down over time.

The other victims gave the same story. Linden met other parents whose outlook on life was changed by the events of the past weeks. There was guilt, shame and anger among them and yet their children's safe return overpowered it all.

The families and the American people who had given their prayers and hopes to find Daisy and the other victims wanted justice. The only people who never once called for justice were the victims themselves.

***

I felt sick with anxiety. Eva couldn't hide her emotions either and I noticed tears on her cheeks several times. Dad was quiet and Harvey returned to his room. There was no news at all, not even a mention. Only on social media were there questions. I refreshed the NASA webpage every few seconds and finally at two o'clock an announcement was made – a live feed from NASA control room was broadcast on their website and social media.

It is with much sadness that I must report that Commander Leslie Peterson will not be returning home to us. He passed away at 7.20 EST this morning, witnessed by Lunar Module Pilot Russell Armley.

Obviously we have limited information at present but it was not possible to return his body to the lunar module in time for its ascent without further endangering the crew. We are closing the live feed for the remainder of this mission and will work with procedural authorities to investigate this tragic incident. Our thoughts and prayers are with friends and family of Commander Peterson. We will hold a press conference in due course.

The screen cut away to a picture of Commander Clifton Peterson in his space suit smiling, with his helmet tucked under his arm.

I broke down. Completely.

– CHAPTER 41 –

The next seven days were surreal. It felt as if my emotions had ridden galactic rollercoasters but nothing prepared me for the nervous tension I felt as Dad and I waited in a central London hotel for Congressman Linden Keld to arrive with his wife and daughter, Daisy. He had asked to meet me in person.

I was relieved that the lunar mission returned to Earth successfully but I missed Clifton deeply and made a vow to tell his story as he had trusted me to. My name didn't break in the news until Monday and after that the pressure was relentless. I'd been interviewed a dozen times and my dad had sought legal advisers. I restricted my story to the press but told everybody that I planned to write a book so that Clifton's legacy of love and hope for humanity could be understood by generations to come.

I recognised Linden and his family immediately. He shook my hand, as did Edina, and Daisy hugged me tightly, which took me by surprise.

'I had to come here to apologise in person and thank you, Aril,' Linden said, almost immediately.

'I don't feel I'm worthy, to be honest,' I said, embarrassed. 'I felt I had a moral responsibility to help and I desperately wanted to understand what was happening.'

'I was horrible to you when you were trying to help and yet you kept your dignity with such grace that you exposed me to my own cowardice. Clifton has landed us both with a moral responsibility now. I've been given control of his entire professional life. The old me would have condemned his name and burned his legacy in the hell I once believed in.'

'Clifton must have trusted you wouldn't. He was brave.'

'A parallel trust, he said. I get it now. I have a lot of learning to do and the biggest lesson of all is forgiveness. That will take longer than Clifton's staff teaching me what they know about his work. I have to learn to trust my faith too, a different faith than I had before – a faith that runs with humanity and not at odds with it. I'm a bad person, Aril, and I didn't even know it. I still have anger and hatred, I'm still greedy and selfish and my personality won't change overnight. I have to adapt to a new way of thinking. But if I don't try, I will never find peace again.'

'You had your daughter taken from you and at one time we all probably believed it was too late to save her,' I said nodding at Daisy. 'All your actions were of a man desperate to find her, they were actions of love.' I caught a smile from Edina.

'Yes, but I was equally motivated by justice and for the first time in my life felt powerless. Clifton played me well and I may never forgive him, but I do respect him. It was important for me to see you face to face. It's the first step on a long road ahead for both of us.'

'I know, sir. I hope we can make a difference.'

'We can only do good by trying. And please, call me Linden.'

We stayed in the hotel for several hours and Daisy explained her own thoughts. Clifton had taught with enthusiasm and passion, he had touched the imagination of all five victims. They were all close and planned to stay in touch and publically speak as a united front in years to come. Our generation really could change the world for the better by our actions and words, by standing up to what was wrong and showing a united voice.

By early evening, it was time to leave. The Kelds were

staying in England for a few days to enjoy being together as a family. As we stood up to leave, Linden Keld reached inside his suit pocket.

'There's another reason I needed to see you, Aril. I'm a man of my word.' He handed me an envelope. 'Go on, open it.'

I was embarrassed but obliged. Inside was a banker's draft for one-million dollars. My hands were shaking. 'Why?'

'We wouldn't have found Daisy without your help. I publically announced the reward for information leading to her safe return,' he said. I noticed his grin. He was enjoying this, as was Daisy.

'I can't, I don't feel…'

'You can and you will,' he said, sternly. 'What you do with it is up to you but you deserve this, Aril. Again, it's another step on that long journey ahead.'

My eyes filled. Even Dad seemed speechless. He put his hands on my shoulder. 'Thank you,' he said.

I nodded, trying to compose myself. 'Thank you, Linden. I'll do good with it.'

'I know you will,' Edina said, with a smile, and held Linden's arm.

***

Thomas and Lucy Riley had been keeping up with the news all week. They toasted Commander Clifton Leslie Peterson as the sad news broke. They were used to being thrust into the limelight, so shouldn't have been shocked by the renewed media attention. Thomas handled it well. Lucy was half-expecting it to trigger his PTSD but he remained fairly calm. They had helped Dale and Aril prepare and recommended legal advisers to help them.

One more piece of the jigsaw came clear as news filtered through that Clifton had ended his own life. Gene Shoemaker, a planetary scientist from America, had his ashes buried on the moon in 1999 by a lunar probe. This had to be connected to the cordwainer reference in his clues. Clifton had planned every detail of this mission; he knew he was staying on the moon.

Lucy joined Thomas at their dining table to help wrap presents. It was four days until Christmas and they were still unprepared. The television played Christmas songs in the background. She had been thinking about a wedding they were attending after Christmas for their friends Amy and Gerard; it was Amy who had gifted them the money to start their company after the Las Vegas treasure hunt.

'Our problem with Clifton's clues was that we were looking for cryptic answers and not taking in what he was saying,' she said. 'He was telling us everything in his own language, yet he knew we wouldn't be able to solve it fast enough.'

'It's like he had enough faith in human nature to stay one step ahead all the time.'

'He bought the trust of strangers. I wonder if the FBI will pursue the people who helped him now. The victims don't seem to care.'

'It's odd isn't it? I still can't work out how the clues ended up scattered all over Britain.'

'I don't think the case will be laid to rest just yet. I'm sure more information will come to light over time.'

The phone went and Thomas answered it. It was Aril; he had been meeting Linden Keld today.

'Well, I can pay you now,' Aril said.

'You can?' Thomas looked confused.

'Linden's given me the reward money. I feel bad about taking it knowing I have a bidding war going on for Clifton's story.'

'I'm glad he honoured that promise. You deserved it. We were talking about it during the week. Money will change you, Aril, but never forget that money is only ever good for what it can do, not for what it buys.'

'I know. I'll be careful and I want to do good with it. I owe it to Clifton. Dad says a million dollars is about £600,000 so

I do want to honour your twenty per cent as we agreed. Then we'll see where the dust settles with the rest.'

'Well, everything was more complicated than we expected so let's call it £100,000 and cap it at that.'

'Thank you. Thank you both. I hope we can stay in touch and if you ever need any help, you know where I am.'

Thomas laughed. 'We will. You take care and enjoy Christmas.'

'Oh, I will.'

– CHAPTER 42 –

It was the dreaded Saturday. I glanced at my clock and it was already midday. Lack of sleep all week had taken its toll and I crashed out when we returned from London. I was looking forward to seeing Unity and Henry but not to the gig.

I hadn't been to college for a week because of the media attention but Dad wanted me to continue, so I would be revising hard over the holidays. Po was already lording over my celebrity status, I think he forgave me for bailing on Thursday's rehearsal but he would have publically lynched me if I let him down again.

I wandered downstairs to find Eva in the kitchen. 'Hey, where's Dad?'

'He's nipped into town with Harvey, he won't be long. I heard about your meeting with Linden.'

'It was nice to meet him and his family. I was shocked by the money. I hope it doesn't become common knowledge.'

'It shouldn't.' Eva stared out the window as she spoke. 'Clifton got his dream in the end, didn't he?'

'He did. Something went to plan for him for once, but with tragic consequences.'

'Maybe they seemed less tragic to him. I envy him sometimes.'

It must have been traumatic for the entire space community. Even Eva seemed deeply touched by what had happened to

Clifton. He was having an impact on the whole world and nobody knew whether we should celebrate or mourn. He was hero and villain, both celebrated and condemned. To me, he was my god, he was my hope and faith and I still believed in him. And I never met him.

I made breakfast then watched the news. Clifton was still the main story: the lunar mission, his death, the kidnappings and his treasure hunt. It was surreal hearing my name mentioned every day on the news. For a while the press were camped outside. Luckily Thomas and Lucy diffused the situation. I was offered six-figure sums for my story but Thomas and Lucy introduced us to publicists who thought it would be better to write a book and then choose specific media outlets for publicity.

The news channel showed a live interview with Clifton's ex-wife, Heydon. She described her husband as dedicated, gifted and inspirational and said he had an infectious positivity that touched everybody. She lamented the breakdown of their relationship and spoke of the sorrow they had both endured because of the demands of his work but she understood his passion. She was asked how her daughter had taken the news.

'I've spoken to Ellie and she is devastated, as you can imagine. She is working in England at the moment. I will see her in the New Year. She has her father's strength and will get through this, but there is unimaginable sadness right now.'

When asked about his body being left in space, she replied, 'He is the man on the moon, collecting sticks for eternity. He'll be in no hurry to come down too soon.'

There was a cry. I looked behind me and saw Eva turn towards the kitchen. In an instant, something hit me.

Eva was crying and I threw my arms around her. She held me for a minute before slowly pulling away. She composed herself enough to speak, though her voice was fragile. 'I'll need to reapply my makeup before your dad gets back,' she said.

'Are you OK?'

'I feel foolish, I'm sorry.'

'I might be wrong here but I'm going to say it anyway. Clifton's mother's pendant is yours, isn't it?'

She looked up at me and sat down at the table slowly before answering. 'Ellerslie Vandalia Aurora Peterson is the name I was born with. Dad called me Eva, Mum calls me Ellie.'

'Oh no,' I said, then reached for her hand.

'Please, Aril, trust me too. I didn't want anybody to know that I'd had any contact with my father. I helped him with the clues but I didn't know about any connection between the kidnappings and your treasure hunt until you did. He was posting the clues to me and I was following his instructions. He told me the truth after you were arrested. There were backup plans that I never had to put into action but he was protecting us too. He was a genius, he planned every last detail.'

'I should have followed my intuition,' I said, trying to grasp what she was saying. 'Does Dad know?'

'No, he doesn't. It's torn me up. Please don't say anything now. Maybe save it for the book and give a chance for time to settle on what's happened. I will look after your father's dream, I won't let him down. Your father's a good man, he reminds me of my father. He has taken care of you and Harvey well. I envy that. Dad was good to me. He was devastated when Mum took me back to Europe. I didn't see him for eighteen years. I resented my mother all that time. My father helped me forgive her. I realised he never stopped loving her and eventually, when I finally talked to my mother about it, realised that she never stopped loving him. They made mistakes and were both too stubborn to admit it and I was the one who suffered. He never forgave himself for that.'

'That's sad. What do you feel about him being left up there? No funeral or resting place. So many people love him.'

'From what I gather there will be a service in his memory after Christmas. As for a resting place, that's a place on this planet where he is likely to be visited once or twice a year. No matter where I am on Earth, we can look up at the skies and remember him every night. It's my father's resting place. He can look down at us like he always wanted to. For Dad, that was always his heaven.'

'And he will be remembered forever…'

Dad's car pulled up in the driveway. Eva smiled, then went to the bathroom to reapply her makeup. I was numb. Eva was Clifton's first victim and he was his last.

***

Po must have texted me a dozen times to make sure I was going to turn up. I told him to chill. I was expecting Henry and Unity in an hour so thought I better start getting ready. I had a shower and chose my clothes, I opted for black jeans with a studded chain belt but wasn't sure whether to wear a band T-shirt or a plain black T-shirt with a mesh neck and sleeves. I was still debating when I heard a car pull up – Unity was here early. I threw on a Young Guns T-shirt and ran downstairs. Unity laughed the moment she saw me and, after a hug, removed her leather jacket to reveal black jeans, studded belt and Young Guns skinny top.

'Twins!' Dad and Henry said, in unison. My cheeks flushed.

We sat for a while drinking coffee and the conversation rarely strayed from Clifton. I had kept Unity in the shadows during the week but kept in touch. She thought I was handling my fame well but I needed to talk to her alone.

'I suppose I better sort my hair out. I'm not sure what to do with it,' I said directing my words at Unity. She connected immediately.

'Need help?' she said.

'I think so.'

We went upstairs. My hair was virtually dry but it was a mess. Unity took control immediately, reaching for my gel and mousse.

'Right, you park your backside there and leave this to me,' she said. How could I argue? 'I can't believe you're famous now.'

'No. Nor can I. Not sure if I like it but I feel I owe it to Clifton.'

'He's landed you right in it.'

'Yeah, I know. I didn't have much choice.' I was enjoying her touch on my hair, it was therapeutic and calming. I loved the smell of her perfume too; my senses were taking her in.

'I needed to talk with you alone. I've been chatting with Dad. When we saw Linden Keld yesterday, he gave me a banker's draft as a reward for finding Daisy.'

'Oh my God, after all he's already paid out?'

'I know right. I didn't want to accept it but he wasn't having any of it. Thomas and Lucy will have one hundred thousand, because we had already agreed a percentage of any treasure.'

'A hundred thousand… How much did he give you?'

'A million dollars, which is about six hundred thousand pounds.'

'Oh wow…'

'Unity,' I interrupted her, 'I want to halve the rest with you. I couldn't have done this without you. I didn't find Daisy, *we* did.'

She was silent for a few moments. Then she cracked the brush against my shoulder.

'Ouch! I said.

'I can't,' she said, 'I can't, I can't, I…'

'You can, and you must. Even if it has to go into trust until you're eighteen or whatever legally, you must.'

'I don't want it to destroy me or destroy my plans,' she said, solemnly.

'Why would it destroy your plans? You've already said you don't know what you want to do. Now you can do anything.'

'I could always do anything, that's the point. I never wanted to rely on anybody, I wanted to remain independent. Go to university, say to my family *I made it, without you.*'

'You still can. You deserve this money,' I pulled her around towards me and looked up into her eyes, clutching her hands. 'You earned this yourself. It's not simply a case of me giving it to you, you earned this. Use it to pay for university and don't touch the rest until afterwards. You've already made it, Unity. You just did it sooner than planned.'

I felt bad because she was obviously fighting tears and I was hoping she would be happy. I was confused. I wanted to understand her logic but there was a battle she was fighting deep inside. 'Unity, listen. You've been fighting all these years. Having this money is payment for the hard work you've done so far but it's where a new challenge begins – it doesn't end here. You still have plans. All it does is give you the time to figure out the direction for your life. You won't be reliant on your mum's plans and her home for your own base.'

'How do you always know what to say?' she said, softly.

'I don't always, trust me.' I smiled.

'Don't let it change me, Aril. I'm happy with who I am.'

'I don't want you to change either.'

***

We all set off for Godmanchester around 7.20. Harvey came along too. I was so nervous, I barely touched dinner. My hair was glam-rock style and I wore every accessory I could find. Unity was amazed that I possessed so many sweat bands, wrist bands and bangles. She managed to convince me to wear eyeliner. I hardly recognised myself in the mirror.

Unity thanked me for my offer of the money. She told Henry in front of Dad and explained her hesitation at accepting it. Henry thankfully mirrored my words, and he shook my hand and thanked me before we set off.

The pub car park was packed as we tried to turn in. There were cars everywhere so we had to pull in down the road and walk back. We were not supposed to be on stage until ten. As I entered the building horror struck – there were cameras and all eyes watched me enter.

'Oh no,' I said.

There were so many people everywhere. I could see Po and the gang in the corner. Po was beaming from ear to ear – the sod – he must have tipped people off. My nerves were crippling.

It took ten minutes to sit down. Somebody gave up their seats so that we could have a table together and I shook the hands of strangers and had photos taken – including numerous selfies. It was awkward and I must have apologised ten times to Unity. The noise was so loud that conversation was nearly impossible. I wished that we had arrived later. Dad and Henry made their way to the bar. Everybody knew my age, there was no way I could get away with drinking alcohol, but I wanted some to calm me. There was no backstage area where we could escape. Every few minutes somebody asked for my autograph. I cursed Po. He must have known because he kept his distance, which was unheard of.

As the time approached ten, I thought I'd better find the band. I struggled to reach them as people, including journalists, handed me cards and asked questions. Thankfully Po came to the rescue and grabbed me.

'All set, superstar?' he shouted as we made our way down the steps to the stage.

'Remind me to kill you after we're done!'

'I only told a few people,' he said with a grin.

'Local media more like.'

We switched on our instruments and fumbled a little, tuning up and setting up. A wall of people grew silent when the lights dimmed. I could see Unity and Harvey on the balcony at the top of the stairs to the right of the stage with Dad, Eva and Henry behind them with Denny, I acknowledged him with a thumbs-up. I thought I was going to be sick and I hoped I didn't look as bad as I felt. We all had microphones for backing vocals especially for our epic finale. We tested them as the sound engineer put his thumbs up and turned on the stage lights.

Po nodded at me and then said, 'Let's go crazy!' which was

my cue.

I began the opening riff of 'Smells like Teen Spirit' and the place erupted. I don't know if the nerves abandoned me or if I simply surrendered to them but I played my part and put on a show. Unity was jumping and smiling throughout and Harvey buried his hands in his face numerous times. I've no idea what I looked like but after the past few weeks, it was a release.

'Stop the Cavalry' was our festive finishing piece. We punked it up with a guitar solo and encouraged the crowd to join in as we repeated the chorus several times and had another twelve-bar solo before the final line. We trashed the ending into an epic drum-roll-scissor-leap finish. The audience loved it. It was the strangest feeling. Po took his bow and I shook his hand, leaving him to his own fifteen minutes of fame while I escaped to Unity.

'That was insane,' she shouted. I tried to ignore people as we made our way back to our table but I was aware of cameras flashing. I remained smiling throughout even though I declined more autographs and dodged questions. I didn't know if Unity wanted to be in the limelight but it was hard to avoid, though she handled it well. As we approached the table, I guided Unity towards the door where there was a stream of people leaving.

'Come on, let's see if we can get some quiet,' I said. She nodded and we headed out.

The cold air was refreshing as we stepped outside. I texted Dad to tell him where we were, then we walked along the lane away from the noise. Henry and Unity had to head back soon and travel up to Scotland the next day for Christmas.

'You enjoyed that, I can tell,' she said.

'On stage?'

'Yeah, you were a proper rock star – as you've been all week.'

'It's a mask I wear when I'm nervous or embarrassed, I think.'

'Well you looked good. You realise there will be videos of

that all over YouTube and Twitter by now?'

'Oh God, no.'

We turned the corner. The street was quiet, with rows of houses one side and a clearing to the other. We could see the moon and we both looked up as we talked.

'He made it, the silly beggar,' Unity said.

'He did. I hope he's enjoying the view.' We both stopped. The moon was nearly full and seemed extra bright with a frosty haze around it. I felt calmer than I had in many months. 'In his last note, Clifton told me to live my dream and share my journey with those I love and those who love me,' I turned to her. 'Unity, will you come with me on this journey? I don't know where I'm going or what I intend to when I get there, but I do know I want you with me.'

She smiled and gently wiped some hair away from my cheek, and replied softly, 'Of course.'

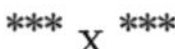

AUTHOR NOTES

Writing *A Parallel Trust* has been one of the most enjoyable and creative journeys I have taken. Everything fell into place. For Cape Canaveral to be on the -52.1775 aggregate line was perfect – and I had no idea it was there when I wrote my initial plan and storyboard. I hoped I would find some connection or observatory and indeed I found Braebrook Observatory which coincidentally had relocated 160 miles north-west to my home town.

All the names (with the exception of Aril, Thomas and Lucy) are place names along the two lines, including all surnames. Unity was perfect for her character – the word's literal meaning of 'one' was ideal for such a solitary and independent girl. Gale (Clifton's mother) is also the name a crater on the moon.

I hope to create my own treasure hunt before this book is released, similar to the one I set up for my book, *Ring of Conscience*. The online treasure is still waiting to be claimed on **www.melodema.net** so feel free to try – now you've read this book, you might understand the final clue better.

You can find me on social media and I have created a mood-board for *A Parallel Trust* on Tumblr: http://aparalleltrust.tumblr.com/

www.jamesstoddah.com
www.aparalleltrust.com
Facebook: http://facebook.com/JamesStoddah
Twitter: @JamesStoddah
Blog: http://melodema.tumblr.com/

9 781910 077528